Nowhere Else But Here

RACHEL COTTON

INK ROAD

First published 2018 by Ink Road
INK ROAD is an imprint and trademark of
Black & White Publishing Ltd
Nautical House, 104 Commercial Street
Edinburgh EH6 6NF

1 3 5 7 9 10 8 6 4 2   18 19 20 21

ISBN: 978 1 78530 163 6
Copyright © Rachel Cotton 2018

A CIP catalogue record for this book is
available from the British Library.

Typeset by Iolaire, Newtonmore
Printed and bound by CPI Group (UK) Ltd. Croydon, CR0 4YY

To my mum, for being the most incredible person in my life.
I love you to the moon and back.

One

One

It had been a sweltering hot summer and even though I couldn't wait for evening, the sun was at least a sign that there was still time to get the job done; the darkness had not arrived yet.

When night fell, we'd have to stop. We'd have to give up on the search for the day.

I posted the flyer through the letterbox. Listened to it drop onto the mat. Tried my hardest to not look at the sombre face in the centre of the paper, below the bold "MISSING PERSON" caption at the top.

These actions felt like routine now.

Once you finished one road it was on to another. Doing the same thing every single time. I wondered how many people would read what I had gone to the effort of posting, how many would actually take a moment out of their lives to think about what we'd written on our flimsy flyers, and how many would just throw them into the bin without a second glance because it wasn't their problem.

And then I'd catch his eyes. The ones on the paper. The ones I had been trying to avoid. His green eyes, glistening from the flash of the camera. His face was contorted into a scowl that showed he clearly didn't want his photo taken at that moment. His dark brown hair, short and messy, fell onto his face.

Theo Lockhart. The boy no one at our school really knew – and the boy everyone now believed something awful had happened to.

There were other helpers waiting at the top of my tenth road, basking in the heat of the evening sun as they took a short break. Their eyes were closed as they rested, taking a few moments to let the fatigue wash over them before they got back to their search. I joined them on the small patch of grass they were lying on, finding my own spot and dropping down onto it.

My feet sang with joy as my weight was taken off them. I closed my eyes and enjoyed the soft breeze that brushed over my skin and blew the hair off my sticky face. But it wasn't long before the moment of peace was ruined, because Grace came bounding over, a frown on her face – that was a sign of bad news to come.

"Here," she said firmly, dumping a wad of paper down onto the ground next to me as she took a seat herself. "Johnny West had to go home, so they've given us the rest of his flyers to post."

She removed her jacket from her shoulders, revealing a black vest top tucked into her denim shorts.

I pushed myself up from the ground and eyed the stash of paper I already had. "But we haven't even made it halfway through our own flyers."

Grace shrugged, using her hand to fan herself in the heat.

"I guess we'll just have to hand in the ones we haven't posted at the end."

"I suppose," I murmured, feeling the last burst of sunlight hit my face before it disappeared for the night. "Was Naya all right with you cancelling your date tonight?"

Grace smiled warmly as she thought of her girlfriend. They had been going out for two years, ever since Grace came out to her parents and me. "She understood how important it was. In fact, I think she might be helping out herself."

"Well, next time you see her, tell her she still owes me that chocolate muffin she stole from me at lunch yesterday."

Grace let out a peal of musical laughter, and I felt my own chest vibrate as I joined her. It was peaceful, just taking a moment to enjoy the last of the summer warmth before it started to turn colder in the next few months. I could hear the chatter of other students who had been helping out and the melody of birds singing in nearby trees. For a moment it was the perfect evening, until I remembered why it was that we were all there.

"I think Tristan wants to come over here." Grace's voice grabbed my attention a moment later. "He keeps looking at you."

And then, almost as if he had heard her speaking, Tristan Meyers called out, "Hey, Rose!" He broke away from his friends and jogged over to us, his face slightly red from the sunburn he'd got over the summer.

Grace shot me a knowing smile, which I chose to ignore. "Hey, Tristan. Everything all right?" I smiled up at him once he reached us. Grace cleared her throat and made to stand up.

"I think my break's over," she said, grabbing half of the papers from our stack.

"I'll catch you up in a minute," I responded. She nodded and, when Tristan wasn't looking, shot me a wink, much to my horror. Before I could reprimand her she was shooting off, making her way down another road.

Tristan let out a small cough, causing my eyes to snap back to him. "I just came over to say thanks for helping out. Not many others were willing to give up their time after school to do this, so it means a lot that you offered," he said, running his hand through his hair. Tristan was Head Boy at our school. It made sense; he was involved in every club our school offered, yet still managed to get brilliant results across the board. Grace always joked that he was going to become Prime Minister one day. Unsurprisingly, he thought he was the boss of Theo's search party.

I started to stand so that we were level in height, his bright blue eyes watching me intently. "It's honestly no problem, Tristan." I pulled my lips up into a small, forced smile. "Any updates?"

"Well, we've searched most of the local area now," Tristan replied. "We've been trying to find any clues as to where he may have gone, but there's been nothing so far."

There was a pause as I took in his words. Not having any clues wasn't a good sign. To me, it was a sign of someone who didn't want to be found – a sign of someone who didn't want to come back.

"Do you think something's happened to him?" I blurted out a second later, my voice barely above a whisper.

Tristan's eyes caught my own, full of concern. "Theo's only been missing for two days, Rose. Let's just worry about looking for him right now."

And he was right. Theo Lockhart, my classmate and

two-year chemistry partner, had only been missing for about forty-eight hours. No one had seen or spoken to him. No one knew why he had disappeared or where he might have gone. The school had asked anyone with more information to come forward, or offer any useful suggestions as to his possible whereabouts. No one did. As soon as he was gone, it became painfully clear that no one knew anything about Theo.

There weren't many ways to describe Theo when asked. He turned up to school. He kept his head down in lessons. I never had him pegged as one for trouble, but I'd heard about a few nasty trips to the head teacher's office that he'd made in the last year. Stupid fights, back-chatting teachers – but nothing out of the ordinary. And sometimes he went AWOL, bunking lessons or turning up late.

He seemed to like chemistry well enough. He'd never told me that, of course. He'd never said very much to me at all to be honest, but he always seemed to do his work on time, and he was helpful during experiments – even if he was pretty happy for me to take charge. It was perfect in a way, because I always wanted to be in charge. I never thought our chemistry lab rapport qualified as "useful information", though, and when Theo disappeared, I realised I couldn't actually think of one thing I really knew about him.

He was an enigma, to all of us, and it seemed that was just the way he liked it. Whoever you were, you wouldn't be able to get much of a conversation out of him; you wouldn't be able to persuade him to sit with you at lunch. It was as though he wanted to be alone. The only time I ever spoke to him was in our chemistry lessons.

Even so, his disappearance had caused some pretty different reactions around the school. Some people posted desperate pleas for his return on Facebook and Twitter – but they tended to be the girls who fancied him, drawn to the drama. Others believed this was all part of some game he had made up, and that any moment he would come striding into one of the classrooms and watch all of our mouths drop open. And then people like me, who didn't know what to think, had offered to carry out the proper search parties, knowing that this was our best shot at finding this mysterious boy.

But the truth was that no one had any idea where he might have gone. Theo wasn't one for making friends, so he didn't have any. And yet he could've had anything. Hell, if he wanted to be popular, his good looks alone would easily have got him there. But he never wanted any of that. He was never one for the attention.

And that was why most people were starting to say something awful had happened to him.

Ours isn't a large town. We are only an hour outside of London, but where we live is quiet, undisturbed, and people know each other. Which, consequently, means that they talk about one another. Theo's disappearance was the first time anyone had gone missing; it was the biggest news to hit our town in years, and it spread fast.

"Well, it's nice that we're able to try and make some sort of difference by doing this. I'm sure Theo's parents are grateful for the help," I said to Tristan, who just shrugged.

"Actually, they didn't seem too bothered about having a search party for him in the first place," he replied.

"What?" My jaw dropped open, and I shook my head in confusion. "Why would they not want a search party?"

Tristan clearly knew more than he was letting on, and I could tell he didn't want others to overhear what he was about to say – he kept turning his head to double-check no one was listening. "A group of us went over to their house a couple of hours ago, and they didn't seem that worried. Then, when the police came round, they were constantly talking in hushed voices so we couldn't listen in." Tristan's voice dropped a little lower. "I think they know something we don't. Like they were expecting Theo to go running off before this happened … Or maybe they're in shock."

A thousand explanations crossed my mind – many of them hopeful, but a few desperate and dark. I had never met the rest of the Lockhart family. Perhaps they were a lot like Theo in that they kept themselves to themselves, but surely they should be more concerned about their son's disappearance?

"Maybe they know he's going to come back." I decided to voice one of my happier thoughts. "And that's why they don't want us wasting our time searching."

"Yes, but then why wouldn't they tell us why he's gone missing?"

It was like my hope was a candle and Tristan had just chucked a whole bucket of water all over it. He must have noticed any glimmer of hope leave my eyes, because he smiled sympathetically at me and gently grasped my shoulder.

"It'll be all right," he murmured. "We'll find him."

"Yeah," I replied, my voice emotionless. My eyes drifted back to Theo's face on the flyer. It captured his essence perfectly – brooding, aloof – and yet there was an unreadable emotion in his eyes that, no matter how hard I studied the photo, was impossible for me to decipher. It was something like sadness. "I'm sure we will."

The town was covered in a blanket of darkness by the time I

arrived home. I shrugged off my jacket and placed it on the coat rack, making sure to switch on all the lights as I walked through the house.

It was empty, of course – my house was practically always empty. Both of my parents had extremely demanding jobs. They both worked at the same law firm – it's a pretty cute story actually because that's where they met and fell in love – and they were made partners a few years ago, which means long days with early morning starts and late finishes. When they weren't at work, they were always checking their emails and calling their clients, or shut away in their study, so I barely saw them anyway. It's busy, it's isolating and it's tiring; there wasn't a time I could remember since I turned sixteen that they came home and we had dinner together like a normal family. I was used to spending most of my evenings alone.

It didn't bother me any more though. I was fine being on my own, and had grown used to my brother being the one who was always there for me, rather than my parents. I knew that if he could, Brent would be home all the time to be with me, but it just wasn't possible with him at university.

There was a stack of homework due the next day waiting on my desk for me when I entered my bedroom, but I chose to ignore it and instead headed straight for the shower to wash the day away. I took my time in there, enjoying the feel of the cool water hitting my face, running down my skin, reinvigorating me. I could have been in there for hours without knowing or caring.

I couldn't block everything out entirely, though. I knew that things were still dark – the fact that we had no links whatsoever as to where Theo could be, the idea that he may not be coming back for good. It troubled me to think that something bad might have happened to him. I caught my expression in the mirror as I got out of the shower; my concerned brown eyes stared back at me. My freckles had become even more prominent over the summer holiday, and my naturally straight hair had grown longer, now hanging past my chin and reaching to the top of my shoulders. At a first glance, I looked sun-kissed and healthy. But there were bags resting under my eyes and I was hunched with the fatigue of the search as I stared back at my reflection.

But for now I had to stop thinking about the darkness, forget my confusion about Theo, and start afresh for tomorrow.

There was a bowl of yesterday's leftover spaghetti bolognese waiting for me in the fridge. I was quick to reheat it, my stomach rumbling in anticipation as I stirred the pot on the stove. As soon as it was done I devoured it, burning my tongue. I still felt empty. Why was I so drained by the last few days?

A glance at my watch as I ate told me that there was no possible way that I could get my homework done for tomorrow without being up the entire night. I cursed out loud and decided to give up, figuring my teachers might be a little lenient once they heard I was out looking for Theo all evening. Instead, I headed back upstairs to throw on my pyjamas and get some much-needed sleep.

But I didn't exactly get what I wanted, because as soon as I got into my bedroom the doorbell rang. I glanced at my clock, disapproval bubbling up inside me as I noticed how late it was. We often had neighbours popping over to have a quick chat, but never at this time of night.

"Coming!" I shouted, hurriedly throwing on the shorts and T-shirt I had been wearing earlier.

The doorbell rang again. And again. And again. Whoever was waiting on the other side of the door sure was impatient.

"I said I'm coming!" I yelled angrily. I padded down the stairs, reaching up to pull my hair into a ponytail as I headed straight for the door.

My hand was on the handle, pushing it down and yanking the door open before I even got the chance to gather my thoughts. I briefly regretted not grabbing a jumper as a cold blast of air hit my body and I shivered involuntarily. But then I looked up, and the thought was wiped clean from my mind. In fact, all thoughts were wiped clean from my mind as I stood there, eyes wide, mouth dropped open.

"Rose Valentine," said Theo Lockhart in a whisper, his eyes filled with an intense, desperate panic. "I need your help."

Two

Then Theo walked into my house like he owned the place. He brushed past me in the doorway, his arm lightly touching mine for a second and sending a gentle flurry of shivers down my spine. He didn't even turn to look back at me before heading into another room, disappearing from my sight.

My feet moved of their own accord, following the direction he had taken without any command from my brain. Realising my mouth had been open the entire time, I quickly closed it, and shook my head as if that would clear my thoughts.

He was waiting for me in the lounge, hair dishevelled, clothes dirty, looking worse than I had ever seen him before. A giant duffel bag that looked practically empty was strapped over his body, and his hands gripped it as if it was his last prized possession in the world.

Theo heard the sounds of my footsteps and tilted his head to watch me as I walked into the room. My stomach jolted as I stared into the same eyes that had looked back at me all day – only instead of being on paper, they were in person. I was speechless, my mind whirling. Theo hesitated, opening his mouth to say something and then quickly snapping it shut again. It seemed he was struggling to find the right words as much as I was.

And then, the world started spinning. My breathing grew laboured as I struggled to get a grip on reality. My hand latched on to the first thing it could grab as I desperately tried to steady myself.

"Breathe, Rose," Theo whispered into my ear, and I realised that it was him I was holding on to; I was clutching him like I was drowning and he was the life jacket keeping me from sinking below the water. "Just breathe."

I closed my eyes to try and make the world stop spinning while he continued to speak soothingly into my ears, his voice as smooth as warm honey. "You're fine. It's just a panic attack, Rose. Focus on your breathing."

I found myself listening to him as I concentrated on bringing the air back into my lungs. He held on to me even when the room came back to normal, and my chest stopped rising and falling rapidly. It was only when I opened my eyes and looked into his worried gaze that he let out a small sigh of relief and released me from his grip.

Eventually Theo broke the silence that had settled between us as he shifted his feet around on the carpet beneath him. "Hey, Rose."

"Hi, Theo," I breathed back, my voice sounding as shocked as I felt inside. Now that I had regained control, I could tell he was waiting for a bombardment of questions, waiting for me to ambush him and grill him until he gave me some answers. And I had plenty to ask him. There were so many words on the tip of my tongue just waiting to be said – but then I really noticed how awful he looked.

A lot can change in forty-eight hours, which was evident when I stared at Theo. His face had lost the tanned colour he normally had; it was now pale and sickly. There were bags under his eyes, much worse than mine – which looked like they could droop shut from fatigue any moment now – and his whole body was shivering, his bare arms covered in goose-bumps. Theo was taller than me, but only by a few inches, so I was close enough to see every detail in his face – every crease of worry – and the golden flecks in his green eyes that were normally dazzling were now dull and lifeless.

I knew I couldn't do it; I knew I couldn't give him hell. The irrational side of me was winning, and I felt myself forgetting about all my questions and instead just wanting to help him, like he had just helped me. The questioning could wait until later.

"You look freezing," I said softly. My breathing was normal now, and my voice sounded less strained. His eyes flickered with surprise, but I cut him off before he could speak by adding, "Do you want a cup of tea? I was just about to make some."

His eyes scanned me to check whether I was serious or not. "Are you sure?" he asked, as though I hadn't thought this through before speaking.

"I'll take that as a yes," I said firmly, before heading off to the kitchen without a backward glance. Subdued, Theo followed me into the next room, his eyes burning a hole in my back.

My hands shook as I grabbed two cups from the cupboard, and after a moment of hesitation Theo flicked the kettle on. He took a seat at the breakfast bar while I organised the tea, and I noticed something inquisitive in his gaze.

Perhaps he thought I might try and call the police, or was biding my time until my parents came home from work so that I could turn him in. Or maybe he thought that offering him a cup of tea was my way of buttering him up, so he'd be more willing to spill the beans when I began my inevitable tirade of questions. It probably didn't cross his mind that I didn't care about any of that. That I, Rose, the girl who never put one toe out of line, had totally ignored every well-behaved instinct I had, and all I cared about in that exact moment was making sure that Theo was okay.

I found myself glancing over at him every so often, like I needed constant confirmation that he was actually sitting there. Every time I did our eyes met, and every time I was the first one to look away.

"There you go." I rested the mug in front of Theo, careful to not spill anything. My hands were still shaking, and I quickly hid them behind my back so that he wouldn't notice. "I'll be back in a second."

I didn't wait for his reply before rushing up the stairs. I threw myself into my bedroom and leaned back against the door as it clicked shut behind me. I closed my eyes and waited for the world to stop spinning again. *What are you doing, Rose?* I asked myself, but the answer was still the same: *I don't know.*

I grabbed the hoodie from my desk chair and shoved it on, then went to my wardrobe and looked through the other hoodies I had until my hands latched onto one that was a few sizes too big for me.

Theo was still there when I returned to the kitchen, casually sipping his cup of tea with a small smile on his face. He hastily put the drink down on the table when he noticed me.

"Here." I tossed him the oversized jumper. "Put this on."

He caught it effortlessly, examining it with a grin. "Normally it's the guy who lends the girl his jacket," he pointed out. "Not the other way round."

"Well, you obviously don't have one in there" – I gestured towards his bag – "so you'll have to wear mine instead for now."

His expression quickly morphed from amused to sheepish. "The only one I've got with me is soaked through. In fact, all the clothes I brought with me are soaked. It was raining earlier when you were at school."

"Give it here then. I can dry it for you."

I grabbed the hoodie from him and tossed it into the tumble dryer, casually shrugging off his mutter of thanks. Theo slipped my hoodie on, and it fit him surprisingly well, if not a bit more loosely than it should have. He looked different somehow, and I had the strange feeling that I'd never properly looked at him until now. He was a few inches taller than me and his hair fell into his eyes, just like it did in the photo on the posters. His brown waves had the usual bed-head messiness that suited him perfectly.

"Hey, we're matching," he pointed out in a low mumble. I looked down and, sure enough, I had picked out almost the exact same hoodie as his, just in a smaller size.

"Oh … yeah. My brother gave me that one when he went off to university," I explained, thrown off by his attempt at humour. Theo's own wary smile disappeared, and he nodded at me, letting out an awkward cough. I took a seat opposite him at the breakfast table, taking a sip of my own tea and letting the warm liquid steady my nerves. Theo kept his eyes on me and took another gulp of tea.

At last he took a deep breath and leaned forward in his

chair, his gaze never leaving mine. "You probably have a lot of questions for me."

"I do." I nodded once before placing my cup back on the table. "But I'm still in shock that you're actually here right now."

"I know," Theo agreed, fiddling with the cords on his hoodie. "I can see how it would be extremely confusing for you. But, before you ask me any questions – before you get your answers – I need you to promise me one thing."

I sat up straighter, my curiosity growing. "What?"

"I need you to promise me you won't call the police. Whether I stay here or not."

I sucked in another breath, my mind working overtime as I took in his words. I stared into his eyes and saw right through his outward calm: I saw his fear at the idea of being caught. And although I knew in that moment that I wouldn't call the police, I still leaned forward in my chair, and faced him straight on.

"I don't think you realise this," I said slowly, reaching to let my fingertips trace around the edges of my empty mug, "but by coming here, you've put your fate into my hands. By coming into my house, you've got me involved in something that I don't even know anything about yet. Whatever happens to you is dependent on me – and if I wanted to call the police I could and you know it."

I saw the panic flash in his expression.

"I knew what I was getting myself into," he said. "And trust me, Rose, I didn't want to get you involved. I still don't want you to be involved. That's why, if you want to call the police … if you want to tell anyone about me being here, then I won't risk sticking around. I'll be out of here before your name can get dragged into this."

"But why are you here?"

"Because I need you, Rose." Theo reached over to touch my hand on the mug. "I need your help."

"With what?" I whispered back, almost inaudibly. But Theo heard me – the room was so silent that it was almost like we were in our chemistry class again, doing an experiment without speaking.

"I need a place to stay for a few nights." His eyes searched my face as he waited for his words to sink in. "And I need you to keep quiet about it."

I yanked my hand away from his and sat up in my seat in pure horror. "You can't be serious? This is insane," I muttered, turning my head away from him. "This really is insane."

But what I found more insane than Theo's request were my own actions. I didn't know anything about the situation – where Theo had been, what he had done, why it was even me that he had come to. Every inch of my body was urging me to turn him in, to do the sensible thing and send him back home. Yet there I was, ignoring all of that and instead listening to him speak.

"I know," Theo muttered. "But I wouldn't be asking if I wasn't desperate."

My breathing became shaky again, and I took a minute to compose myself before looking at him questioningly. "Where have you been these past forty-eight hours then?"

"There are some lovely allotments a few miles away with a great array of abandoned sheds to sleep in."

"You slept in a mouldy shed?"

An image of him lying down in the corner of a dark, damp hut in only a jacket and jeans forced its way into my head, and I shuddered, freezing just at the thought of it.

17

"And then I came back into town in the day." Theo paused for a moment, before adding, "I saw all of you out there helping, you know. You were handing out flyers."

"Because we were all worried about you," I replied. "Turns out that was obviously a waste of time."

He cringed. I felt bad immediately after saying it – it was clear to me that Theo hadn't considered that his sudden absence would put any strain on others' lives. Nevertheless, he sat up straighter a second later, his eyes filled with stubborn determination.

"Sorry … I guess. But I'm not going back home, Rose," he said, his eyes boring into mine so that I could see the pure honesty they were filled with.

"Why can't you go back?" I asked. "What happened?"

And, just like that, I watched Theo withdraw from me. Any barriers I may have opened between us were suddenly shut as he released my hand and moved backwards, closing the conversation off before it had even really started. "I can't tell you that."

"Why not?"

"Because you don't want to be involved, right? It doesn't matter now anyway, I just need to figure out what to do next."

I stilled, a thousand different scenarios filling my head.

"Why me then?" I felt my cheeks flush with warmth the moment I said it, and I saw his eyes flicker to the ground.

"What do you mean?"

"I mean …" I struggled to get my words across. I wanted to know why he had come to me – why he was asking for *my* help – but I was hesitant to ask, not sure if I wanted to hear his answer. "Why did you pick me if you aren't even going to tell me why you're running away? Why do you think I'll help you?"

A sad, bitter smile tugged at Theo's lips. "Think about it, Rose. I don't exactly have many people I can turn to." Before I could respond, he added, "Besides, even if there were others, you would have been my first choice."

"But why?" I started to feel insecure underneath his piercing gaze. "We barely spoke to one another at school. I didn't even think you *liked* me ..."

I thought back to all the times at school when Theo had ignored me and everyone around him. I'd always felt something a bit like pity for Theo, but maybe it had stemmed from my need to be liked. Within our first few chemistry lessons together I realised I was never going to get more than a few words out of him at a time. When I'd asked if he wanted to sit with me and my friends at lunch and he had politely refused, only to proceed to his normal solitary spot in the corner of the dining hall, I knew that this was probably how Theo wanted things. Theo liked being a loner; it suited him, and he'd rejected my friendly advances because he wanted to stay that way.

But he wasn't uncomfortable to be around. He paid interest to me during chemistry experiments, his eyes intently watching me when I spoke and his attention never breaking. He'd clearly sussed my control-freak tendencies, and would always retrieve the equipment we needed for each experiment and wait for me to tell him how he could assist. He would often copy my homework when he thought I wasn't looking, but I'd always thought it was kind of cute. I remembered that sometimes, just sometimes, it did actually seem like Theo wanted to get to know me, and even though our conversations were always short and snappy, I felt like we understood each other.

"I dunno, I guess you're ... different." Theo shrugged. "You just always seemed like a nice person. I figured if anyone was

19

going to hear me out before sending me away, it would be you. You've always been nice to me at school, and I know I'm not always the easiest person to be around."

"Well, I think everyone should get a chance to explain themselves," I mumbled, averting my eyes in embarrassment.

In that moment, I prepared myself to say no. To tell him that I couldn't help him – I didn't even know where to begin and it wasn't my problem. And that I didn't feel comfortable breaking the rules, especially when I didn't even know what he had done in the first place. I could be harbouring a criminal for all I knew!

But instead, as I opened my mouth to tell him that I simply wasn't the right girl for the job, I spluttered, "So what ... what do we do then? Do I hide you up in my room away from my parents until you can go back home?"

There was a long silence. I watched Theo in his chair; disbelief and shock crossed his features. He looked so bewildered that I thought it might be a while before he'd be able to speak again, but his words filled the room a second later.

"You're going to help me?"

I shrugged helplessly, still astonished at the decision I had made. "I can't just let you sleep outside in the cold for ever, can I? And I know you won't let me just call the police –"

"If you do that, I'm out of here," Theo cut me off. "Seriously, Rose, if you want to do that –"

"I don't. Didn't I just say that I want to help you?" I interrupted him sharply.

And I did. I knew this was ridiculous; I knew the consequences of my actions, the effort that it was going to take, and how hard it was going to be to keep the secret. For once, I didn't know how things would turn out. I didn't actually know anything – how long it would go on for, why it was happening. Yet I still found myself agreeing to it. There was something in Theo's eyes – that same something that had transfixed me earlier that day – that told me that I had to help him, that turning him away would be the wrong decision.

Perhaps I hadn't thought it through enough; perhaps I would regret it later. But I had never done anything risky before in my life, and maybe now was the time to live in the moment. Maybe it was time to start saying yes.

"This is only temporary, right?" I confirmed. "I don't want you to end up staying here for weeks on end, when my parents could literally catch you any second."

Theo shook his head firmly. "It'll only be a few days, I swear. I just need some time to get my head straight. And besides, Rose, I promised you before that your name wouldn't get dragged into this, and I'm going to keep my word."

I nodded once more, clicking my tongue on the roof of my mouth. He watched me just like he had before, but there was something else in his eyes this time. Hope. Hope that maybe I would be different, hope that maybe, just this once, I would break the rules, and all for him.

"Are you sure there's nothing I can do to persuade you to talk to your parents? If you just went back home and faced up to whatever you've done wrong –"

My voice trailed off.

"I can't do that, Rose. I just can't." He sounded so distressed that I reached forward and took hold of his hand.

As soon as we made contact, Theo stiffened up again, and I wondered if he would pull away from me. But instead, he just gripped tighter, his shoulders relaxing.

"It's all right," I said softly, giving his hand a squeeze. "We can talk about this later."

"Thanks," Theo said. His voice still sounded strained, but his eyes, catching mine, were filled with relief and gratitude.

And, in that moment, it all seemed fine. I had found the boy who was lost, and I was actually glad he was with me. In that moment, I was actually proud of myself for taking a risk, for pushing myself out of my comfort zone.

I should have known that feeling wouldn't last.

Three

It was only after we had made our agreement and Theo mentioned he was tired that I realised just how awkward the whole set-up was going to be.

He followed me up the stairs, and we padded to my bedroom. I immediately went over to the curtains and yanked them shut, blocking out the twinkling stars in the night sky, then turned to the fairy lights that hung around my room. I flicked them all on so that they illuminated the room with their glow.

"I can sleep on the floor," Theo said. His voice was soft, but it still made me jump.

I suddenly noticed how little space there was in the room. My double bed took up most of it, and the wardrobe and desk took up what was left, meaning the only area left big enough for Theo to squeeze into was right beside my bed.

There was no other room in the house he could have slept in. My brother Brent's room had been turned into an office by my parents when he left, and we had no guest rooms.

When my parents had both started making more money they had considered moving to a bigger house, but at the time I'd rejected their offer, liking the cosiness of our little house and the comfort it provided when I was home alone. Right now I regretted that decision.

"All right," I replied, turning around to face him. He lingered in the doorway, seeming unwilling to enter without my permission. "You can come in and make yourself comfortable. I'll just go to Brent's old room and see if I can get you a sleeping bag and some pyjamas."

Theo had now entered the room and was scanning my extremely full bookshelf with curiosity. As I spoke, he turned to me and said, "Just the pyjamas please. I've still got my sleeping bag from the allotments." And, as if to prove his point, he reached into his giant duffel bag and pulled it out proudly.

"Right." I forced a smile at him, and then moved towards the door. "Be back in a sec."

My brother had taken most of his clothes with him to university, so there wasn't much to choose from as I riffled through the only remaining chest left in the room after the refurbishment, but I did manage to grab a pair of tracksuit bottoms and a shirt that would fit Theo. I grabbed myself another shirt to wear (I'd decided I didn't want Theo to see me in my normal pyjamas, which were a bit on the skimpy side), and then headed straight back to my own room.

Theo was making himself comfortable when I got back, his sleeping bag already out and unrolled, ready for him to climb into. He looked up as I entered, a smile forming on his face.

I tossed him the clothes and, after muttering his thanks, he examined them with a frown. "Oh, I don't need these." He handed me the tracksuit bottoms. "I only wear boxers to bed."

I shook my head at him, and shoved the tracksuit bottoms back into his open arms. "Not in my house, you don't."

For a moment he just stared at me, as if he was trying to work out whether I was joking or not. But then he just shrugged and stripped down to his boxers, changing his shirt and shoving on the bottoms a second later. I tore my eyes away from his bare chest a second too late, glimpsing his lean muscles ripple when he reached up to pull the shirt over his head. He changed so quickly that I didn't even have the chance to blush at the fact he'd literally just stripped in front of me.

I blinked in surprise. "Right. Well, I'm just going to go and change myself." I motioned to the bathroom. "I'll be one minute. Don't mess anything up while I'm gone."

He smirked and muttered something back but I didn't listen to him as I strolled into my bathroom, shutting the door behind me and locking it for good measure. I changed quicker than I ever had before, cringing when I caught sight of myself in the mirror and saw my bushy hair and flushed face. I attempted to brush the messy knots out, regretting not drying my hair straight like I normally did, and then threw it up into a loose bun. I felt a strange rush of adrenaline coursing through me as I stared back at myself. What was I doing?

Theo was clearly waiting for me as I walked back into my room. He looked up at me, a small smile tugging at his lips. "Do you always wear clothes that are too big for you?"

I looked down at the giant T-shirt that I had picked earlier. "It's more comfortable." I shrugged. "And they're not mine – most of what I wear at home used to be my brother's."

"Do you miss him?" Theo asked.

I felt my eyes shift over to the corkboard hanging by my wall. A photo of Brent and me that was taken last year rested in the middle. We were both laughing in it. His arms were wrapped around me in a hug and our faces were carefree and happy. "The house is a lot emptier," I admitted, before adding, "But I'm used to it now. He comes home as often as he can anyway."

He nodded in understanding, although as an only child I'm sure he probably didn't get it so much.

When my brother left for Durham University a year ago, I have to admit, it was a lonely experience. My parents' jobs had become increasingly demanding since they had been made partners at the firm, and Brent and I had learned to take care of ourselves. It had been just the two of us for as long as I could remember, and he always took care of me, no matter how much of a pain I may have been. So when he was gone I spent many months lonely in an empty house, wishing he would come back. But it was a natural part of growing up, and we had both known the day would come when I'd have to fend for myself. And fend for myself I did.

But with Theo in my house, I would no longer be taking care of just myself – I would be taking care of him too. We might be the same age, but he wasn't going to be able to do anything for himself; he was going to be confined to my room for a few days, and I was the only one who was going to know about it.

"Right." I cleared my throat, heading over to the duffel bag he had tossed onto my bed and shoving it underneath instead. "I think a few ground rules need to be set. Number one" – I gestured towards my bed – "you aren't allowed on my bed at all."

Theo grumbled something under his breath, but I chose to ignore it and continued on. "Number two" – I lifted up the covers at the corner of the bed to show him the space underneath it, where his duffel bag was currently placed – "if anyone tries to come in here, you need to get under there immediately."

"And number three" – I had saved the most important for last, and I hoped Theo would realise it too – "in the time that you are here, you can never leave my bedroom. There's too high a risk of you getting caught."

"All right." Theo shrugged like my conditions weren't a big deal. "But what if I do break any of these rules?"

I knew he was baiting me – I obviously wasn't doing a good job at being the slightest bit intimidating. But I found myself playing along, and I stepped closer to him with what I hoped was a dark expression.

"You don't want to know the answer to that, Theodore."

A smirk started to spread across Theo's lips but, being as practised at hiding his feelings as he was, he managed to fight it off his face. I saw amusement dancing in his eyes and wondered if my own looked the same.

And then, for a split second, I could have sworn that his eyes dropped lower, resting on my lips. But then, in the next blink, they were back on my eyes, leaving me to conclude that I must have imagined it. It must never have happened.

Theo opened his mouth to speak, but the noise of a door opening cut him off. Or, more specifically, the noise of my front door opening.

Because my parents were finally home.

It was like all the panic I had pent up inside of me was suddenly released as I stared into Theo's equally bewildered expression. Both of us remained frozen, listening intently to the noises downstairs. I could hear the faint murmur of my parents chatting, and the sounds of footsteps as they walked around.

Theo suddenly grabbed my arm. I jumped on the spot and snapped my head towards him.

"Does your room have a lock?" he asked quietly.

I nodded, unable to make a sound, and he padded over to the door and turned the key in the lock, trying to make as little noise as possible.

"There," he said softly. "As long as we can keep them out of this room, they'll never need to know I'm in here."

I found myself nodding, but my feet still didn't move. I was trapped on the spot. The sudden realisation of what I was doing – of what *we* were doing – had hit me, and I wondered if I'd be able to hide a secret this big.

Theo picked up on my emotions right away and stepped closer to me, before deciding against his actions and awkwardly shuffling backwards again. "Hey, it's all right," he said, his voice hushed and soothing. "It's going to be fine, Rose. They're not going to find out about me being in here. You're not going to be involved in this."

"But I can't lie, Theo. I can't lie to save my life," I admitted, finally finding my voice. "What am I going to do?"

Theo's expression told me everything: it showed me the clear, cold truth. "Then you'll just have to practise, Rose. Or else we'll be in a lot more trouble than we ever anticipated."

I had always been, by nature, a very controlling person. Rules and planning were what grounded me, what made me feel like I had some kind of control of my life when everything else felt unstable. I was the type of person who overanalysed everything too – the type who left post-it notes all over the pages of every book I read, jotting down hints at a character's personality and trying to figure them out. And that's what I was trying to do that first night; I was trying to analyse Theo in excruciating detail, because I needed to figure him out – I needed to have more information – to feel like I had some control over the situation after all.

But, in reality, it was more likely because I'd never been able to understand the enigma that is Theo Lockhart, and it really frustrated me. He was like an intricate puzzle – one of those jigsaws that had hundreds of thousands of pieces and could make your head spin when trying to fit them all together.

Rolling over in bed later that night, I snuck a look at him. His brown hair was sprawled out across the pillow on which he rested his head, his eyes were closed and a murmur of light snores escaped his mouth. He looked snug wrapped up in his sleeping bag on the floor of my bedroom, and it hadn't taken him long at all to fall into a deep slumber.

I, unfortunately, wasn't finding sleep as easily. This was a common occurrence for me – sleep and I were never on the best of terms. It would take me hours of tossing and turning in my sheets every night before I could finally fall into oblivion, and I would often find myself tired the next day because of it.

But that night was a whole new experience, a whole new chapter of insomnia. And, as I watched the time on my alarm clock flicker as it changed every minute, I couldn't help but let my eyes drift over to Theo's sleeping form every now and again.

So maybe the feeling of my eyes burning a hole into the side of his head was why he suddenly turned over, his head lifting up from his pillow and his green eyes shining as he whispered softly, "Stop overthinking it, Rose."

My entire body stiffened, although my head was still able to linger on the pillow as I looked back down at him. "How did you know I was still awake?"

"Because I can literally hear the cogs in your brain working overtime." There was a pause, and I wondered if he had perhaps fallen back to sleep. But then I heard a loud exhale, and glanced over to see him drop his head back down onto his pillow. "You don't need to worry about everything right now. It's all going to be fine."

It was like he was able to read my mind. I was taken aback for a moment, unsure of what to say, but I quickly blurted, "Do you not realise how many things could go wrong with this? For starters, you seem to forget that there are two other people living in this house who don't know about you being here."

"And I told you before – you don't have to worry about being involved," Theo whispered back, his voice sleepy but intense. "I already told you that I won't let you get involved."

I rolled on to my back and stared up at the blank ceiling. There was some shifting and shuffling from the room next to mine, and I felt my breathing hitch as I worried that we had made too much noise. Nothing seemed to follow after that, though, and I felt myself relax again.

"But how will you make sure I'm not involved?" I asked Theo.

"Go to sleep, Rose."

And I thought that would have been the end of the conversation for the night. But then Theo raised his head to look at me once again, mischief lacing his features. "Unless you want me to join you up there?"

I was grateful for the darkness – as Theo couldn't see how

red my cheeks flared. "Of course I don't!" I snapped, but I felt a flutter in my stomach.

"Are you sure?" His grin widened, and he sat up further. "Because I've heard that a lot of people who have insomnia often only need a snuggle buddy –"

"A snuggle buddy?" I felt myself laugh. "What are we, five years old?"

Theo snorted. His messy bedhead curls fell on to his face as he moved around in the sleeping bag to find a new comfortable spot, but I could still see his eyes, and the wicked glint he held in them.

"Well, I'm just saying. The floor isn't exactly comfortable."

"Doesn't seem to me like you've got any other options," I cut him off flatly. "Goodnight, Theo."

Theo was still grinning when his head hit the pillow and his eyes closed automatically. "Goodnight, Rose," he mumbled back, before I watched him fall straight back to sleep once more, leaving me to stare into the darkness on my own, even more wide awake than before.

The next day was filled with lies.

The first lie occurred literally just after I woke up. My parents were still home when I got up, both of them dressed for work as they struggled together to make breakfast for us all. I had to make up a lie about being starving when I was too nervous to even eat a single bite myself, just so I could get some food into the napkin that was grasped in my hands under the table and bring it up to Theo afterwards.

After that, it was just more and more lies – so many that my brain was already starting to ache from the worry about all the ways this could go wrong. And none of it was for my benefit either.

It was all for Theo.

"If you want to call it quits, Rose," he had said softly earlier that morning, "if helping me gets too much for you, just say the word and I'll be out of here in five minutes."

But I knew I couldn't do that. I knew that whatever had made me open the door to Theo, whatever had made me agree to let him stay, hadn't disappeared overnight. He was desperate, I could see that. But part of me wanted him to stay so that I could help him, so that I could find out what he'd done. I wanted to understand him. And so the lying continued on throughout the day.

I'm sure I looked exhausted as I entered my house after a long day of school and helping with the search for the missing boy who was currently sitting in my bedroom. I'm sure I looked as awful as I felt, but Theo didn't comment as I opened the bedroom door.

"You all right?" he asked instead, his features laced with concern.

He was sitting on his sleeping bag and had clearly just showered, as his wet hair was dripping. My television, which was attached to the wall, was turned on, and he held a book, which he must have plucked off my bookshelf earlier.

"Fine," I replied curtly, not bothering to look at him as I headed over to my wardrobe and pulled out a towel.

He dropped the book onto my bedside table, stood up and lingered on the spot for a second, looking sheepish. "You know, you don't have to keep searching for me –"

"I do," I cut him off. "If I stopped helping the others search for you, they'd know something was up."

32

"I know," Theo replied, his voice quiet. "I just ... never mind."

I didn't bother trying to pick up on where he had left off, instead going over to one of my drawers and pulling out a new bottle of shampoo. I slung my towel over my shoulder and finally turned around to look at him properly. "I'm going to have a shower. Do you need anything before I go in there?"

He shook his head, and with that, I walked briskly out of my bedroom and into the bathroom. I slammed the door shut and leaned against it for a moment, letting my eyes close as I took a chance to catch my breath. The fatigue was slowly settling in, and already one day of carrying around this secret had ruined my mood.

I could barely stand up in the shower, my feet constantly slipping on the wet tiles. I blindly stumbled back out again and wrapped a towel around me before heading back out to Theo in my room.

His eyes widened when he noticed I hadn't yet got changed, and he cleared his throat awkwardly. "I'll just go in there to give you some space," he barely managed to say before he sprinted to the bathroom.

My cheeks reddened as I snapped back to my senses, and I quickly grabbed the first appropriate clothes that I found in my wardrobe and shoved them on, calling out to Theo when I was decent. He slipped back into the room, his cheeks a cute shade of pink.

"What do you want for dinner? I can cook for the both of us," I said, stifling a yawn as I headed over to my door to go back downstairs.

Theo stepped in front of me, placing a hand on each of my shoulders and walking me backwards towards the bed. "You need to sleep, Rose," he said.

I tried to move sideways but he grasped tighter.

"I'm fine. Seriously, Theo."

"No, you're not," he mumbled, holding my gaze.

I protested half-heartedly under my breath as he led me over to my bed and sat me down on it. Calm and firm, he lifted my legs up onto the mattress so that I was lying down.

Theo was a boy I felt like I barely knew and yet there he was, gently putting my pillow under my head and covering me up with one of my blankets. "What are you doing?" I asked sleepily, already feeling myself start to drift off.

"Helping you out," Theo said gruffly, as he reached over to cover my shoulders with the top of the blanket. "It's the least I can do considering all that you've done, and are doing for me right now."

I could barely keep my eyes open. It was a struggle to keep a grip on everything that was going on around me, but I managed a dozy smile as I looked up at him. "Thank you."

And, as I started to fall further and further, I could still sense that Theo hadn't moved from where he was standing. He was there next to me, and I drowsily wondered whether he was watching over me, making sure I was actually going to go to sleep. It made me smile because, even though it was a small gesture, it showed to me that Theo actually cared, and that mattered to me more than I thought it ever would.

Four

I ended up sleeping most of the night, a gift which left me feeling more rested than I had been for days. I woke up early, and after an endless hour of tossing and turning and trying to fall asleep again, I decided it was futile. So, instead, my feet hit the soft rug that covered my bedroom floor and I lifted myself up, before heading over to my window and yanking the curtains open.

I opened a window and the sound of birdsong filled my ears. I smiled and listened, the sound of their cheeps and chirps calming me.

"Rose." Theo's voice interrupted my thoughts, and I jumped before turning round to look at him. He was sprawled out in his sleeping bag, his hair wild, and his half-closed eyes sleepy and irritated.

"Morning, Theo," I said cheerfully, a grin making its way onto my face.

He grumbled and sat up, his body still wrapped in his sleeping bag as he turned towards me. "What the hell is the time?"

I glanced at the clock on my bedside table. "Six thirty."

He blinked. "Then why the hell are we awake?"

I couldn't stop my smirk from widening, and I let his crude language slide as I stepped away from the window and headed over to grab a sweatshirt from my dresser so that I could cover my bare arms. "Well, I'm going to go downstairs and grab some breakfast because I can't sleep any longer, and it's been about" – I paused to calculate in my head – "twelve hours since I last ate."

"Aren't you worried about waking your parents up?" Theo asked, reaching up to rub at his eyes in a lame attempt to wake himself up more.

"Oh, they're already gone." I gestured towards the window, where I'd already observed that their cars were missing from the drive. "Or else I wouldn't be going downstairs, because they go crazy when I disturb their sleep."

"How nice of you to consider that others are still asleep before you go and make a disturbance that wakes them up too," he muttered dryly. I shrugged and walked out of the room before he could make another surly comment.

I had expected Theo to go back to sleep once I left the room, but his voice rang out from upstairs as I headed into the kitchen to make myself some toast.

"Hey," he called down, his voice echoing through the house. "Since your parents aren't here, am I allowed to break that rule about me never leaving your bedroom so I can grab a bit of breakfast myself?"

I shrugged, not seeing the harm in it, before I realised he couldn't see me. "I guess so," I called back. "But this is not a common occurrence. Don't start getting cocky and coming down here all the time just because my parents aren't in the house. They could come back at any second."

Theo practically bounded into the kitchen, looking excited to be in a different space to the one he had been cooped up in for the last two nights. He headed straight over to me and grabbed the bread out of my hands, before shoving the two slices into the toaster.

"I was using that –" I started to protest, but he cut me off.

"I'm making the food today. No offence, but I can't imagine you being the best cook."

I was actually a pretty good cook, but I let his comment slide as I felt a smile make its way back onto my face for the second time that morning. For the first time in ages I sat back and let somebody else make me some food. And it was nice to take a break – or at least it was, up until Theo managed to burn my toast.

There are some moments in life that you can never predict.

Life is fragile. It has twists and turns that can leave you breathless and render you powerless, until you no longer feel like you have control over your own fate. Our lives sometimes feel too intricate to have happened by chance; they're too complex to be a simple string of random events, and yet it doesn't feel as though we have any control over them ourselves.

I think that's what I struggled with the most: I hated feeling powerless. I hated having no control. But sometimes, I was discovering, it was impossible to have any control.

Like I've said, I was the kind of girl who loved planning – the kind of person who loved to set everything out in great detail. I liked a routine, I stuck to the rules, I had a plan for the next five years of my life. I'd always known what I wanted; I planned for everything long before others had even thought of it. When our teachers told us to start looking at universities, I had already researched subjects, schools, and selected my top three choices. My homework was always the first to be handed in, I never missed a day of school so that I wouldn't fall behind on any lessons, and I'd decided that I wanted to be a teacher when I was only seven years old. Everything was all lined up; I just had to stick to the plan. I guess you could say that made me boring, but I didn't enjoy searching for the unknown – and my brain felt like it was too set in its ways to be knocked off track.

But after Theo arrived, something felt different. Something about Theo had made me want to leap into the unknown. I wasn't thinking about my five-year plan – all I was thinking about was how to get through the next few days without our frankly bizarre situation exploding on us. Theo and I were like two ships that were used to passing each other without any interaction, but now we had crashed into one another and were trying desperately not to sink.

"Here you go." Grace and Naya grinned together as they watched my expression change once I caught sight of the double chocolate muffin they had placed on the lunch table in front of me. Hands still intertwined tightly, they plopped themselves down onto the two seats opposite me, but I barely noticed – I was too busy reaching out and yanking the muffin towards me.

"You know," I said to Naya through a mouthful of muffin, "I think this is the first time you've ever paid me back for something."

Naya shrugged, flicking loose strands of her long, straight black hair out of her face. "You've been out of sorts this whole week, so I thought it might cheer you up."

I brushed a few crumbs off the table, swallowed loudly, and replied, "I have not been out of sorts. If anything, your constant PDA has been putting me off my food."

But we all knew it was more than that. The contentment I had felt earlier in the morning eating Theo's burnt toast was now long gone, disappearing in the chaos of school and draining away further with each lie I had to tell.

This included lying to my two best friends. It was too risky for me to tell them about Theo hiding in my bedroom. But he had been in there for two nights now, and it was getting difficult to explain my odd mood as the days wore on.

"You know PDA is banned at school," Grace reminded me, raising one perfectly shaped eyebrow. "So that's not the reason."

I shrugged, looking away from them and back down at the table where my half-eaten muffin rested. I didn't have to look up to see the exchange of glances Grace and Naya shared with one another; I knew them so well, and they were so in sync, that I could easily predict how they would react to any sort of situation.

"Have we done something to upset you?" Grace asked softly, her tone making me snap my head back up to meet her worried gaze.

She took her hand out of Naya's and reached across the table to grasp mine instead. "Because if you've been feeling like a third wheel, then all you have to do is tell us. We won't be offended. You can even come with us on some date nights if you want, it wouldn't be weird –"

"Grace, it's not that. Really. You and Naya going out without me hasn't ever been a problem, and it never will be," I interjected.

Grace's shoulders sagged with relief, but Naya's expression was still laced with concern. "Then what is it?"

"Nothing." I had to break my gaze away from them when they both shot me the same flat look. "It's seriously nothing," I continued. "I'm more than fine. Neither of you need to worry about me."

It was clear neither of them believed me as they sat back and scrutinised me. They were polar opposites in looks. Grace had blonde hair, blue eyes, and fair skin that was marked with moles and freckles, whereas Naya was of Indian heritage and had black hair, brown eyes and a darker skin tone. But their personalities were extremely similar. Both of them were smart and practical thinkers, and while Grace was more dramatic and defensive, Naya's calming nature grounded her. They were a couple that I was envious of, and I aspired to have a relationship like theirs with someone one day. I had been friends with both Grace and Naya for years – before they even started dating – and they were always able to tell when something was up with me.

The only thing that worried me, as I tried to avoid their stares, was that eventually they'd be able to guess what that something was, and I knew that if they even got close to the truth there was no way I'd be able to lie to them about it. I comforted myself with the fact that the truth was so ridiculous it would never even cross their minds, but it didn't do much to cheer me up.

So, instead of panicking, I forced a smile and grabbed my muffin once again, taking a big bite and closing my eyes in mock satisfaction. But the chocolaty dough was like glue in my mouth, and I struggled to swallow it as my guilt bubbled to the surface.

"All right." Grace finally gave up, shaking her head like she always did when something got too much for her. "We'll let it go." She leaned forward so that she could catch my gaze once again, and there was no mistaking the sincerity in her eyes as she added, "But we're always here for you, Rose. So when you're ready to talk about it, you know where to come."

And, just like that, the guilt consumed me whole. I was touched by how much my two friends cared for me, but felt so bad that I couldn't tell them what was bothering me.

Because I knew I couldn't, not then. Not with everything that was at stake. I didn't know what I was gaining from keeping Theo's secret safe; all I knew was that I felt deep down that there was too much to lose if I didn't.

It's fair to say that I was shocked to find my mother waiting for me in the lounge when I came home later that day.

It had been a common occurrence when I was younger – she would come home early every Friday when I was at primary school and wait until I came bursting through the door so that she could hear all about my day. We'd watch films and cuddle together on one sofa, stuffing our faces with chocolate and popcorn, talking about everything and anything.

It had been a tradition, a time for us to bond without any boys. My brother and father were never invited to our cinema sessions: they were our thing and our thing only.

But as I got older and progressed to secondary school, and my mother's career really took off, our film Fridays were just one of the things that fizzled out between us. And with that, our relationship deflated as well.

And yet there she was, wrapped in a blanket in her old spot on that same sofa, her legs curled up and her hands already

41

claiming chocolate buttons to pop into her mouth. A box of old films rested on the coffee table, a packet of popcorn placed next to it. It was a completely nostalgic moment for me, seeing her sitting waiting for my arrival.

It only lasted a minute though, and then I snapped back to reality, remembering that I wasn't that same little girl who used to watch films every Friday with her mother – and that she wasn't the same woman who did that with me.

She looked up as I walked tentatively into the room, a large smile brightening her face. "Hey, you," she said cheerfully, beckoning me over. "Fancy watching a film?"

"What is this?" I asked as I took a few steps closer towards her, like a wary animal approaching a hand outstretched in greeting. "Aren't you meant to be at work?"

My mother shrugged, shifting on the sofa to make more room for me. "We finished our case early, and I thought I'd take the rest of the afternoon off so I could come home and do this with you, just like old times."

Back then, I was used to my parents being at work more often than they were at home. They'd always been very career-driven, and they'd always worked long hours. But it was only in the last few years, as Brent and I got older and they were able to focus more on their work and less on their kids, that I realised we had drifted apart completely. Sometimes it felt like we lived on different planets; we never spent any time together any more, and even though we lived together we didn't have anything to do with each other's lives. They didn't take the time to call Brent at university, and I was pretty sure they couldn't name a single one of my friends or teachers. In the same way, we didn't ask about their work any more. Neither Brent nor I would be able to say what our parents were working on right now. We were strangers living under the same roof, and that realisation stung.

So, seeing her at home, actually trying to spend time with me, made me hesitant. I narrowed my eyes slightly, staring at her and feeling lost for words. She seemed to notice my uncertainty, but didn't let it faze her as she patted the space next to her on the sofa. "Come sit."

I moved forward and took a seat, feeling weirdly stiff and awkward. She grabbed the remote to turn on the TV then leaned forward to rummage around in the box on the table.

"We've got all sorts of things in here," she murmured, pulling out a couple of old DVDs and handing them to me. "Any preference?"

I looked down at one of the disks in my hands, an unfamiliar emotion starting to rise deep inside me – a strange mix of nostalgia and longing. "Actually, I believe it's your turn to pick," I replied, my voice thick. We always used to take turns to choose the film we watched, so as not to be unfair, and I could still remember picking the last film – *The Little Mermaid* – before we stopped our tradition for good.

My mother's mouth dropped open in shock. "You still remember that?" she asked, her eyes twinkling with the recollection.

I simply nodded.

"All right then." My mother turned away from me again to look back into the box. She spent some time rummaging around, muttering a few things under her breath as she tried to make her decision.

I realised how hard she was actually trying – how much she wanted to make this work. To her, picking a film wasn't just simply picking a film; it was the only way she knew how to connect with me again. And that made my heart swell. It made me feel like I was still loved. She was trying, and that was more than enough for me.

My mother then turned to me, and her smile morphed into a wicked grin as her eyes flashed with excitement. "These are all quite old films," she said, and I could tell where this was going. "How about we watch something else instead?"

"What were you thinking?" I asked, but I knew my mother well enough to already guess what her answer was going to be.

And then I watched as her eyes flashed again, making her look younger, making her look almost exactly like the woman who used to sit next to me in the same exact spot, picking the movie of her choice. It didn't matter that she was in a suit, and it didn't matter that her hair was wrapped into a tight bun on the top of her head, instead of loosely cascading down to her shoulders like it used to. Because she was there, and I could see now that she was still the same woman of my memories. I just didn't get to see that woman as much.

"I was thinking a horror film?" she suggested, and I felt a grin make its way on to my face.

It was the perfect choice. Because while it might not have been a choice she would have made before, it showed how much things had changed. I was no longer that ten-year-old who would only watch Disney films – I was an adult. Yet that little girl was still inside me – just like the mum I knew was still inside her.

"I can't think of anything better," I replied, and her smile immediately mirrored mine.

Despite my promise not to, I couldn't help but let out a loud burst of laughter when my mother hid her face behind the cushion she had picked up earlier, her face pale but her eyes glimmering with tears of laughter.

"Oh God, I can't look," she muttered.

"It's not that bad," I responded, but even I was struggling to keep watching the screen. "At least it's only one of her eyes that's missing."

My comment only made my mother squirm in her chair and let out another loose giggle. Her hair was starting to fall out of her bun and her suit looked crinkled. I laughed along with her, throwing my head back and wiping my eyes.

And then the moment was ruined.

My mother and I both screamed, and her hands reached up to clutch her chest. Her face was pale with horror, and I felt my own heart pounding from shock.

My mother snapped her head towards the stairs, her eyes wide. "What was that?"

It was a loud bang that had come from upstairs.

I had admittedly forgotten about Theo when my mother and I were bonding and messing around eating chocolate and scaring ourselves silly – all without a care in the world. But as soon as she spoke, reality came crashing down on me, forcing me back to the real world and the very real stowaway hiding right above our heads.

"I don't know," I replied.

She went to stand and my heart leaped inside my chest. I knew if she went upstairs, then it was probably all over – she'd go into my room, see Theo, and everything would be finished. I reacted instantly, standing up with her, losing my balance slightly and tipping forward.

"I'll go," I said, touching her arm to get her to stop. "Something probably fell in my bedroom. I'll just go and check it out."

To my relief my mother stopped moving, but she frowned at me. "I don't mind checking."

I was being obvious, but I was too worked up to try and control it now. I shook my head, trying to cover my nerves with a forced laugh. "It's fine. I'll be back in a minute."

Theo was standing right by my bookcase when I opened my door, one hand tugging on the ends of his hair and the other clasping a book at his side. He turned to me as I walked in, his expression guilty, as if he already knew I'd be coming up and could guess what I was going to say.

"What are you doing?" I hissed, glaring at him as I closed my bedroom door.

"I'm sorry. I was grabbing this and some other books fell with it," he whispered, holding up the book in his hands to show me.

"My mum is downstairs," I said, "and she could come up –"

"Rose?"

I stopped talking, my words getting lodged in my throat as I heard my mother at the bottom of the stairs calling up to me. Theo's eyes widened and he sucked in a breath. Neither of us dared to move or even speak. I raised a finger to my lips, and half ran out of my room to where my mother was standing at the bottom of the stairs, looking up at me.

I was convinced she could detect the panic in my eyes, and she looked at me in confusion. "Everything all right?"

"Yes," I said breathily, desperate to keep my voice neutral. "Just something that fell off my bookcase. Want to watch another film?"

She narrowed her eyes at me, but didn't comment. "Okay," she said. Her tone was suspicious, but she turned around and headed back into the lounge again.

I looked at Theo one last time before shutting the door, my heart beating in double time. He stared me dead in the eye, saying the same thing I was thinking with just a simple look. *That was close.* I knew now that every time my parents were in the house, keeping Theo's existence a secret was going to be twice as hard. We were walking on very thin ice, and it was inevitable that, soon enough, one of us was going to make it crack.

Five

When Theo decided to tell me later that evening that he sometimes talked in his sleep, I was worried. Scenarios of my parents hearing a boy muttering things in my room late at night immediately crossed my mind and made every little thing seem much, much scarier. As it stood, the only time we were safe from discovery was at night when everyone was asleep.

"You worry too much," he muttered when I started drilling him with questions about his sleeping habits, my mind going into overdrive. He was sitting on my chair, his feet propped on my desk. He turned the page of the book he was reading, as he tried to ignore my constant pacing around the room. "I hardly do it any more anyway. It's only when I'm having a particularly good or bad dream, that's all."

Maybe I did worry too much, but it was a habit of mine. We all have bad habits – mine definitely overthinking – but it's easier said than done to try and turn them off.

It was Theo's sleep talking that woke me up early the very

next morning. At first, it sounded like rubbish. He muttered a couple of things – quite loudly – and let out another snore before quietening down again. I closed my eyes every time he stopped, hoping to fall back to sleep, but less than a minute later he would start back up again, spluttering out more incoherent gibberish that did little to soothe my worries.

But the longer he talked the more sense his words made, until he said something that was so clear in the quiet of the morning that I felt my own heart stop beating for a second.

"Rose ..."

I jolted up in my bed at the sound of my name escaping from his lips, my eyes flicking towards him to see if he was still sleeping. Sure enough, Theo lay in the exact same spot as before, his eyes tightly shut and his mouth open. He let out a few easy snores before he muttered my name again. "Rose."

It was the way he said it so softly and delicately – like I was at the centre of a good dream – that unleashed a flurry of butterflies deep inside my stomach, and I smiled in spite of myself.

It helped me piece together another part of the jigsaw puzzle that was Theo Lockhart, a puzzle I had been doing since he came to stay three days ago. The picture was getting clearer, and I realised that the more I found out about him, the more I wanted to know. I wanted to know the little things about him. I liked knowing that he can't drink hot chocolate right before bed because it was like a shot of coffee for him, keeping him awake all night. I liked knowing that he was constantly making up rhymes in his head for every little activity, and that he often hummed them to himself as he moved around my bedroom. And I liked knowing that he sometimes talked in his sleep.

I wanted to know everything about Theo. He was a puzzle I was intent on solving.

But he wasn't easy to figure out. Theo Lockhart, despite his new status as my roommate, was still a mystery to me. He always kept to himself. I could see in his eyes that he wanted to keep himself closed off from me, and when we spoke he chose his words carefully, as though afraid he might give too much away. He wanted to remain an enigma because that's what he was used to, what he'd always been. No one really knew him – those who thought they did only really knew *of* him.

To think I didn't even know why he was in my room – I didn't know why he had run away and why he had asked for my help. That was a scary realisation. I was putting everything at risk for him, breaking so many of the rules I'd always followed, and pushing past all of my comfortable boundaries. And I didn't even know what for.

Well, that wasn't quite true – I knew that it was for Theo. It was all for Theo.

I watched him roll around again in his sleeping bag. He muttered my name a few more times before falling back into a deeper slumber, his breathy snores filling the room. But I knew then that sleep wouldn't come for me – and that the butterflies in my stomach wouldn't go away.

"He's looking at you again," Grace muttered into my ear as she shoved a wad of flyers into my hands, her gaze lingering on a spot behind me.

I inclined my head to the left and let my eyes drift over to the side, seeing Tristan standing there in the corner of my vision. He seemed to be hovering off to the side while his friends chatted among themselves as they waited to be sent back off on their search.

"So? Does it matter?" I asked, trying my hardest to keep my voice down.

Grace rolled her eyes and looked at me sternly. "He wants to ask you out."

"W-what?" I spluttered, my cheeks turning a vibrant shade of red. "No he doesn't."

But I knew it was true. It had been like this all week – him watching me whenever he was close enough and coming over to spark up conversations with me. Grace was a constant tease, always making fun of me whenever Tristan wasn't around and making kissy faces behind his back when he was.

"Do you like him? Are you going to say yes if he does ask you out?" she pressed, her eyes never leaving mine.

I opened my mouth and automatically closed it again, at a loss for words. I lowered my gaze and caught sight of the boy looking back at me on the front of the flyer.

"Oh gosh, you do like him." Grace's mouth dropped open. "You're blushing like crazy."

I looked away from her and down at the floor, desperately trying to hide the evidence of my red cheeks by brushing my hair over my face. But it was too late.

"Who would have thought that a boy could make you blush this hard." Grace shook her head, wielding a teasing smirk. "This boy has really got to you."

I started to object to Grace's comment, but the sound of Tristan deciding to call over from his spot cut me off.

"Hey, Rose!"

Grace shot me a coy wink as he headed over to us. She grabbed half of the stack of flyers out of my hands, held them tightly to her body.

Tristan only seemed to notice her a few seconds after he

came over, and his face flickered with a twinge of disappointment. "Oh, hey, Grace. You all right?"

"Never been better thanks, Tristan." She grinned. "In fact, I think it's time for me to go and do my rounds again – I'll see you in a bit, Rose?"

Tristan barely gave her another glance, and she headed off, but not before shooting me yet another horribly obvious wink. I couldn't help but roll my eyes in response and she stifled a giggle before scampering off to catch up with the others doing their rounds.

"So, uh" – Tristan awkwardly raised his hand up to scratch his neck – "are you all right?"

"I'm fine thanks, Tristan," I said, as I glanced at my wristwatch. There wasn't long before the town would be engulfed in darkness once again, and I wanted to make sure I posted all my flyers so I could get back home to Theo as soon as possible. "Did you need my help with something?"

If Tristan was acting awkwardly before, then it was nothing compared to how he was acting now. His feet shuffled constantly on the ground and he stared down at them, licking his lips nervously.

"Actually, I was just making sure that you were doing okay," he said, gathering enough courage to look back up at me. "With everything that we talked about the other day, I mean."

I frowned. "What thing were we talking –" I started, but then my eyes fell back down to the flyers in my hands, and Theo's sombre face answered my question for me. Tristan's gaze followed mine, and I felt him glance back up at me to scrutinise my expression.

"I can't believe it's already been five days since he ..." He

52

trailed off, his sentence hanging unfinished in the air.

I refused to look away from the flyer, my breathing heavy and my heart pumping at an increasing speed with every second that passed. I felt a rush of guilt for knowing that this boy was waiting for me back at home when everyone else was out searching for him, and I supressed a shiver when Tristan took a step closer to me.

"They've been thinking about doing a press conference with his parents," Tristan said, his voice a whisper. "They want more people out looking for him. This might end up becoming much larger than anyone originally thought."

And it was only in that moment right then that I realised just how little time I had left with Theo. All the worrying I had been doing was purely about getting caught – there hadn't been much time to worry about anything else. But the longer that Theo decided to stay, the more attached I felt myself becoming to him. I hadn't really given any thought to the inevitable moment when he would have to go home again; it was almost like I wanted him to never leave, when at the beginning him leaving was the only thing I had wanted.

"Are you all right?"

My head snapped up. I looked into Tristan's concerned eyes and forced a smile. "I'm fine."

He nodded. "You know, I find it touching that you're so worried about him when you two weren't that close. Not that that should have anything to do with it." He cleared his throat. "But not many people are like that, you know? You're a very selfless person, Rose."

I could tell what was coming, and I desperately tried to swerve it any way I could. "Oh, I don't know about that –"

"You are. It's actually one of the reasons why I like you."

Tristan's eyes gleamed with a newfound confidence, and the corner of his lips turned upwards into a small smile. "And it's also why I wanted to ask you out on a date this Friday."

He stared hopefully at me, desperate to gauge a reaction that would answer his question. And yet I found myself unable to look at him in return. The only thing my eyes were able to focus on was the now-crumpled flyers that were still clasped in my hands.

"I'm really sorry, Tristan," I started, finally bringing myself to look back up at him, "but I'm going to have to say no."

"Oh." Tristan tried to mask his surprise and disappointment, but it was hopeless. "Is there a particular reason why?"

"It's not anything to do with you," I assured him, awkwardly, trying to show him the sincerity in my expression. "I just don't think of you in that way."

Tristan looked at me for a moment, an expression that I couldn't translate on his face. And then his eyes flashed with understanding, and he said, "You like someone else."

My mouth dropped open. Tristan smiled knowingly at me, almost as if he thought he could read me better than I could read myself. Before I could object, he held his hand up. "You don't have to explain anything to me, Rose. I don't want to know the details. But it's pretty clear you like someone else."

I was still lost for words, my emotions unknown to me despite them apparently being obvious to Tristan as he looked at me. There was no hint of disappointment on his face any more – just a smug smile as if he knew he'd caught me out.

My mind was whirling. But it was clear Tristan didn't want to hang around and wait for me to work out my feelings for myself, because he spun around a second later to head back to his group, who were calling him over.

"And, Rose" – Tristan stopped and glanced back at me – "you never know – if you stop being in denial and just tell him your feelings, you might find that he likes you back."

Theo pulled himself up from the floor and moved over to my bookshelf to replace the latest book he'd read.

"You know," he said, turning around to look at me lying sprawled out on my bed, "I don't think I've ever told you this before, but I really like your bedroom."

"Is that a joke or something?" I asked, flipping to another page in my biology textbook and scanning through the dense text.

"No," Theo quickly clarified, his eyes still on me as I started answering one of the homework questions. "I just meant that your room is a lot different to what I expected from you – but in a good way."

My bedroom was plain – there was no other way to describe it. Bare walls, all the same shade of cream, a double bed with a white duvet, and a small blue rug covering the centre of the wooden floor. The rest of the furniture – my wardrobe, desk and bookcase – was cream. It wasn't a small room, but I had so much oversized furniture that it all felt crammed into the space. The dominant feature was my bookcase. It was a monster – larger than my wardrobe and crammed full of books of all shapes and sizes. Even the pony magazines that my ten-year-old self had adored still had their place on the shelves.

"Really?" I threw my pen down and sat up to look at him. "What were you expecting?"

He grinned guiltily. "Honestly? Lots of pink. And I thought you'd be a lot more organised than this." He gestured to my desk, which was messily stacked with bits of scrap paper and various pots of pencils and odds and ends. "But it's refreshing to see that you're as much of a scatterbrain as I am."

He walked over to my bookshelf and picked up the first novel on it, flipping it to one of the pages where I had scribbled thousands of annotations. "I never thought you were the type to write all over the books you read, either. In fact, I thought I was the only one who did that."

I shrugged. "To be fair, I would never do it with the books that I absolutely adore, so not all of them are scribbled in. But my mother always used to do it, so I guess I picked up her habit. I only ever use pencil though – no biros or highlighters."

Theo nodded and continued to walk around, stopping when he reached my desk, his eyes scanning over all the bits and pieces littered on its surface. He picked up a couple of pens and placed them back in my pencil pot, and examined the covers of some of the textbooks.

"My room at home is smaller," he said absentmindedly, as he picked up another pen and read the logo on it. "My parents never let me design my own room and because I'm a boy they made everything grey. *Grey?* I never had the heart to tell them that I actually hate the colour." He let out a short laugh.

"Well, this is exactly what the room looked like when we moved into the house," I offered, my own gaze trailing to the cream walls. "I just tried to make it my own, and it ended up becoming really messy instead."

"No," Theo corrected me, "it looks lived in. My father's a bit of a neat freak, so if he saw I'd left a mess anywhere, he'd have a fit. But I think that's part of what makes it your room, you know? You should be able to have it how you want." He turned to me, forcing a smile. "Sorry. It's pretty lame of me to be going on about bedrooms when you're trying to do your homework."

I was, in fact, actually extremely interested to hear about Theo's own bedroom, because it was a chance to hear about his home life for once. But I tried to act casual instead, simply shrugging and picking my pen up to write in my notebook once more.

"Your parents are pretty controlling, then?" I asked a second later, the thought playing on my mind.

"My dad more than my mum," Theo explained. "I think they're probably just as controlling as most parents, but I never wanted to stick to their rules as a child, so we always fought a lot. It's one of the reasons I –" He stopped and shook his head. "Never mind."

A sudden desperate urge to ask him to continue rose inside me. I got the impression that whatever Theo was going to say had something to do with the reasons why he'd run away, and curiosity gripped me.

"Theo –"

I was interrupted by my phone buzzing.

Theo's eyes lingered on my desk, his hands reaching out to pick up the phone placed on the corner. He turned and held it out for me. "For you, Miss Popular."

"It'll just be Grace," I deadpanned, my voice sounding deflated. "You can check it if you want."

He tapped a button, the screen lighting up his face as it turned on. I sat up and watched him as he read the text, his eyes completely blank, not giving anything away.

And then he stiffened. He stood in silence, and I opened my mouth to ask what was wrong when his head snapped up to look at me.

"Grace wants to know if Tristan finally asked you out," he said in an unrecognisable tone, his eyes drifting away from my face. He tossed the phone in my direction. "You should probably let her know."

I caught the phone effortlessly, clutching it in my hands. *But what do you want the answer to be?* I asked in my mind, not having the courage to say it out loud.

The air was thick with tension as I texted Grace back, Theo refusing to look at me as I did so. He turned around on the spot, once again looking at my bookshelf with faux interest as he stayed away from me. I summed up just about everything that had happened earlier in a one-line response to Grace and set my phone back on the side, biting my lower lip. I had no idea what to say.

"So did he?" Theo asked casually.

I looked at Theo, aware of a frown forming on my face. He still had his back to me as he picked up another book to read its blurb.

"What?"

"Ask you out, I mean." He inclined his head to gaze at me. "Tristan. Did he finally ask you out?"

I felt my throat constrict. "Yeah, he did." Theo's head sharply turned back to the book in his hands. "But I didn't say yes."

He walked back to his sleeping bag with the book. His legs crossed over one another as he sat down. "You said no? Why?"

I scooted over to the edge of my bed so that I was facing him on the floor, my legs hanging over the side. "I'm not interested in him in that way." I shrugged. "Besides, I don't have time for dating. Especially right now."

Almost as soon as the last words escaped my lips I flinched, waiting for Theo's reaction. I didn't want him to worry that he was being too much of a bother to me, or that he was affecting my life more than he intended – but, of course, that's what he immediately did think.

He sat up straighter on the floor, his face full of concern. "Rose, I'm not the reason why you said no to Tristan, am I?"

"Of course not," I said straight away.

But I knew, deep down, that there was something behind his words – something else that he may have been asking at the same time.

"Good." Theo broke the silence a second later. "Because I'd hate to be the one who got in the way of your dating life."

I couldn't help but let out a small burst of laughter. "Trust me, you don't have to worry about that," I said. "Besides, I said no to Tristan because I don't like him that way."

"You don't?"

"No, I don't." I shook my head, grabbing my notebooks and pens off my bed and transferring them on to my desk. "So there's no need to worry, Theodore."

I examined the mess that was still there on my desk, contemplating tidying it. But out of the corner of my eye I could see Theo staring at me with a small smile playing at the edge of his lips.

"What?" I asked, feeling self-conscious.

Theo shook his head. "Nothing."

"No," I immediately said in response, pushing him to tell me what was on his mind. "What is it?"

"It's just … you're the only person to have ever called me by my full name. Theodore," he admitted.

"Oh. Sorry." I hadn't even been aware that I was doing it half the time. "I won't –"

"I never said that I didn't like it." Theo's face had grown slightly heated. He turned to face away from me, blocking himself off again.

"Okay." I chose not to comment on his obvious embarrassment. "I'll keep calling you that then."

Theo nodded, and that was it. I slipped on an oversized hoodie from my wardrobe and padded over to peer out of my window. The sun was just starting to make its descent into night, and the sky was splashed with pinks, yellows and oranges that blended with the clouds in a beautiful watercolour sunset.

"My parents should be home soon," I said, glancing down at the watch on my left wrist. "I better go and make dinner for the both of us."

I knew it was frustrating Theo that he wasn't able to leave the room, but the morning he'd been allowed to come downstairs was a one-off moment – not one I wanted him getting used to. I was worried that letting him come down too often would make him cocky, and if he got more confident with coming down when he thought my parents weren't around, it only made it more likely we'd be caught.

I decided to make enough food for a bigger group of people than two, meaning I could take the leftovers from the meal up for Theo to eat the next morning. I knew Theo loved lasagne, so I settled on that. I'd found out that his love of eating and my love of cooking was the perfect combination, especially when it meant I didn't have to cook dinner for just myself.

I kept an eye on the clock the entire time I was downstairs, but my parents didn't show – they were both probably still stuck at work.

Theo was still in the same spot when I came back, waiting

patiently for me. I handed him the plate of lasagne straight away, shrugging off his thanks.

We sat in silence for most of the meal, until Theo rested his knife and fork down on the plate and cleared his throat. "It's really nice," he said, gesturing towards his almost empty plate.

"Thanks."

There was a pause as I continued eating and Theo stared at me as if trying to decide if he wanted to say anything. Eventually he cleared his throat and said my name to get my attention. "Rose."

"Yes?" I asked, concentrating on shovelling a bit of mince and pasta on to my fork.

"Do you think I'm stupid for doing this?" He paused, before clarifying, "Hiding, I mean."

I tried to conceal my surprise that he was the one bringing the subject up. Theo had avoided the topic of his disappearance as much as he could ever since he'd turned up on my doorstep, and the fact that he'd decided to raise it now distracted me enough that I stopped eating.

"Theo," I started softly, "I have no idea why you're doing this, so I can't pretend to understand your reasons for leaving. And I might not know you extremely well, but I know enough to tell that you're not the type of person to run when things get a little bit tough. So no, I don't think you're stupid. I just think you're lost right now."

There was a long pause as Theo stared down at his plate.

"I've told you more than anyone else, you know," he said quietly a moment later. "About myself, I mean. I just –"

"You don't need to explain it to me, Theodore. I understand," I cut him off, shooting him what I hoped was a small, understanding smile.

61

He looked back at me, his face blank. His eyes pierced into mine, and he absentmindedly flicked back his hair. "Do you really think I'm lost?"

I thought about it for a second, not really knowing what to say. But then, the words came to me.

"When I was ten, I ran away from home," I started, moving to take a seat next to him on his sleeping bag. "Brent and I got into a massive argument and my parents, who were home at the time, both took his side. I was so bothered that they had taken his side that I threw a tantrum, accused them of not caring about me, packed a bag and left straight afterwards.

"But what I didn't think about were the consequences of my actions. I had nowhere to go, no one else who could care for me. I ended up walking around the streets for ages, until finally my parents found me sitting at the side of the road, crying my eyes out.

"And after they took me back home, I asked my mother why she even bothered searching, and she said to me, 'Rose, whenever you're lost, whenever you can't find the way and you need my help, I will always be there for you. Because as long as you have people who love and care for you, you will always be found whenever you are lost.'

"So I guess what I'm trying to say here is that no matter how you may feel right now, Theo, you'll always find your way back home – because you have people who care about you."

Theo was silent for a moment as he took in my words, and his shoulder gently pressed against mine as we sat next to one another. It was a peaceful silence, and I realised that I was the most relaxed I'd been since I agreed to help Theo.

In fact, the only times I had felt even remotely close to relaxed recently were when Theo was in my presence. He was like a pill, making me feel completely at ease, while wedging himself further into my life every single time we were together. Despite the constant fear of Theo's discovery, we had a good time together. It was surprising, actually, how well we got on. He was funny – much funnier than I'd ever realised at school. I found myself being glad that he dodged any discussion about how serious the whole situation was, because when we talked about nothing in particular I felt like I knew him best. The moments when we discussed our particular preferences in food, or when he tried to explain the plot of one of his favourite books to me, or how awful he really was at chemistry, felt like a welcome distraction from the outside world. And it was in those moments that I realised I may be becoming addicted to having him here. Theo had become my drug, my guilty pleasure.

He turned his head, his striking eyes locking with mine, sucking all the air out of my lungs so that I found it hard to breathe.

"Does that mean that you care about me then?" he whispered, the smoothness of his voice like a melody in my ears.

I could barely think straight with him looking at me like that – the intensity of his gaze piercing into me – and yet I managed to nod my head.

"Yes," I whispered back. "I do."

Six

If there was one person in my life who I knew I couldn't lie to, it was my brother Brent. He knew all the signs that I apparently show when I'm not telling the truth, from my left eye twitching, to both the tips of my ears turning bright pink. Whenever I did something I wasn't supposed to, he would always find out immediately – which admittedly might be part of the reason why I became such a rule-follower.

But Brent wasn't around, although we spoke regularly on Skype. However, on this occasion I decided to phone him. There was a chance I could get away with lying to him over the phone, because he couldn't see me to tell that I wasn't being truthful.

Or so I thought.

"You're hiding something from me." Brent's voice crackled on the other end of the line, but it did little to hide the accusation that laced his tone.

How can you tell? The words were on the tip of my tongue

and yet all I could do was splutter and try to deny everything. And that didn't work on Brent.

"Rosaline Gertrude Valentine," Brent drawled, and I could tell he was smirking on the other end of the line. "Are you breaking some rules right now?"

I cringed at his use of my full name, and shook my head before realising that he couldn't see me. "I have no idea what you're talking about."

He hummed on the other end, and I waited for him to press on and continue. "All right," he simply said instead, letting it go. And that was why I loved my brother more than anyone else in the world – because he understood. He wanted me to break through my boundaries, and he didn't care how I did it. He just wanted me to live my life.

"Anyway," I said, eager to change the subject. "How's uni life?"

"Terrible." Brent sighed dramatically. "I've literally run out of everything already: books to read, new clothes to wear, clean underwear –"

"Ew, okay, okay, too much information," I cut in, with a dramatic shiver of disgust. "I would say that I feel sorry for you, Brent, but you've only got yourself to blame for not taking enough stuff with you."

I walked over to the oven and, using my shoulder to keep the phone pressed against my ear, quickly opened it, pulling out the fresh batch of cookies I had baked. The smell wafted into the air and I smiled in satisfaction and dumped them on the side, preparing for Brent's next burst of outrage.

"Hey," he started, his voice full of sorrow, "it's not my fault that you wouldn't let me borrow any of your books to take away with me."

65

"I gave you some!" I protested.

Brent scoffed. "Yeah, like three – which I burned through in the first week, by the way."

I started transferring the cookies on to a cooling rack, rolling my eyes at his words. "Well, get your own books then."

"What's the point of that, Rose? Your room is literally like a freaking library."

"Language," I scolded him, not bothering to object to his comment. Even Theo had commented on how many books I had in my room, but he was steadily burning through them each day, and I was starting to wonder if I needed to buy more just to keep him quiet and out of trouble.

Brent let out a laugh again on the other end of the line, and I found myself smiling affectionately. There was something about his laugh that had the power to send me back in time, to the years when we would joke around and play games as kids. He was the guardian of all of my most happy memories, and his laughter was the key to unlocking them.

"I miss having you around," I admitted, feeling a sudden pang of loss.

There was a pause on the other end of the line, like Brent didn't want to ask the next question. "Mum and Dad still aren't home much then, huh?" he finally asked, although his tone implied he didn't really want to know the answer.

I didn't need to give him an answer. It hurt both Brent and me to know that our parents prioritised their work over us, but we had both learned to get used to it. I would be lying if I said I wasn't still angry about it, though. At first, it had been tough when they weren't around, but Brent soon took over the parental role – making my dinners, talking to me about school, deciding my bedtimes. It brought us closer together,

66

which inevitably made it even harder for me when he had to go off to university.

Brent tried to change the subject by saying, "Well, I should be able to make a trip home soon."

"When?" I asked eagerly, feeling my mood lift.

Brent laughed. "Can't say, or else I'll end up disappointing you. But in the next couple of months, when the workload has eased off, I'm sure I can make a trip back home to see you all."

We soon ended the call with promises to talk more often and try and plan when he could next come home. The cookies still lay on the side, now a lot cooler, so they didn't burn my mouth when I scoffed a couple. I quickly plated them and headed upstairs to my room where Theo was waiting for me.

"That's another one done," he said with a sigh as I entered the room, tossing the book in his hands on to my bed and watching it land neatly on the white duvet.

His eyes then landed on the plate in my hands, and he sat up straighter in the chair right by my desk like a well-behaved puppy. I bit down on my lower lip to stop myself from laughing.

"Are they ...?" Theo trailed off, his eyes lingering on the biscuits.

I walked over and carefully set them down on my desk. "They're chocolate chip, which I know is your favourite. You can have as many as you want, my parents don't like –"

Theo was already lunging forward, his arm swooping out and grabbing hold of the first cookie he could get his hands on. I watched as he bit into it, and his eyes closed with satisfaction as he ate it within seconds.

He didn't say anything until half the stack was gone. "Did you make these for me?"

67

I shrugged. "I always bake on Sunday mornings. And I know how much you've been missing your daily binge of Oreos, so I thought these could make up for it before I go to the store and buy you some."

Theo looked like he was about to say something, but decided against it, instead smiling at me gratefully. He turned away a second later, going back to the plate and grabbing one more cookie. "These home-baked ones are nicer anyway."

His words crept under my skin, settling in my rib cage and causing a flurry of butterflies to erupt. I told myself to stop being so ridiculous – all Theo had done was compliment my baking skills – and I picked up a cookie of my own just so that I would be too busy chewing to say anything stupid.

"Do you know what I do miss? Crisps," Theo continued, his mouth still full. He swallowed and added, "Especially Frazzles."

I went over to my bedroom door and closed it, rolling my eyes at Theo's comments. "I'm not a fan of bacon-flavoured crisps, so they're the only ones we don't have," I said, shrugging. "But I'll buy you some when I next get the chance."

Theo placed a hand to his heart. "I seriously do not know what I would do without you, Rose Valentine."

Despite his joking tone, he shot me a look that made my own heart stop beating. My stomach jolted, and I let my hair fall into my face to try and conceal my cheeks, which were growing hotter and hotter by the second. If Theo noticed me blushing then he didn't comment – but he also didn't stop looking at me in that intense way that had me struggling to think straight.

I cleared my throat. "Anyway, do you fancy watching a film or something today?"

68

Theo snapped out of the daze that he'd been caught in, shaking his head. "Uh, yeah. Sure."

The cardboard box of DVDs that had been sitting on the bottom of my wardrobe since I started secondary school was filled mainly with all the films Brent had given me over the years. He was a real movie junkie and was often watching new things, and when he ran out of room to store all the discs that he had, the older ones would go to me. I hadn't gone through them in a while because of my obsession with Netflix, but I couldn't bear to get rid of them and face the wrath of Brent if he found out I'd given any away.

The box was heavier than I thought when pulling it out, but Theo was more than eager to help me get it on to the bed, and he rummaged through all of them as soon as we'd put it down.

"There's a lot to choose from," he commented a moment later, pulling out all sorts of films and discarding them to the side. He picked one up and scanned the cover, his eyebrows rising. "I didn't know your brother was into Hungarian art-house films."

"I don't think there's any type of film that he doesn't like," I responded. "He even went to the cinema once and ended up seeing a documentary about coin collecting. He bought it a few months later and tried to get me to watch it with him."

Theo let out a snort of laughter. But the look of amusement on his face was quick to disappear as he lifted up something entirely different from the box, and his eyebrows quickly knotted together.

"You left a photo frame in here."

I immediately knew which one it was, and moved to the windows to open them so Theo wouldn't be able to see my face. "Did I?"

"Yeah." He picked it up to get a better look at it. "Was that taken at the winter dance when we were fourteen?"

I didn't need to look at the photo to say yes, but I still turned around and looked at the frame Theo was holding up for me. There I stood in the red dress I had spent months looking for, with my hair curled to the side, wrapped up in the arms of a boy whose grin was almost as wide as mine.

"Well, I'm with Xander in it, so yeah." I felt my throat constrict.

"Oh yeah. Xander Everett." Hearing his name roll off of Theo's tongue felt so wrong to me. "Didn't you two date?"

I so desperately didn't want to talk about it, but I still nodded my head in answer. "Yeah, we started dating after he asked me to the winter dance."

There was a pause in our stilted conversation as Theo stared at the photo in silence. His eyes trailed over both our bodies, lingering on the hand Xander had around my waist. It seemed he couldn't look away.

I started talking again, daring to say the words that had been on my mind ever since he pulled the photo out. "I guess I actually have you to thank for that," I finally said, the words leaving a bitter taste in my mouth.

He frowned, glancing up at me. "You do? Why?"

His ignorance felt like a blow to my chest. He turned away and went back to the desk chair. The photo frame remained in his hands, but he dropped it facedown on the surface in front of him and gave me his full attention.

"You don't remember? I asked you to the winter dance before Xander asked me," I said meekly, not daring to look him in the eyes. I looked everywhere else – anywhere else – trying to focus on something that wasn't anywhere near the sparkling green irises that were desperately trying to read me.

The image of Theo entering the school hall with a blonde girl on his arm came flooding back into my mind.

He seemed to have remembered himself because he swallowed, his Adam's apple bobbing, before he said, "And I rejected you for Hannah Marshall."

"Yes," I breathed, my voice so quiet I barely heard it.

I could see her clearly in my mind. Her strawberry blonde hair, always perfectly curled and hanging down her back. Her bright blue eyes, unblinking and captivating, able to sway any boy in her direction with a single glance. Her cherry red lips, always smirking. She used to smirk like that just before hurling an insult at an unsuspecting victim. She made lots of people her victims, including me.

And I used to let her insult me. I used to take it in my stride; I used to try and ignore her jibes and cruel comments when she'd call me a nerd, or tease me for being such a control freak and the teacher's pet. But deep down inside, I burned with a hatred for Hannah Marshall that I would never be able to quite put out, and when Theo rejected me for her I had been more than hurt.

Theo laughed then to break the silence, but it sounded bitter, forced. "Only because she demanded I go with her first."

I stayed silent. The memories were all flooding back into my mind, and an unpleasant feeling sat deep in my stomach and refused to go away. I still couldn't even look at Theo, and pathetically turned my head away from him, in an attempt to block him out.

I can still remember those moments clearly. Going up to Theo, where he had been sitting on his own. Gathering up all of my courage to ask him out. I can still remember the way he looked up at me, guilt flashing in his eyes, and the way he hesitated before saying, "I'm sorry, Rose, but I already have a date."

I'd got away as quick as I could after that, heading to the gym to find a space so I could face my humiliation alone. Theo had been my first proper crush and the pain of being rejected by him had reduced me to tears. I'd never admitted it to him, and I never would. But Xander Everett was the only one I couldn't hide it from, because he caught me right in the act.

Xander Everett, the golden boy who was loved by everyone. Xander Everett, the boy who had the charm and wit to make a whole class erupt into laughter. Xander Everett, the boy whose eyes would crinkle every time he laughed at my reactions to his constant teasing.

We sat near one another in class, and had a love-hate relationship – he used to drive me insane with his incessant teasing and joking. He found me amusing, and I thought that was the only reason he ever spoke to me. As it turned out, he liked me more than that, which is why he was more than happy to be my saviour after my humiliation.

"Go to the winter dance with me instead, Valentine," he'd said to me, his thumb brushing along my tear-stained cheek. He always called me by my last name, Valentine, and I didn't realise how much I loved it until that moment.

I hadn't told anyone about Theo turning me down – not Grace, not Naya, not even Brent. I was so humiliated that I couldn't bear to mention it to anyone, and if it hadn't been for Xander, I don't think I would have managed to go to that winter dance at all.

Theo noticed me turn away almost straight away, and I could feel him staring at me even when I was facing away from him. "Hey," he said soothingly, his voice like velvet. "You're not still upset about that, are you? Because I was a fourteen-year-old idiot back then, and if that happened –"

"It doesn't matter, Theodore," I interrupted him, my voice hard.

I swallowed, desperately trying to remove the bitter taste of old hurts in my mouth. "Besides, it all worked out in the end, didn't it? Xander never would've asked me to go with him instead, and we never would've dated if things had happened differently."

I refused to look at him. I refused to look at him and see the past humiliation that I had tried so hard to bury away. I refused to let his words soothe me.

"Yeah," Theo mumbled, but his voice was distant now. "I guess it worked out for all of us."

I didn't tell him how broken fourteen-year-old Rose had been at the time. I didn't tell him how he had always piqued her interest. And I definitely didn't tell him how desperate fourteen-year-old Rose had been for him to notice her, and how gutted she was when he noticed the popular, pretty, bullying girl instead.

I wondered if that moment of rejection had anything to do with why Theo had picked me for help. Did he think that I liked him? Perhaps he thought I still harboured feelings for him. The way I was acting probably suggested as much – from the way I blushed when he said my name, to my small shudders whenever our skin made contact.

He never gave anything away, but that was Theo for you – a total enigma. And he'd been that way since we were fourteen.

"Do you miss him?" Theo chose to break the silence between us.

"Sorry?"

"Xander," he clarified. "He moved away when you were still dating, didn't he? Do you miss him?"

I honestly didn't know how I felt in that moment, and Theo was making it even harder for me to assess my own feelings.

"That was a long time ago. But yeah, I guess sometimes I still do."

Xander and I had left things between us on very bad terms, and the scars of the relationship had taken a while to heal. I didn't want to talk about him. I didn't want to remember the pain of losing my first love. And I think Theo could tell this too, because he coughed awkwardly and looked away.

"How about this film then?" he said, reaching over to the box on my bed and picking up the first case he could get his hands on. He held *The Breakfast Club* in his hands. "A true classic."

I laughed lightly. "Sounds good."

I stood up, ready to open the case and pop the disc into my DVD player. But Theo cleared his throat, taking my attention away from the task at hand. I glanced over to see what he wanted.

"Hey, why don't we go downstairs to watch it instead?" he suggested hesitantly, his eyes trying to gauge my reaction.

I froze. "Downstairs?"

"Yes. You have a lounge, right?"

"Well, yes, but –"

Theo smiled, as if he'd known I was going to be reluctant. As if he could read my mind and see my response before I even had time to react.

"But it's against the rules?" he guessed. He laughed when silence was my only answer, and I felt myself blushing again.

"Rose, you know nothing bad is going to happen if you break the rules every once in a while, right?"

"No, actually, I don't know that," I said automatically. What I did know was that being downstairs was too much of a risk; it would be too easy for him to get caught.

"Rose, your parents are never here! You can do whatever the hell you want. You don't have to be such a goody-goody all the time."

I froze at his words. That's what he thought? That I was lucky my parents were never around? That I was too boring and sensible to make the most of my freedom? I felt tears pricking at the corners of my eyes, and I turned away from Theo.

Undeterred by my lack of response, he carried on. "Rose, you have the freedom every other teenager dreams of. You can do whatever the hell you want, but you're so strict with yourself. About everything. I don't get it!"

"No, Theodore, you don't get it," I snapped without thinking. "I don't want this freedom! I'd give anything not to have it. I'd rather my parents actually gave a crap what I did."

Theo didn't respond straightaway, and I felt embarrassed at my outburst. I took a deep breath, trying to regain some composure. I felt Theo's gaze on me, but I couldn't bring myself to look at him.

"Rose," Theo said quietly.

I cut him off, shaking my head and forcing a smile. "I'm fine. It's all fine."

"No, Rose, I'm sorry. That was thoughtless of me."

I shrugged and looked at my feet, afraid the tears might reappear. "It's just – I don't know why I am the way I am, okay? Perhaps I just find it easier to get by if I make rules for myself. It's not like anyone else is making them for me. But, yeah, I know that makes me a boring old *goody-goody*."

Theo cringed. "I didn't mean it like that. It's not such a bad thing." He reached out and squeezed my arm. "Hey. Look at me, Rose. Let's stay up here. We can watch a movie here."

I gave him a small smile, and his whole body seemed to relax. I noticed he hadn't let go of my arm. Catching me looking, he quickly pulled away. Neither of us said anything for a moment, but it didn't feel awkward. It felt nice.

"I suppose my parents won't be back until late ..." I began, my smile widening at the sight of Theo's eyes sparkling again.

"It'll only be for a couple of hours," he assured me. "As soon as the film is over I'll come straight back up here. Please? I feel like I'm going crazy in this room."

His eyes shone with hope, and I found it impossible to say no to Theodore Lockhart when he looked at me like that.

"Okay. Come on then."

I led the way downstairs, Theo following eagerly behind. He offered to make some popcorn but, after the mishap with my toast the other morning, I soon took over to avoid the risk of him burning the kitchen down.

I sat on the sofa with the bowl of popcorn in my lap, watching Theo in amusement as he struggled to get the DVD player to work. Having a little bit of time off from being cooped up in my bedroom was clearly a treat for him; his face was brighter, his body more relaxed. He looked carefree.

He came over to where I was sitting and, instead of choosing to sit at the other end of the sofa, plopped right down next to me, so close our thighs were touching.

"Ready?" he asked, turning to look at me, his breath fanning my neck.

"What?" I said stupidly, too distracted by the proximity between us. "Right, sorry. Sure."

Theo's lips twitched as he watched me tumble over my words, a blush quickly blossoming on my cheeks. "You all right?" he asked, his voice teasing.

I only nodded, not trusting myself to speak. He bit on his lip to contain his laughter, but made no comment and started playing the film.

Neither of us spoke for what seemed like for ever, Theo concentrating on the film while I tried to distract myself from the fact that I could feel him pressing against me. Occasionally he would reach over to take some of the popcorn out of the bowl on my lap, chewing quietly. While he laughed at the film, I could barely hear what was being said, for the blood was pumping too loudly in my ears. If Theo noticed, he chose not to say anything. It was only when I got up halfway through the film to make some more popcorn and then strategically put more space between us when I sat down again that he finally turned to me.

Wordlessly, he pushed himself across the sofa towards me, closing the distance between us.

"What are you doing?" I croaked, as he got so close I could barely breathe again.

He glanced at me, confused. "What? Do you want me to move closer?"

"I don't think that would be physically possible."

"Oh, sorry. Do you want me to move away?" He started to shuffle back across the sofa.

"You don't have to," I answered too quickly.

Theo immediately stopped moving and looked at me, amusement in his eyes. He looked happy at my answer, and he bit on his lip as if trying to stop himself from smiling.

"You do want me closer to you then?" he asked teasingly.

I took a breath, trying to relax my whole body, then rolled my eyes and crossed my arms over my chest. I met his eyes, bright green and sparkling. "Don't flatter yourself, Theodore," I said.

He laughed again, longer this time. He moved back to close the space he had put between us, one arm snaking around the back of the settee and resting on my shoulders, pulling me to him. My heart fluttered below my ribcage.

"You're too easy to wind up sometimes, Rose," he breathed, his mouth just above my ear. "It's cute."

I smacked him lightly on the chest in retaliation, but made no comment. We both went back to watching the film that was still playing, but Theo's arm didn't move from my shoulder.

It almost felt right being in his arms like that. If the situation that had got us there wasn't so weird, it would've been normal. Being with Theo like that felt like the most natural thing in the world. It was our moment, only ours, and there was nothing to interrupt us, nothing that could spoil it. I didn't want it to end.

But of course, once the film was over, reality settled back in. Theo removed his arm from around me and stood up. A small smile appeared on his face as he picked up the empty bowl of popcorn from the coffee table. "Want some more?"

I knew it was time to tell Theo to go back upstairs, to remind him that our agreement was that he'd go back up as soon as the film was over, not play for time by making more popcorn. And yet the only thing I could say was, "Sure."

It was getting later. My parents hadn't told me what time

they'd be home, but I knew that we were going to be cutting it close if I let Theo stay downstairs. And yet I made no protest as he walked into the kitchen, only followed blindly behind him.

Sure enough, it was only a little while after that we heard the sound of keys jingling in the door.

Theo's whole body froze. We stared at one another in silent horror as the front door creaked open and slammed shut, and my father's voice rang out in greeting.

"Get upstairs!" I snapped at Theo as quietly as I could. "Now!"

"How?" he asked in a furious whisper, gesturing towards the stairs, which were right by the front door that my father was coming through. It was impossible; he couldn't get back upstairs without being seen.

I sprang into action then, rushing to the front door where my father was busy removing his coat and scarf. He seemed surprised when I came to greet him at the door, and even more shocked when I leaped into his arms for a hug.

Theo must have realised what I was doing because he took advantage of the moment. He moved as fast and as sound-lessly as he could, sprinting up the stairs and giving me a quick thumbs-up as I watched him dash past. I tried my hardest to keep my father in my grasp, hugging him for the first time in years. The hug lasted for what seemed like for ever, and when my father hesitantly brought his hands up and patted my back, I couldn't wait for it to be over. He coughed a moment later, as if signifying that he wished it to be over too, and I pulled away, glad that Theo had now managed to get by without being seen.

I'm sure my mother must have commented on me acting

strangely the past few days, which would explain why my father looked so freaked out as he stared, his lips parted but no words coming out. I was normally so calm, so detached from both of them. I never hugged them, never welcomed them home – I hardly ever saw them. I was always in my room and they were always at work. But I just had to hope he was going to be too tired to try and get out of me what was going on. And, to judge by the dark circles under his eyes, it seemed I might be lucky after all.

"Welcome home!" was the only thing I could think to say as he stared at me in confusion, looking as if he couldn't really believe what had just happened. He looked stunned and clearly nervous about it, while I felt embarrassment wash over me.

I didn't wait around for his response. I followed the path Theo had just taken up the stairs, getting out of the hall as fast as I could.

Seven

The days had ticked by, and October would soon be approaching with its bitter winds and cold temperatures. I knew I needed to talk to Theo about going home.

It had been a week. A week since he had disappeared. People at school were getting more and more edgy with each passing day, the rumours growing more and more outlandish, and I knew this was going to turn from a missing person search into a dead person search if I didn't do something soon.

But I found myself wanting more time, wanting more than the few days we'd spent together with him hiding in my home. I knew it was wrong – I knew I shouldn't be letting everyone else worry when I knew exactly where he was – and yet I just kept putting off talking to him about going back home.

Theo seemed to be doing the same as me, never bringing the situation up and always changing the subject whenever we got remotely close to talking about his disappearing act and the impact it was having on other people. And I found myself letting him, because I was almost as desperate as he was to put the inevitable off and save any trouble that might come our way for another day.

There was something about being alone with him in my bedroom – something that brought a false sense of security, distracting me from the mess that we'd both created and making me forget about all of my worries. When I was out of the house, I found myself constantly desperate to go home, eager to spend as much time with Theo as possible before it would all stop. Before we'd have to face the consequences we both knew were coming.

But I couldn't just stay in the happy bubble that I was in whenever I was with Theo because, unlike him, I had to go into the outside world, and I had to hear the things that people were saying about him.

They were quiet, the whispers that floated through the hallways at school, but if you listened hard enough you could hear everything. Every guess about where Theo Lockhart had gone, every speculation about who he really was, and every murmur about which of the rumours about him were true.

Some of them were absurd and made no sense, like the rumours that he'd committed a heinous crime that no one knew about yet. Some were ridiculous clichés, like the one about him being in a gang on the run from the police. But some of them could very plausibly have been true. Some were so believable that even *I* found myself wondering if there was any truth behind them.

I'd heard rumours about Theo before, so I knew what people thought about him. At school, he hadn't willingly interacted much with other students, but his striking good looks and the few nasty fights that he'd ended up in had drawn attention to him anyway.

No one from our school had ever gone missing before – in fact, it seemed that no one in the whole town had ever just disappeared without a trace. It was such a novelty that everyone was still talking about his disappearance, and the speculation as to where he'd gone was a large part of people's conversations. But I hated hearing people talk about him. Now that I knew what Theo was really like, the other versions of him created by the gossip and rumours at school made me desperate to defend him. I felt protective of him, and I wanted to stand up for him when he was unable to do it for himself, but at the same time, I couldn't help but wonder if anything the other students said was *true*. Especially when I knew that when I got home he'd be there, waiting, and when I looked at him one thought would flash through my mind: *What's the truth behind the rumours of all the fights?*

"Are you sick?" I asked Theo on the eighth day as I passed the bowl of cereal I'd brought upstairs into his hands.

Theo coughed again, a noise that had become all too familiar since it woke me up hideously early that morning. "I'll be fine. It's just a cold."

"You sure? Because I can get you some medicine from downstairs, there's a cupboard full –"

"Rose," he cut me off, offering me a soft smile. "Don't worry about it."

I shot him a flat look. "You and I both know that's easier said than done."

He laughed loudly, the sound filling the room before it turned into a hacking cough.

83

"Why don't we do something today?" he suddenly said, sitting up from where he was lying on his sleeping bag and looking at me.

I froze, confused. "Like what?"

He shrugged. "I don't know. Anything. I'm tired of being cooped up in this room all the time."

I sighed and started, "Theo, you know the rules –"

Theo rolled his eyes at my hesitation. He cut me off before I had the chance to finish my sentence. "C'mon, screw the rules. Did no one ever tell you rules are for breaking?"

"Even if we could, I can't today. I've got school –"

"And you couldn't miss just one day?" he pressed. "Rose, you've got perfect attendance."

I was trying to make him see my side of this – the side that was practical. I knew that Theo took more risks than I did. He was clearly more reckless than me, which was why he was sitting in my room in the first place. But I couldn't be like that, and trying to make him understand why was a challenge, especially now he was getting so restless.

"Me missing school would only draw attention to us," I tried to reason with him. "Don't you think people would ask questions about where I was and what I was doing ..." I trailed off when I caught sight of his defeated expression.

"Yeah, you're right," he said shortly, waving a hand dismissively in my direction and turning his face away from me. "Forget it."

I frowned, trying to reach out to him again. "Theo –"

"Have a good day at school, Rose," he cut me off sharply, before pushing himself off the floor and walking over to my bookcase to inspect it for yet another read.

And so I left for school, despite the feeling deep in my gut that something wasn't right. The day dragged after that, my worries about Theo being sick replaced by the effort of trying my hardest to act like everything else was normal. It had become increasingly easy to lie to my friends and family, but as the days went on and Theo's whereabouts became more and more mysterious, I had to test out my lying skills in almost every conversation throughout the day.

"It's funny, isn't it?" Grace commented dryly as we waited in the line for lunch. "No one gives a crap about him when he's here and yet when he's not he's the talk of the whole school."

"That's just how it goes." I shrugged, picking up a burger and placing it on the plate on my tray. "It would be the same for you and me as well."

Grace shook her head in disgust. "It's just so wrong. None of them even cared about him but now that he's suddenly so *interesting* they're desperate to find him."

She did have a point – as word about Theo had spread round our school, the number of people signing up for the afternoon search parties had increased day by day. Girls who didn't even know his name before he went missing were suggesting places he could have run off to, and others were upset over a boy they didn't even know.

"At least we have fewer flyers to post now," was all that I offered in response, moving away from her and the lunch queue before she could get another word in.

Hannah Marshall was one of the many girls extremely worried about Theo. Although limited, her knowledge of him from their time together at the winter ball all those years back was far more than what most others had. I'd told Theo about it, and he'd simply rolled his eyes. "Good to know she's still the same drama queen," was his only comment on the subject before he asked me to drop it.

By the time it was decided to stop searching for Theo that evening, everywhere was dark. Only our torches lit up the streets. I was more than eager to escape everyone and head home to a certain someone else, so I was quick to hand back the few flyers I hadn't managed to post and walk off without saying goodbye.

"Theo," I called out as soon as I came in through the front door. "I'm back." I took my jacket off and hung it on the coat rack, listening out for his call of greeting. When he didn't bother responding, I headed on upstairs anyway.

I held the packet of Oreos I'd bought after school in the corner shop as I walked into my bedroom, opening the door and expecting to see him sitting there waiting for me.

All I saw instead was darkness.

My hands immediately went to the switch, flicking it upwards and watching as light flooded into the room, highlighting just how empty it was.

"Theo –" I started, my eyebrows knotting together. Then I felt the draught, and my eyes automatically locked onto the window, which was wide open. Wide enough for a body to fit through.

I was paralysed for a moment, unable to do anything except stand there. My heartbeat quickened and my chest tightened to the point where I thought I might pass out.

I walked over to the window. As my fingertips traced the sill, I pictured Theo clambering out to make his escape.

I caught sight of my expression in the glass: bewildered, shocked, hurt. My hair was wispy and all over the place, my eyes were wide and my cheeks flushed from the cold air. But I had no reason to feel like this – I had no reason to feel like I had been betrayed when both Theo and I had known that this was going to happen.

I just thought he'd tell me before he decided to leave.

My hands quickly came up, grabbing the window and pushing it down, sliding it shut and blocking out the bitter, insistent breeze that blew into my bedroom. I flicked the latch that locked it and pulled the curtains, turning away. Because looking back wasn't going to bring Theo back.

I did everything that I normally would have. I ate my dinner in my bedroom. I had a shower and got changed in my bathroom. I got into bed and wrapped myself in my covers, mumbling goodnight to no one.

But it all felt wrong. I'd trained myself not to let loneliness overwhelm me and yet without Theo there I felt more alone than I ever had before. He'd only been with me for five nights, and yet I felt like I couldn't function without him now.

Sleep didn't come. I tossed and turned for hours, watching the hands of the clock tick by, wondering where he was, what he was doing, if he was okay ... I didn't want to think of him. And yet I couldn't stop myself.

Everything was quiet – too quiet. I was used to the soft sounds of someone snoring on the floor next to me, the light murmurs of my name or other words that came with it. The night was still, but I didn't find it peaceful. I just found it painful.

So when the first tapping noise sounded, I ignored it. I told myself it was nothing, that I was going mad, that it was my mind making things up. But as the tapping continued, I found I couldn't ignore it any longer.

I threw the covers off and hesitantly headed to my window, where the noise seemed to be coming from. I grabbed the curtains and yanked them back – to reveal a smirking Theo Lockhart waiting on the other side for me.

He was just about secure, standing on the ledge just under the window, but his body swayed from side to side dangerously. I pulled open the window and stared at him, my mouth hanging open in shock.

"Rose Valentine," he drawled. The words were slightly slurred and his smirk was crooked. "I need your help."

I was tempted to shut the window on him.

It would have been so easy to shut it and walk away. To leave him out in the cold, with no other option than to go home. He'd broken my rules, he'd left me hanging, and he didn't deserve my help any more.

But even I knew things weren't that simple.

So I helped him inside. He grabbed hold of my arm and I heaved him in. He fell facedown onto the floor and lay still for a second. As I stood over him, he managed to get back on to his feet. A flurry of giggles escaped his mouth in the process and he wobbled as he stood.

"Where have you been?" I asked, my voice harsh even as a whisper. I didn't want to wake anyone else up, but I also couldn't control my anger at Theo.

"Relax, Rose. I was just outside," Theo said, waving his hand absently in the direction of the back of the house before clarifying, "at the bottom of your garden."

"All this time?" My eyes flicked down to the bottle in his hands, noticing it for the first time. "Where did you get that?"

Theo only giggled for a moment, hiccupping slightly. The

harsh smell of alcohol fanned across my face. "Your parents have a special stash in the cabinet in your dining room. I just helped myself to a drop of their finest Russian vodka." At the shock on my face, he smirked. "Did you not know that?"

I was too angry to speak. All I could do at first was shake my head, disbelief and rage washing over me. "I can't believe you right now," I said, my voice low. "I really can't."

Theo stared at me for a moment, not saying a word. He stood still, his eyes following me, as I started to pace the room.

"Why are you mad? Do you not get how bored I am in here?" he finally said, his tone impatient. "I just sit in this room all day, staring at the walls ..."

Then I lost my temper with him.

"And why do you think you're doing that? Because you asked for my help! Do you not realise how much I'm risking to do this for you?"

"I do. And I really appreciate it, Rose," he said. His tone was sincere, but the alcohol on his breath and the way he slurred the words only gave the opposite impression.

"Because stealing from my parents' drinks cabinet and scaring the hell out of me by climbing out of my window really shows that," I said sarcastically, reaching a hand out for the bottle. "Give that here. I need to go and put it back."

He handed it over without another word. I held the bottle in my hands, wondering if my parents would notice that it was now considerably emptier than it was last time they'd seen it. There was a long pause – a really long pause – before, finally, Theo said in a soft voice, "I'm sorry, Rose. I wasn't thinking straight."

I sighed, closing my eyes for a moment to try and control the anger that was still threatening to overpower me.

He'd taken advantage of me. All the rules I'd set in place, all the things I had done to try and keep this secret ... and Theo had risked it all because he was *bored*. He'd disregarded everything I had said, and I had every right to throw him out.

And yet, I couldn't help the other feeling that was there, behind all of the anger.

Relief.

Relief that he hadn't left me for good, relief that it wasn't all over yet. It was that relief that had me lightly take his arm, as I decided against kicking him out. For now.

"C'mon. You need to sleep it off," I said, trying to guide him over to the sleeping bag that was still unrolled on the floor.

But Theo was too drunk to be fully aware of what he was doing. The moment of sobriety he'd had when he was apologising to me had faded fast and now he was just standing on the spot, swaying and refusing to move his feet no matter how hard I tried to pull him. I tugged harder, but he shrugged my arm off, covering his mouth with his hand.

"I feel sick," he said, his voice muffled. I instantly panicked, looking around for something to grab and hold out for him to vomit in, but there was nothing. Not even a bin.

Theo let out a giggle a second later as the feeling passed. He grinned sheepishly at me.

"I'm going to get you a bucket," I grumbled, turning away from the drunken smile that was doing all sorts of things to my heart. "Wait here."

All of downstairs was dark. I stumbled into the kitchen, not bothering to flick on the lights as I grabbed the bucket normally used for cleaning the floor. I could feel my mind going into overdrive, but I tried to stay calm and rational, heading back up the stairs with the hope that Theo hadn't been sick in the time I had left him.

He hadn't. Instead, I found him curled up on my bed. Now he was breaking rule number one. The covers were wrapped around him and his eyes were closed as he snuggled his head into the pillow. His hair was messily falling into his face, and his breath was slow and heavy.

I stopped in my tracks, staring at him in disbelief. "Theo —"

Eyes still closed, he pulled a sleepy smile at me, making my heart stop altogether. "I left enough room for you too."

Every part of me wanted to climb into the space he'd left me, to curl up and sleep beside him, yet I hesitated at the thought of it. The idea of being so close sent my brain into a frenzy.

I walked over and lifted the covers up. There was enough space for me to get in and lie without touching him. Carefully, I slid under the covers, my body stiff. I turned over so that I was looking at Theo. We were so close that I noticed details about him I hadn't before.

I could see the freckles on his nose, small and dainty, barely visible. I could see his dark lashes, long and thick, fluttering every time he breathed out. I could see his chapped lips, red and wet from the tongue that had just dashed out of his mouth to lick them.

I could see everything. And it felt like so much more than just looking at him. It felt like I was looking through him – like I was able to see the inside of his soul. I'd never felt this close to anyone else in my entire life.

"Rose," Theo mumbled, his eyes opening to lock on to mine.

"Yes?" I breathed back, my voice soft in the night.

And then the moment was ruined.

Theo opened his mouth and said the words I had been so desperate to hear, but no longer wanted to know. The truth about why he ran away in the first place.

"I got expelled from school."

"What?" I sat up in the bed, looking at Theo's expression. His bloodshot eyes were full of guilt as he looked up at me, desperation distorting his features as he tried to gauge my response.

"That's why I went missing. I was hiding from my parents because I couldn't face their reactions. You don't understand, Rose. And ... I just panicked and ran, but now I've messed it all up and I don't know what to do next. I can't go back home. I can't start over. I've screwed everything up, Rose."

As his confession poured out, I could see why Theo had never told me why he had run away before. I'd heard the word "expelled" whispered in the school corridors, but dismissed it along with all the other rumours. Mostly, everyone had assumed something terrible had happened, yet the real reason he was hiding in my room was that he couldn't face the consequences of his behaviour. He'd dragged me into this and made me think something unspeakable had occurred. I could see his distress, but I couldn't excuse his actions. I couldn't work out whether I pitied him or was angry with him. I felt guilty for hiding Theo all this time when nothing truly awful had befallen him, and furious at myself for being so gullible – for tricking myself into believing that maybe it had. The rush of confused emotions building up inside me was overwhelming, and I could only stare at him, mystified.

And then I laughed.

Theo's mouth dropped open as giggles escaped from my lips. My head fell back as I laughed harder.

"Is this a dream?" he asked. "Why are you laughing?"

"What do you mean?" I replied, finally managing to get a hold of myself. I wiped away the few tears that had escaped from my eyes.

"I mean, I thought you'd be mad. Hell, I thought you'd never want to see me again. Why are you finding this so funny?"

His eyes were unmoving, trying to scrutinise me, to see what was going on in my head. But even I didn't know what was going on in there, and the longer I laughed, the more I questioned my sanity.

In the end, I shrugged my shoulders at him helplessly. I was so overwhelmed with anger and the absurdity of the situation that laughter felt like my only possible response. "What's the point in getting mad about it now? Being angry isn't going to take back the past, and it's not going to change the fact that I've already helped you. What's done is done – you had your reasons for running away, and I had my reasons for helping you. There's no point in arguing over it, because it's not going to change anything."

There was a pause as Theo took in my words. And then he whispered, "You're amazing, you know that?"

I ignored his comment, despite the way it set the butterflies fluttering in my ribcage again. "What did you get expelled for anyway?"

"I knocked Luke Baker unconscious," he admitted. He broke eye contact with me for the first time since he'd told me the truth.

"Why?"

"It doesn't matter."

"Yes it does, Theodore," I urged, desperately wanting to reach out and touch his face. "People don't just knock each other out in school! So something bad must have happened or –"

"He made a comment about you, okay? He made a comment about you and other girls in our school that I didn't like, and I saw red and punched him. It's just ... I dunno, guys shouldn't think they can treat girls however they want. I just feel like those sort of dumb comments are something people should stand up to."

His words stunned me to silence. I struggled to think for a moment. My eyebrows knotted together and I pursed my lips. "I hardly think that punching him solved any problems." Then curiosity got the better of me. "What did he say?"

Theo scoffed like the idea of telling me was preposterous. "I'm definitely not telling you that. Your pretty ears shouldn't ever hear that kind of talk." He drawled the words out teasingly, but I still rolled my eyes at the comment.

I wanted to pester him. I wanted to force the answer out of him, to know exactly why he put his neck on the line for me and the other girls too. But instead I awkwardly blurted out, "You think my ears are pretty?"

Theo looked at me again. His eyes flashed with something unrecognisable as he whispered, "Rose, I think all of you is freaking beautiful."

I couldn't speak, but I didn't need to because a second later Theo's eyes fluttered shut and he was fast asleep.

Theo Lockhart is a cover hog.

It'd only been a few hours since he'd climbed drunkenly through my bedroom window, and then climbed into my bed and fallen asleep, but I hadn't managed to get even a little bit of sleep. My duvet completely covered his body, and there

94

was none left for my own. I reached out to grab it from his grasp, but his sleeping form just grumbled and yanked it back before I could get a proper hold, leaving me cold, tired and angry with him.

I sorely regretted letting another rule get broken. Theo had already left my bedroom when he wasn't supposed to, and now he was on my bed – *in* my bed – making that the second rule he'd broken in a matter of days. And I was the one letting him get away with it.

And, ultimately, I was letting him break down the walls that had taken me for ever to build up so he could worm his way into my heart, capturing it and claiming it for his own.

But there was something comforting about him being there next to me, something soothing about having his body pressed to my own. It made me feel safe. It felt right. And that was what scared me the most.

He stirred for a second, and I glanced at him from under my lashes. His body shifted slightly on the bed, rolling closer to my own. His lips moved as he mumbled something in his sleep. I failed to catch what he said, but a second later his arm was sliding around my waist.

He wrapped himself around me, pulling me into his chest and leaving no space between our bodies. His legs intertwined with mine a moment later, and I suddenly noticed the covers were back on me as well.

"Rose," he murmured a heartbeat later, his voice dozy and sleepy as though he had just woken up.

I paused, waiting to see if it was just him talking in his sleep.

"Rose," he repeated impatiently, filling the silence that I had created.

"Yes?" I whispered back, my voice shaky and weak in the darkness.

"Do you know why I really chose you to help me hide?"

His words held a double meaning. I knew he was talking about asking me to help him out, but there was an unspoken sense that whatever he was about to say would explain much more than that.

"For all these years, you've been so nice to me and you always thought I didn't notice," he continued, and while his voice still held a drunken slur, I could also feel the raw emotion in it. "But I noticed everything, Rose. Always. I always noticed you."

Then, before I had the chance to ask him what he meant, his light snores filled the room once again.

Eight

I knew as soon as I woke up the next morning that I had overslept.

The sun was shining brighter through the open curtains and the birds were chirping just that bit louder. The sounds of my parents slamming cupboard doors and rushing around downstairs to organise their things for the day made it clear they were both pushed for time as well. I knew I should be getting up and joining them.

And yet I wasn't even bothered about being late for school at that moment, because as soon as I caught sight of the boy sleeping in my bed next to me, all thoughts fell out of my mind like water falling from a tap.

We were wound tightly together, our legs still intertwined from the night, my head tucked into his chest and his arms around me, pulling me closer to him. I moved my head back to look at him, but there was little I could do to be released entirely from his tight hold.

Theo was still sleeping soundly, his mouth wide open and

his face relaxed. All I could do was stare wide-eyed at him, my body unable to move and my brain unable to think.

"Rose!" my mother called from the bottom of the stairs, making me jump. It seemed to do the trick waking up Theo as well. His eyelids fluttered as he opened them, his gaze landing on me.

He didn't freeze; he didn't panic. His eyes searched mine for a moment, and neither of us spoke. I thought about asking him how he was feeling, but the words were left dangling at the tip of my tongue.

And then, he moved closer to me. Our breath mingled and our eyes stayed locked. I opened my mouth again to say something – anything – but some part of me wanted to see what would happen. Some part of me never wanted to break the hold we had on each other in that moment.

I don't know how long we lay there looking at one another. It could have been seconds, minutes, hours. I didn't care. I just didn't want the moment to end. But what I didn't know was that it had only just started.

Because Theo chose to make the first move in the best way possible. His hand came up to gently tilt my head back, and his lips came crashing down on to my own.

It was like someone had pressed the stop button on a clock. It felt like the kiss would last for ever. The only thing I could register was Theo. Theo holding my hips, pulling me closer to him. Theo winding his legs tighter around mine, locking them together like two intricate jigsaw pieces. Theo moving his lips against mine, pushing his tongue into my mouth and kissing me with passion.

He became everything in that moment: my oxygen, enabling me to live and breathe; my blood, burning with desire and racing through my veins; and my heart, beating wildly against my ribcage with every passing second.

It was Theo. There was only Theo.

We broke away only when we needed to breathe, our chests rising and falling rapidly. My entire body had been sent into overdrive, and as my eyes locked with his once again, I could tell he was feeling the same.

"What are you doing to me, Rose?" Theo whispered, and my insides melted. He grabbed my hand softly and pressed it against his chest, letting me feel the heart that was pumping beneath his skin.

The moment was perfect – everything about it was perfect. And even though it wasn't my first kiss, I couldn't help wishing it had been, because no other kiss would ever compare to it. I had never believed in feeling sparks, but the tingling all over my body made me second-guess myself. I found myself getting sucked into the fairy tale of it; I found myself falling further and further into the world of Theo Lockhart, and in that moment it felt like nothing could ever be more perfect, more blissful.

But reality would always intervene – and this time it was in the form of my mother shouting, "Rose! You're going to be late for school if you don't come downstairs right this minute!"

So I was forced to break away from Theo. I was forced to get out of bed, out of my room, and out of the world of Theo Lockhart. And, as he watched me leave the room, I desperately wished I could go back into that moment and live in it for ever.

If only I had known how precious it was then, I would have held onto it a little bit tighter. I would have ignored my mother. I would have refused to go to school. I would have stayed with

Theo all day. I would have savoured every single second until they all ran out, and the memory would be etched into my mind for ever, to live in my system and flow through my veins for the rest of my life.

I didn't know that time had run out for Theo and me, but I did feel a sense of foreboding, deep in the pit of my stomach. Time was falling away, bringing us closer to the inevitable end. Once the truth was out, there would be no more moments, no more secrets to hide or kisses to share. As I left my room that morning, I pushed my worries from my mind. I refused to think about what would happen when the end finally came.

It's magical how one kiss can change your entire perspective on everything.

I felt lighter. All my worries had evaporated the moment our lips had touched, leaving me with no other cares in the world. That feeling lingered with me for the rest of the day. Everything felt effortless – the smile that I couldn't seem to shake, the lightness of my steps as I walked. It felt like life couldn't get any better.

If I'd known a kiss with Theo Lockhart would make me feel like that, I would have done it much sooner.

"You look happier today," Naya commented as I strolled into our first lesson five whole minutes early, plopping myself down at the desk next to her.

It was so hard not to say anything; it was so hard not to beam like a fool at her. If I thought keeping quiet about the fact that Theo was hiding in my house was hard, it was nothing compared to not telling anyone that he had kissed me.

Theo had kissed me.

I repeated the thought to myself – it still hadn't yet sunk in.

"It's just a good day," was all that I said in response, shrugging as I tried my hardest to keep my face impassive.

Others were starting to come into the room and I looked for Grace amid the sea of people, but Naya didn't seem able to draw her gaze away from me. Her eyebrows were drawn together in confusion.

"What are you talking about? We're at school," she said, still looking at me as if I was insane. I just shrugged again and picked up my pen, pretending to scribble something down just so I could let myself think about a certain green-eyed boy.

As the lesson started, I felt myself drifting away. My hands absentmindedly rose up to touch my still-tingling lips, feeling their smoothness and remembering the sensation of Theo's lips on them. I could feel Grace – who had walked into the room late – looking at me out of the corner of her eye, but I didn't care. I was too lost in the moment.

The lessons flew by for the rest of the day. Admittedly, I didn't spend many of them focused on what the teacher was saying, for my mind was hopelessly filled with daydreams and memories, and only paying attention to the flurry of butterflies that rested deep in my stomach.

But there was also a feeling of dread, like something terrible was just over the horizon. It was the same feeling I'd had earlier that morning. I knew that time was running out, and soon there'd be no secrets left to keep. The end was just beginning.

Nine

I had never seen someone look so close to falling apart until that afternoon when I saw Theo's mother walking down the school corridor with his father.

They walked together and yet seemed so far apart. His hands were gripping her arm, but they didn't seem to offer her any support, and he kept a watchful eye on her at all times even when the head teacher, who was with them, was speaking. But Mrs Lockhart paid no attention to her husband as she nodded her head at what Mr Humphrey was saying. Her eyes were filled with an intense, dreadful worry that I had never experienced myself, and hoped to never feel for as long as I lived.

Other students were walking past, throwing them pitying and curious glances, but the couple didn't notice as they concentrated on their conversation. Mr Humphrey tried his hardest to ignore the looks, but his eyes kept drifting over to those who were watching, his lips pursed in annoyance. Mrs Lockhart didn't stop looking at him, and Mr Lockhart didn't stop watching her. I wondered if they were at school to discuss Theo's expulsion in more detail.

My body froze as they drew closer to me, a few people bumping past me as I unexpectedly came to a halt in the hallway. My brain stopped working to the point where I couldn't get my body to move any more. It was surreal, seeing the parents of the boy who had earlier kissed me, and who was hiding in my room, while they worried themselves to death about him.

The sight was a stark contrast, I realised, to the picture Tristan had painted of them and how they were coping when Theo had only just gone missing. The words "actually, they didn't seem too bothered about having a search party for him in the first place" rang in my head. Theo might have gone AWOL on occasion in the past, but this was the longest he'd been away. Theo's parents certainly seemed more than worried now, which meant something had to have changed, or they were really losing hope that their son was going to return unharmed home to them.

They didn't notice me, of course. Neither of them looked in my direction despite my obvious staring. Even if they had seen me, it's not like it would have given anything away. It's not like they would have known that their son was hiding in my room – they didn't even know of my existence. But it was then that I felt guilt consume me whole. There I was, feeling the happiest I had ever been in my life. All because of the boy who was causing them so much pain. And all because of me, the girl who had promised to keep the truth from them. It was horrifying. It was frightening.

It was like looking into a nightmare.

Mr Humphrey seemed to finish what he was saying, because

he reached out to shake Mr Lockhart's hand and to pat Mrs Lockhart on the shoulder, offering them one final, pitying look before heading back to his office. Theo's parents stood there for a little longer, talking to one another in hushed voices before they moved away too, heading in my direction.

I panicked. I tried to jump to the side to make space for them to walk by, but the bodies of other students hurrying to class hemmed me in and I was sent sprawling into Mrs Lockhart. I knocked her bags to the ground, scattering her things everywhere.

"Oh God," I immediately cried out, reaching down and gathering a hold of whatever I could. "I'm so sorry."

"It's all right." Mrs Lockhart's voice was muted. Her husband simply stood where he was and watched as she bent down to help me.

We both stood up at the same time, and I anxiously reached down to straighten my skirt. Mrs Lockhart and I looked at one another in awkward silence for a moment before she cleared her throat and looked away, thrusting the books and papers that were mine into my hands.

"Er, thanks," I mumbled, glancing down at the work and willing my cheeks to not turn scarlet like they were threatening to.

"Is that your chemistry teacher's name?" Theo's father suddenly said. His eyes were narrowed and he was studying the textbook on the top of the pile.

I'd forgotten he was there and his voice made me jump on the spot. I inclined my head to look at him, but the accusation and suspicion in his eyes had me quickly directing my glance back down at the pile in my hands. I was conscious of my grip tightening to the point where the books were scratching the skin on my palms.

104

"Yes," I mumbled, my voice barely audible.

Mr Lockhart practically burned a hole in the side of my head with his sharp stare. "So you know our son then?"

"I'm sorry?" I glanced up at him, deciding to pretend I was confused instead of revealing to them the panic that I was feeling inside

"Our son has the same chemistry teacher as you. Theo Lockhart – the boy who is missing. Do you know him?"

His tone was accusatory and it sent shivers rolling down my spine. He made it sound like Theo was his possession, inconveniently misplaced. He didn't sound caring, worried or loving, just stern and authoritative.

I struggled to string any words together, suddenly feeling very intimidated by him. "I –"

"You look about his age too," he said, cutting me off in an equally harsh, demanding tone. "Surely you were in the same class?"

Mrs Lockhart could clearly see the discomfort her husband was causing me, and she reached over and touched him on the arm. "Christopher –"

"We were chemistry partners, actually," I admitted, cutting Mrs Lockhart off.

She was more surprised than her husband at my words, her jaw dropping open as she eyed me in complete and utter bewilderment. "You're Rose," she stated, and I looked back at her in matching bewilderment, not knowing what to think.

Mr Lockhart seemed as confused as I was at her recognition. "That's your name?" he asked abruptly, before looking at his wife. "How on earth did you know that?"

Mrs Lockhart didn't seem unsettled by her husband's cutting tone, but she shifted her bag on her shoulder and subtly angled herself away from him to create some space between them. "Theo mentioned her once or twice," she said softly, trying to keep her voice casual.

Mr Lockhart's jaw tightened. "And you didn't think to tell me about this before?" he asked, but his calm tone sounded forced as he tried to control his obvious anger.

"It didn't seem necessary –"

"Of course it didn't," he almost mocked his wife, "to you."

There was a pause and we all stood silently, the tension rising with every short breath that Mr Lockhart puffed. Mrs Lockhart looked down at the ground, and I could tell she was holding all her tension and worry across her shoulders, which were as stiff as a board. I found myself wanting to say something, but seeing Mr Lockhart reach out towards his wife stopped me. I watched as he grabbed her hand in his own and gave it a reassuring squeeze.

"Sorry," he said, and I couldn't tell if he was speaking to her or me. "Under all of the current circumstances, I'm afraid it's becoming harder to keep our desperation to find our son under control." He looked at me again, his face much calmer than before and his eyes filled with nothing but curiosity. "Did you two talk much?"

"Only about classwork," I answered, shifting awkwardly as I tried not to give anything away in my eyes.

"And nothing else?" he pressed, speaking with urgency at the prospect of gathering more information about where his son could be.

Some instinct told me to keep as quiet as possible when speaking to Mr Lockhart, and looking into Mrs Lockhart's eyes briefly assured me I was right as I saw the fear in them.

"No. Nothing else," I lied even as the guilt burned a hole

into my stomach. But I didn't say anything. I knew I couldn't say anything. I had made a promise to Theo Lockhart, and I knew I couldn't break it now.

Because breaking that promise would mean breaking my own heart too.

The search for Theo had now been marked as futile.

I was no longer required to help hand out flyers. Everyone now knew about the disappearance of the boy who only lived a few roads away from them, and it seemed that almost everyone had come to the resounding conclusion that he was gone for good.

"There's no point in handing out flyers with his name on to people when they all haven't seen him," Gregory McAllen, one of the volunteer helpers in charge, said when Grace and I went to grab a stack of flyers from him. "And there's no point in walking around everywhere searching for him when we've covered all possible places near here that he could be."

I raised my eyebrows at him in disbelief, but he didn't look fazed. He regarded me and Grace with tired eyes.

"So that's just it then?" Grace asked.

"Look, Theo's either left town – and I wouldn't blame him for wanting to leave this shithole – or something much worse has happened to him. It's time to leave it to the authorities," he said in a bored tone before walking away from us.

I admittedly didn't know what the police had been doing about Theo's disappearance; I didn't watch the news, and I hadn't exactly tried to pry information from anyone else about what was happening. Honestly, I think part of my mind was blocking that all out in a desperate attempt to dislodge myself from reality, from the world outside my four bedroom walls.

But I was unable to stop all the guilt I had tried to bury from clawing its way back out, and it was only the concerned expression on Grace's face that brought me out of the darkness that I was sinking down into.

"So I guess that's that then," she murmured, her eyes downcast and her tone thoughtful. "Theo Lockhart's done a runner."

And, in that moment, I almost told her everything. I almost told her exactly what I had been keeping from her, everything that had happened and everything that I was risking for the boy whose name had just fallen from her lips. But I held my tongue; I promised myself that it wouldn't be long before I would be able to tell her, when Theo would return home and all this madness would end once and for all. Even though I didn't know when that would happen, the thought of it still made me feel a little bit better on the inside.

"Well, we should probably go home then." Grace broke out of her thoughts, looking up at me and forcing a smile. "I'll see you tomorrow, Rose."

"Yeah," I murmured as she started walking away. "See you tomorrow."

I stopped by the supermarket on my way back to grab a few necessities before going home to Theo. The store was quiet as always, the few other shoppers not bothering to talk to one another as they hurried to fill up their baskets and be on their way. I picked up a box of pasta, my eyes wandering over to the crisp section and landing on the giant packets of Frazzles placed at the centre of all the other brands of crisps. The sight of it brought a smile to my lips and I went over and grabbed a couple of packets, throwing them into my basket before heading over to the counter.

My parents' cars were both parked in the driveway when I arrived home, but the house was silent when I let myself in, meaning they had probably gone out for dinner somewhere in town, leaving me home alone once again. Still, I waited until I got upstairs and was outside my room before I called out to the boy hiding in my room.

"Theo," I sang softly, tapping on my bedroom door. "I actually went out and bought you some –"

When I opened my bedroom door, I stopped. I dropped the Frazzles in a heap on the floor.

Theo was nowhere to be seen.

But there were my parents, sitting on my bed, their expressions full of disappointment and anger.

Ten

It was like the world had suddenly come to a standstill.

Everything stopped: my brain, my breath, and my heart. I simply stood there with a blank expression for who knows how long. My gaze drifted around the rest of the empty room, my entire body numb from the waves of dread and trepidation that rolled in and hit me again and again.

"Where is he?" I managed to ask, my voice cracking at the end.

My parents stood up from the bed at the same time. They exchanged a look, their expressions cautious. I could see they were assessing the best way to deal with the situation, but I was starting to lose my patience.

"Rose –" My mother reached her hand out towards me, before suddenly pulling back as though she'd changed her mind.

I felt panic rise inside me as a thousand different scenarios of what had happened to Theo flashed through my mind. "Where is he?" I repeated, unwilling to talk about anything else.

The answer was painfully obvious, but I still needed verbal confirmation.

"He's not here. He's gone."

Those words sparked something inside me. I stared at them, fear igniting under my skin.

"Where?"

My parents stayed quiet for a moment. Finally, my dad cleared his throat. "We sent him back home," he explained, his voice as cold and robotic as it had been for the last ten years.

For a moment I couldn't gather what his words meant, or what they meant for me. Then everything came crashing down.

Theo was gone. He'd been discovered. He'd been sent home – the game was up. My parents knew everything. And it was like every single moment I had with Theo – every single conversation we had, every memory we shared – was out in the open. It was like we'd been written down and our past together was a book that everyone else was able to read. And seeing my parents' faces, knowing that they now knew everything that had been going on for the past week, sent a shiver down my spine.

It was like my mind was refusing to let their words in. I shook my head as the word "no" formed on my lips but fell short of being said. "How did you –"

"He was in your bedroom, Rose. Of course we were going to find out eventually. Considering how strangely you've been acting these last few days, I'm surprised we didn't find him sooner," my mother cut me off, her tone snappy and impatient. She didn't hesitate to turn on me then, looking at me with disapproval. "What were you *thinking*?"

There was nothing I could have said to justify my actions. So I stood there, staring at them, and stayed silent. They waited, both of them looking angrier with each passing second, but still I kept my mouth shut and decided not to say a word.

I had expected my mother to be the one to speak first, to be the one to let out her rage. But it was my father who decided to say something, and his voice was so calm and chilling that I wished my mother had spoken – had even shouted violently at me – instead of him.

"She wasn't thinking, was she?" he said to her. Then he looked at me, his expression cold. "Rose just did exactly what she wanted."

I felt my eyes grow heavy with tears as I turned away from them, not willing to face their disappointment any more. "There's a first time for everything," I mumbled, but I doubt they even heard me.

And then I was moving, grabbing a jacket and wrapping it around myself as I started to head down the stairs. My parents sprung into action and were quick to follow me.

"Where are you going?"

I could feel my mother's breath on the back of my neck. I felt suddenly suffocated, and I increased my pace.

To see him. The words were on the tip of my tongue, but I didn't say them. I didn't know where Theo was – I didn't know his address, and besides I was sure I wouldn't be welcome at his home. I knew I couldn't see him, but part of me was still clinging onto the hope that he hadn't really gone, that I'd still be able to see him, that I'd still be able to find him. And I clung onto that hope like it was my lifeline.

"I can't stay here," I managed to get out in response, my breathing laboured as the panicky feeling of being trapped rose inside me. "I need to get out for a bit, to clear my head –"

"Rose."

My mother reached out for me properly this time, touching my arm. I recoiled away from her, creating a large space between us.

"Rose."

I wasn't listening any more. I pulled my hair into a ponytail, zipped up my jacket and tried to get around my father to the front door. But my mother wasn't done yet.

"Rose," she persisted. "I know Theo's home situation is very tough right now, but his mother told me today when I drove him home that she's dealing with it –"

I stopped and spun around to look at her. A sudden nauseous feeling filled my body. "What?"

I froze. I felt like I was living in a nightmare, all by myself, with no Theo there to face it with me.

My mother blinked, surprise seeping into her features. "I – I thought you knew," she stuttered.

"Knew what? What's been going on at Theo's?" I pressed, unable to think about anything else.

"Rose," my mother started, looking into my eyes as she said the words that would break me and everything I had known apart. "Theo's dad ... he's been ... Well, he's violent. Towards Theo. Apparently it has been going on for years."

I couldn't breathe.

I was falling apart right in front of my parents' eyes and they had no idea what to do. They stared at me, waiting for the truth to sink in and for me to act normal again, but I knew things would never be the same.

My brain was moving back in time, searching through my

memories for any time when Theo may have shown signs that he and his father had a more complicated, unpleasant relationship than I had thought.

"How long have you known?" I managed to rasp out, still not looking at either of my parents.

"Since this afternoon. When we were talking to Theo about going home I knew that something was off. I managed to get it out of him," my mother said. I could feel her stare burning into the side of my head.

I braved one glance at their faces and regretted it instantly. My mother, who was always so prim and proper, looked dishevelled, the lines of her wrinkles prominent and her body hunched rather than upright. My father had black circles under his eyes from all the stress. His face was drained of colour and his gaze was unfocused. Watching him try to process what was going on made me realise it was the first time I'd seen him with real emotion on his face. The situation must have been surreal for both of them. I knew all of this was going to shock them, but I had somehow prayed that they wouldn't find out so soon.

"What did you do?" I asked, but the answer was already clear to me, despite how much I wished it wasn't true.

"I took him to his mother, Rose," she said softly, her voice weak and feeble.

Anger flared up inside me. "You took him back home! You should have told someone, gone to the police –"

"The police are already involved, Rose. Theo's mother has pressed charges and moved in with her brother. Theo is there now. He's safe, I promise you. It's over."

I was stunned into silence again.

My mother reached up and took her hair out of her bun, letting the loose waves fall down past her shoulders. She let out an exhausted sigh. My father stood in the exact same position, his face unreadable and his body slumped over.

"The police will deal with Theo's father. The important thing is that Theo and his mother are out of that house and safe. Apparently, she'd been preparing to leave for a long time – I suppose Theo's disappearance was the final push she needed. She has the situation under control and she's going to do what is best for her and Theo. They are going to live with her brother until they're back on their feet. So there's nothing I – nothing *we* can do, Rose, except leave it be."

I could feel my shock brimming to the surface as I tried to get to grips with everything I had just learned. I tried to find reasons for Theo not telling me about his family situation. What could have stopped him from telling me something so important? I should have pushed him for answers – I should have known there was something darker, more fragile behind his disappearance. And I should have done something. I could have done something. Now I just felt utterly helpless and completely out of my depth.

Why could he not just tell me the truth? In the end I could only see one possible reason.

He didn't trust me.

It was clear now. To Theo, I was just someone who could help him out. While he may have liked me enough to ask for my help, he plainly didn't like me enough to tell me his secret. He hadn't trusted me like he'd never trusted anyone else before – I had to find out from my parents. I had been naïve enough to assume that he came to me because he saw something in me, but he obviously didn't respect me enough to be honest with me. My eyes stung as I came to the bitter realisation that he had only chosen me because I was reliable. Because I was boring and safe. Because I had liked him enough to ask him to the dance once.

"I just –" I tried to speak, but my throat felt raw and I had nothing else to say.

My mother was still watching me carefully. I felt her notice the tears glistening in my eyes, and saw her bite down on her bottom lip thoughtfully. "Theo never told you?" she asked.

I shook my head.

"Then why did you agree to help him?" My father's voice sounded hoarse.

I stayed silent, no explanations in my mind. It was like someone had turned the switch in my brain off. I was motionless, staring at a spot on the wall as everything washed over me.

"Are – are you in love with this boy, Rose?" my mother said quietly, like she didn't want to hear the answer. It sounded like she was scared of the response it might bring.

"No!" I said, my answer an automatic lie.

There was a pause. It felt like my parents were trying to work out what I was thinking, like they were trying to figure out the limits of what they could say in front of me without pushing me over the edge and out the door.

"Well, do you like him then? More than a friend?" my mother decided to press, her voice delicate.

"I don't know." I shrugged. I felt weak and pathetic; my body was tired beyond belief and the desire to leave home and go and find Theo was well and truly gone. I just wanted to go to bed and sleep for ever, or at least until the news and the shock had sunk in. "I guess maybe I do."

In the past, whenever Brent or I were disobedient, there would

116

always be a confrontation, a shouting match and then bitter remarks from them for the next few weeks.

I would rather have endured all of that than what I got the next day when I woke up and went downstairs: silence.

They sat at the breakfast bar together, sipping their coffees and reading a section of the newspaper each. They always split the paper in half and then swapped once they were done with their section, so they could read at the same time.

I hadn't expected them to still be in the house; I had expected them to have gone off to work so they could avoid me altogether. They had no idea how to deal with me any more, that much was clear. And part of me thought they couldn't be bothered to go through the rigmarole of disciplining me, not when they were so busy at work. But it seemed to be part of their punishment, forcing me to sit with them and eat my breakfast while they pretended I didn't exist. And it definitely worked as a form of torture too.

The only noises in the room were of chewing: me with my toast, my parents with their bowls of Weetabix. Occasionally my father would clear his throat, or my mother would sigh at something she read, but other than that it was silent. A cold, unfriendly kind of silent.

After I finished eating I grabbed my bowl and washed it up. Then I braced myself and spun back round to look at my parents. They were still immersed in their papers and the food in front of them.

"I better go and get ready for school," I said, my voice ringing out through the silence. I prayed it would cause some sort of reaction. But they both continued to stare at their newspapers without glancing up at me.

I felt tears prick at my eyelids, but I forced myself to swallow down my hurt and frustration and instead headed away from them. After all, I was the one who'd caused all of this mess – and I had no idea if it had even been worth it at this point. Only Theo had the answer to that.

So for once I hurried to get to school. I got changed quicker than I had ever done, and left the house earlier than usual, desperate to get away from my parents. School would be my sanctuary for the day.

If only I had known what was in store for me. Because maybe then I would have been sensible enough to stay away and give myself a day off before my heart was broken all over again.

Eleven

There was nothing more shocking than coming into school to find Theodore Lockhart sitting in all of his normal lessons, acting as if nothing had happened.

The news that he was back had spread like wildfire, and soon everyone knew about Theo's return whether they cared about it or not.

According to the rumours, the school had decided they were too rash in their punishment of Theo, and his mother had managed to persuade the board to give him one last chance due to "special circumstances". Some people were shocked that he was allowed to come back – it wasn't the first fight Theo had got into, but it had been one of the worst, as the punch he'd thrown at Luke Baker was strong enough to knock him unconscious. No one knew what had been said before the fight; they just saw Luke Baker sneer at Theo and then fall down when Theo whirled right around and threw a fist at his face.

As for me, walking into my chemistry class and seeing Theo

in his old seat right next to mine was like walking into a parallel universe – one that I didn't want to be in.

He looked up as I entered the room, his eyes instantly locking on to mine. I sharply sucked in a breath, looking at him for the first time since everything had happened. I was overwhelmed by the sense that there was so much between us now – so many secrets had been revealed, and so many new feelings of longing now ran through my veins.

But when he broke eye contact and looked back down at the desk, he made it clear that I was wrong. There was nothing between us any more.

I stopped walking, confused by his reaction. He must have felt my gaze still aimed towards him but he ignored it and continued to look down, his fists clenched on the desk.

I felt tears start to prick at my eyes, and shook my head to try and repel the pain that was starting to claw at my insides. I stiffly made my way over and I held my breath as I sat down, once again glancing over at Theo to see if his reaction was any different.

"Theo?" I ventured. He just shifted his chair to make more space between us and acted like I wasn't there.

The teacher started the lesson as normal and I tried my hardest to concentrate, but it was no use. The urge to run from the room was strong, and I willed myself to remain seated, desperately trying to act like there was nothing wrong.

We didn't have to pair up for experiments – and I was beyond grateful for that. Theo remained expressionless the entire hour, not looking at anyone despite knowing that they were all studying him.

I was thankful for the bell as soon as it rang. I grabbed my things and didn't bother to put them in my bag as I rushed to get out of the classroom and away from the source of my pain. I felt Theo's eyes on me as I practically sprinted past the teacher but I didn't dare to look back, terrified of letting him see the agony he was inflicting on me.

He didn't care any more – that much was clear. There was no other reason for the way he was acting towards me, no other cause that I could think of. The deal was finished, over, so he didn't have to worry about me any more.

There were so many things I had wanted to say when I first saw him sitting there in chemistry. I had wanted to reach out to him. I still wanted to reach out to him. I wanted to be there for him. But he'd put up a wall between us; and with that wall he'd demolished any kind of relationship we had, and as he cemented the divide between us, the tiny cracks in my heart grew bigger and bigger.

Theo was everywhere and yet nowhere at the same time, haunting my dreams, stalking my thoughts ... There were traces of him everywhere I went.

I caught glimpses of him all the time at school – in the classroom, sitting on his own in the lunchroom, laying down on the grass outside – but every time I desperately wanted to go over and talk to him, he would turn away as if he couldn't stand to look at me.

To say it hurt would be an understatement. It felt like everywhere I went, I was carrying the pain with me. It weighed heavily on my shoulders and dragged me down with every step I took.

There was so much that I wanted to ask him, but I would have settled for anything. A nod in my direction, or even a hello in the corridor would have been enough. Just some acknowledgement that we knew each other, that we'd shared something. The longing I had to speak to him increased every time I saw him, and I couldn't bring myself to be the one to talk to him, when he was clearly avoiding me.

Why did you not tell me about your dad?

The words were on the tip of my tongue whenever we happened to make eye contact for a single second, and yet at the same time I didn't want to know the answer – because I had an idea of what it would be already.

Theo didn't trust me. And while I couldn't blame him for not sharing something like that with me, I couldn't deny that it hurt.

What was he thinking? There were times when I just stared at the back of his head, as though if I looked long and hard enough I would be able to see right into his mind. But as much as I tried, I knew Theo Lockhart was still a mystery to me – one that I would never figure out.

But there was one thing I was sure that I did understand, and it was the thing that bothered me most of all.

I had been convenient. I had been available and predictable; if Theo was hard to figure out then I clearly wasn't. He picked the girl that he saw right through. He saw kindness in me – affection, too. But he also saw loneliness. And while I'd maintained the illusion of control, I had actually been the gullible one.

And it stung. Seeing him in class, seeing him in the hallways, seeing him everywhere ... all of it hurt. Because it was a reminder of what we'd been through. A reminder of how little it had meant to him, and how much it had meant to me.

"Rose." Grace snapped me out of the trance I was in. We were sitting in the large canteen surrounded by other students, and I turned to look at her. Her eyes wandered over to Theo, who I had been looking at before, but she flicked them back to me. "Are you all right?"

I swallowed, nodding my head. "I'm fine."

"I only ask because you haven't touched your food for the last half an hour."

I looked down at my plate and saw that it was indeed full, but none of it looked appetising. Grace and Naya both kept their eyes on me, and their expressions filled with concern as I pushed the plate away.

"I'm not hungry today," I said.

"You weren't hungry yesterday either," Naya pointed out. "Or the day before that."

I kept my head down, refusing to make eye contact with either of them.

"Does it have something to do with Theo? Because he hasn't stopped staring at you," Grace commented, and I abruptly turned my head in his direction. Smooth, I know.

Sure enough, Theo was looking at me, an unreadable expression on his face. Once he caught me staring back though, he quickly turned around and acted as if nothing had happened.

I sighed, letting my hair fall into my face and making no effort to sweep it back. And then I looked up, and I told them both everything.

It was a relief to share it with someone else. I knew I could count on both Naya and Grace to keep it to themselves, and I made sure to keep my voice quiet as I filled them in on everything that had happened during that week in my bedroom. But I didn't tell them about the kiss – it hurt too much to talk about it now, and it wasn't relevant any more – and I definitely didn't tell them about Theo's dad. If Theo wouldn't even tell me, then that secret wasn't mine to share.

When I was done they both sat back in their seats, dumb-struck.

Neither of them said anything for some time, both looking at one another as if having a conversation just with their facial expressions. Soon, I decided I'd had enough.

"Are you mad?" I blurted, looking to Grace for confirmation.

She broke eye contact with Naya and ran her fingers through her hair, sighing. "You could have told me. You know I wouldn't have said anything to anyone else."

I opened my mouth to desperately try and make an excuse, but she broke in before I could speak. "But I do get why you couldn't say anything. The chances of you getting caught were too high."

"We're your best friends," Naya added, frowning. "Who were we going to tell?"

"I know," I said guiltily. "I'm sorry. I don't know why I didn't say anything. I know I can trust you both."

"But you wanted Theo all to yourself," Grace said, her bluntness taking me by surprise. "You wanted to have something with him that was just yours and his. A secret between just you two."

Grace always had known me better than myself. She was assertive, and she understood people; she saw the motives behind people's actions, and she saw through me right then.

I still frowned, feigning ignorance. "What are you trying to say?"

Grace paused and smiled at me for a moment, her eyes knowing. "You like him, Rose. You like him more than you want to admit."

For a moment, I didn't know what to say. Naya just watched me, as though trying to read me, trying to figure out if any of what Grace had just said was true. Finally, I sighed and said, "I do. I do like him." I raised my eyebrows at them. "There, I've admitted it. Now, will you please forgive me? Can we all be okay?"

They exchanged a glance. Then, after a dramatic sigh, Grace grinned and said, "We're all good."

But the smile on my face was quick to fade when I caught Theo's eyes once more. He stood in the lunch line, his tray grasped firmly in both hands. A flash of pain crossed his face at the sight of my smile. As soon as he realised I had noticed him watching, he dumped his tray on the counter and walked out of the canteen without turning back.

"But why is he ignoring you now? What happened to make him act like that towards you?" Grace suddenly cut in, her tone soft and filled with confusion.

"I don't know, Grace," I replied, my voice quiet as I continued to stare in the direction that Theo had gone in. "I really don't know."

Every single time I saw Theo my heart clenched. I imagined his lips on mine again, his voice whispering in my ear, his legs wound around mine …

And then I'd be taken back to cruel reality.

There were more times when I caught him looking at me. I'd turn and see his eyes lingering in my direction, then he'd panic and turn away. But I knew he was watching. He was always watching, yet always pretending I didn't exist.

My mum had told me that he wasn't still living with his dad. But I didn't know what had happened after he'd gone back home. I didn't know if he was doing okay. And it killed me to know that I couldn't ask him.

Chemistry was the worst subject, the most painful class of them all. Every lesson I would enter the room and he would be there, fists clenched and eyes downcast. We both struggled to concentrate in the lesson, and we only spoke when the teacher gave us some chemistry issue to discuss.

I didn't know what I had done wrong; I didn't know why Theo wasn't willing to share anything with me any more.

A week after Theo's return, we were sitting in chemistry ignoring each other, listening to our teacher deliver instructions.

"The Bunsen burners are located in the cupboard at the far right side of the room. I need you to work with your partners to fill out the table on the sheet in front of you, and we'll discuss what we find as a class later." The teacher's voice broke me out of my trance, and the hustle of students getting up from their desks a second later almost made me jump out of my skin. Theo also got up; he walked stiffly past me to the cupboard everyone else was crowded round.

I could hear him speaking to one of our classmates. His voice was quiet, but I could still hear the relaxed tone, carefree and easy, and my heart panged at the sound. I snuck a glance at him out of the corner of my eye, letting my hair fall forward onto my face so I could peer without being spotted. I watched as he grabbed hold of the Bunsen burner and headed back towards me, his body growing tense as he drew closer to me.

I was in charge of the experiment on the whole, but when following the instructions I made sure I was slow enough for Theo to keep up. I wasn't too bad at chemistry, so it didn't matter that I couldn't talk to Theo about the answers I put down, but I could tell that he was struggling to keep up with the classwork, especially because he had missed over a week's worth. Normally, I would have offered to help him – normally, he would have asked for my help. But now there was just silence, apart from a few small groans from Theo when he got to a section of the table that he didn't understand.

After a while sitting there in silence, as the other students chatted in their pairs, I opened my mouth to ask Theo if he needed any help, but quickly snapped it shut and looked back down at the sheet on my table. Every part of my body was urging me to speak – to break the awkwardness and at least try to fix things – but it was a lot harder than I thought.

Surprisingly, it was Theo who decided to speak to me for the first time since he'd gone back home, and his choice of topic was unexpected. "I didn't want to tell the police about you giving me a place to stay," he said, his voice quiet. "I didn't want to get you into trouble."

I jolted my head up from my work. "What?"

"I lied when I was asked where I had been all that time I was missing," Theo explained, looking straight at me. "I promised you I wouldn't drag your name into this mess, and I didn't. But my mum knew the truth, and made me tell the police. I had to."

My heart sank when he didn't say any more. He didn't offer me an apology or seem willing to discuss anything else that had happened between us. And so I swallowed my hurt, straightened my body up, and grabbed my books, as it was almost the end of the lesson and everyone was packing up. "Well," I said, breaking eye contact. "Thanks for letting me know." And then, just as the bell rang, I rushed away to put as much distance between us as possible, although my wildly pumping heart told me that it wouldn't be so easy to get over Theo for good.

Twelve

Weeks passed and still I felt the same: broken and worn down, unable to stop my thoughts from taunting me.

I didn't know if Theo felt the same as me; I didn't know if he felt lost about everything that had happened, but the circles that had formed and darkened under his eyes made it clear that, whatever he was thinking, he wasn't able to sleep peacefully either.

But he seemed to have found a new table to sit at during lunch. One day I walked into the lunchroom and saw him sitting next to Hannah Marshall. Her hand was wrapped around his arm as she chatted animatedly to him. I almost fell apart.

I knew she had been trying to latch herself onto him since he'd come back to school and become the new centre of attention, but from what I had seen he'd been trying to avoid her, practically running away whenever she came near. But now it seemed she had worn him down, and her whole face was lit up with triumph as she looked at him like he was a sparkling trophy that she had won.

I was unable to move, my eyes fixed on the two of them, my vision growing blurred and my hands shaking by my sides.

It was hard to come to terms with what I was seeing; it was hard to face the pain as it hit me in the face, sharp and fast. It was strange to feel like I had been betrayed, even though Theo and I hadn't spoken in almost a month and he should be able to sit wherever he wanted. But the fact that he was sitting next to *her* of all people was what made it so hard for me to bear.

Theo must have sensed me looking at him because his eyes flicked over to me, catching me in the act of staring. He awkwardly looked away as soon as our eyes made contact, and pulled his arm away from Hannah's grip. But she latched back onto him a second later, and he made no attempt to push her off him again.

A hand touched my shoulder then, making me pull my eyes away from the torturous sight.

"Everything okay?" Tristan asked kindly. His expression was gentle and I noticed a flicker of understanding cross it.

I forced myself to nod, swallowing the bitter taste I had in my mouth. "Everything's fine," I managed to say in raspy response, and I let him lead me over to the lunch table where Naya and Grace were already sitting.

Tristan sat down next to me when we got to the table, taking us all by surprise. He turned and offered me a smile. Then, noticing that I was shivering, he reached into his bag and pulled out a hoodie.

"Here," he offered, holding it out to me. "Wear this. It'll keep you warm."

"Oh, no." I quickly shook my head. "I'm fine."

The look that he shot me made it clear that he didn't believe me. "I can see the goose bumps on your arm from here."

The first genuine smile of the day spread across my lips as I shook my head again, but this time in defeat. "Thanks," I said, taking the jumper from him. "But aren't you going to be cold now?"

Tristan shrugged as I pulled the hoodie over my head, immediately feeling warmer as the soft fabric touched my skin. It was massive on my small frame, but I always enjoyed my hoodies being too large on me, so I revelled in the cosy bagginess. I could sense Grace and Naya watching the two of us carefully, but I chose to ignore them. Tristan had distracted me enough to forget about everyone else in the room, including *him*, and I was more than grateful for that.

I was surprised that he'd chosen to sit next to me. I rarely saw Tristan at school outside our lessons together, but today he seemed to be hanging around, like he'd somehow known what I was going to see when I entered the lunchroom, and how much it was going to affect me. It was a relief to have him there. He never struggled to start a conversation with me, making it easy for me to become distracted.

"I don't really ever feel the cold," Tristan explained. "My whole family is warm-blooded."

I laughed, pulling my ponytail out from underneath the hood. "I wish I could say the same for myself, but I'm always freezing."

He let out a light burst of laughter, and the sound made me smile wider in response. The sleeves of his hoodie fell further down my arms, covering my hands, and I clutched the excess fabric in my fingertips.

"Anyway, I better get going." Tristan suddenly stood up, grabbing his half-empty lunch tray. "I have band practice, and I'm already late."

"Oh," I said, taken aback. "Well, do you need this back?"

My hands reached down to grasp the bottom of the hoodie, ready to take it off.

"Keep it." He shrugged again, that same dazzling smile playing on the corners of his lips once more. "I have plenty more at home, so I can spare that one for you." And, with a final friendly wave, he walked off.

As soon as he was gone, the same knot I'd had in my stomach for weeks came right back. I snuck one more glance behind me, back at where Theo had been sitting. But the space next to Hannah Marshall was empty and her face disgruntled.

And my eyes lingered on the tray Theo had left behind, still full of food.

My pencil rhythmically hit the table, creating a soft tap, tap, tap sound that filled the silence. My eyes constantly flicked to the clock on the wall, scanning the time to see if it had miraculously sped up in the few seconds that I had been looking away from it. Nope, it still read 2:48 p.m. Two minutes until the lesson was over.

Theo awkwardly cleared his throat next to me. I sensed him look up at the clock, scanning it anxiously too, waiting for the bell. I didn't dare so much as glance at him.

When you're eagerly awaiting something to happen, time always seems to slow down to the point where it becomes non-existent. I could hear the clock constantly ticking and yet time didn't seem to pass, the moment threatening to stand still for ever, torturing me. The room was suffocating; being next to him was suffocating.

The other students also sighed when finally it did ring, signifying another lesson was over and we were one step closer to the end of the school day.

131

The next few steps were simple. I threw my bag over my shoulder and scooped all the books off my desk. Time was of the essence – every second that went by was another second of awkward torture in Theo Lockhart's presence. I made sure to get out of the room as quickly as possible.

My plan was never foolproof, though. I'd often have to go back into the classroom at the end of the day, looking for my reading glasses or my pencil case. And today was no different – but this time I wasn't the one to notice that I had left something behind.

"Rose!"

I turned around to see Theo heading towards me. I'd only managed to make it halfway across the classroom and he was striding towards me, catching me up in only a few steps.

"Oh," I mumbled as he approached, barely able to get any words out at all.

"You forgot your book," he said, holding it out to me. "I mean you left it behind, and I didn't think you actually wanted to leave it behind –"

"I didn't," I cut him off, forcing a small smile at him. I tucked my hair behind my ears, suddenly feeling self-conscious. "Thanks."

"No problem," Theo replied in his smooth voice, the sound almost making me melt. It made me realise how much I missed him talking to me – how much I missed hearing that voice – but at the same time it made me want to get away from him as fast as possible.

There was a lull, and both of us just stood in the same place for a moment, not daring to move. I hesitated, not knowing how I wanted to react. One part of me was filled with anger, but another part wanted answers and thought that now might be the best – and maybe the only – time to get them. I frowned in frustration – frustration that he still hadn't explained himself, or told me why he was treating me like this. Like we were strangers. Or acquaintances. Not like I was someone who had helped him. Who had kissed him.

"Listen –"

"Theo!"

My voice died on my lips as Theo and I turned to see Hannah Marshall standing outside our chemistry room, waiting eagerly for him to join her. She waved when she saw us both, throwing me a cold glance, and then beckoned Theo over.

My heart dropped into my stomach. Theo sighed beside me, because he knew the damage was already done – both of us were quickly closing back up. I cleared my throat awkwardly. "You better not keep her waiting," I advised him, causing him to glance back at me. "I heard she threw a temper tantrum the last time her boyfriend didn't race to her side when she called for him, and then she refused to talk to him for the rest of the week."

"I'm not her –" Theo said quickly, but I raised my hand to stop him from speaking.

"Doesn't matter." I shook my head, trying to act like I wasn't bothered. "Thanks for the book, Theo."

"Theo," he repeated quietly, almost like he was testing his name out.

I turned away from him.

"See you later," I said. He didn't reply as I walked off.

It was only once I turned the corner, and he could no longer stare at my back, that I realised I hadn't called him Theodore like I used to. Why that bothered him, I didn't know, but Theo was not my Theodore any more.

He was just Theo now.

Thirteen

December was soon upon us, bringing with it plummeting temperatures and biting winds but also its merry spirit. You could feel the excitement that lingered around school strengthening as it got closer and closer to the holidays, and everyone looked that little bit happier.

It was my favourite time of the year out of all the seasons. Snow had always seemed so magical to me, and something about it always brought good luck into my life when it appeared. As I watched the first snowfall of the season tumbling outside the window, a cup of hot chocolate in my hands, I couldn't have stopped the smile from spreading across my cheeks even if I had tried.

"Here," Grace said to my right, and I glanced over at her. She reached into one of the cupboards in her kitchen and pulled out a packet of marshmallows, tossing it over to me. "I knew I had some in here somewhere."

"Thanks," I said gratefully, ripping open the packet and dropping a few into my cup. "And thanks for letting me crash here last night."

She smiled brightly, coming over to me and taking the seat at her dining table right next to mine, to watch the snow fall with me. "No problem." She raised her own mug to her lips, taking a sip, before asking, "Are things still bad with your parents, then?"

I nodded, not bothering to elaborate. We both knew why things were still tense with my parents. But, months after everything had happened, I hadn't expected the atmosphere to still be so tense in the house. But my parents were dead set on punishing me for my actions and their chosen method of doing so was to make my home life even more uncomfortable by being there *all the time*, constantly watching and yet ignoring me at the same time.

"Things will get better," Grace assured me, nudging me with her elbow. She grabbed the packet of marshmallows in front of me, re-opening it and popping one into her mouth.

I stayed silent, watching the flurries of snowflakes descend softly down to the ground, some getting caught in a small gust of wind and blowing around, suspended in the air. I was mesmerised, enthralled, awestruck. It was so magical to me.

"Well, they better improve soon," I mumbled. Grace offered me the packet of marshmallows, and I reached over to grab another for myself. "I can't stand the way things are at home right now."

I'd talked to Brent about the situation at home, but closed up when he started asking about what had happened to make things so tense in the first place. It was awkward, talking about a boy with my brother, and while I knew he would be there for me if I needed him, I didn't want to discuss something so raw and personal with him right now.

"Are they really that bad? Or is this because of Theo too?" Grace prodded, glancing at me with a concerned expression.

I didn't reply, instead just continuing to stare outside the window.

"Well, if anything, the snow is a sign," Grace continued, nudging me with her elbow once more. I turned towards her, taking in her wide, hopeful smile. "Trust me, it shows there are good things to come. Maybe a chance at a fresh start."

"I hope so," I murmured, not really believing it. I took another sip of my hot chocolate and glanced at my watch. "Do you think school will be cancelled today because of the weather?"

Grace shook her head, her neat curls flying around her face. "It would have to be a full-on snowstorm for school to say that we don't have to come in." She looked down at her own watch, before standing up and taking her empty mug over to the dishwasher. "We still have some time before we need to leave. Do you want some pancakes?"

I also stood, finishing off my drink and handing my mug to Grace to put in the dishwasher. "Actually, I think I might go for a walk in the snow for a while," I said, walking over to the coat rack and grabbing my scarf.

"Okay," Grace replied. "I'll see you in a bit."

I threw on my coat and wrapped my scarf around my neck. My thick jumper felt itchy on my skin. My hair swept around my face as soon as I opened the front door, the stray straight strands getting caught in my lipgloss and turning sticky and messy. But none of that mattered as soon as I stepped outside into the winter wonderland.

The wind was bitter enough to make my face sting, but it was worth the pain to see my footprints making a path in the snow, and my shoes getting coated in a layer of white that went all the way up to the tops of my ankles. I brushed my hand across the top of my car, letting the snow coat my fingertips and watching as it melted quickly in the palm of my hand. It was the happiest I'd felt in a long time, standing outside with the snow falling all around me, creating a blanket of white over everything and making the whole world beautiful again.

And that happiness lingered inside me even when Grace and I arrived at school, my car skidding on a patch of ice as we pulled into the car park. We met up with Naya, who had walked in wearing her wellies and thermals, before going inside and sighing as we were met by a blast of heat from the school's tropical heating system.

It was hard to concentrate in class that day, as the snow showed no signs of stopping any time soon. I was constantly distracted by the view outside the window. I wished I could be out there, enjoying the weather while it lasted. I was so distracted that I barely looked at where I was going between classes.

But I hadn't realised just how slippery the ground was underneath the snow, meaning I had a few close calls with falling over face-first into the white. I knocked into one person so hard that I would have gone flying if they hadn't grabbed my arm in time and steadied me against their body.

"S-sorry," I gasped, looking down at my feet to make sure they were placed firmly on the ground before glancing up at the person who was still holding me for protection.

Theo's eyes caught mine, sparkling bright and green in the white all around him. His whole body was coated in a layer of snow, including his hair – until he brought a hand up to run his fingers through it, causing all the flecks of white to fall on to his shoulders.

"It's fine," he managed to reply, a small, almost nervous smile flickering on the corners of his lips.

He looked so breathtaking in that moment that I struggled to

137

think properly. I still felt unsteady and all I could do was stare at him in wonder. His lips were pinker than normal, slightly swollen in the cold. The few freckles on his nose seemed to be highlighted, and the dimples of his cheeks also seemed more prominent than ever. It was so easy to get lost in him, until I remembered where we were and who we were to each other.

I pulled myself out of his grip and tugged at my coat so it wasn't ruffled up any more. I cleared my throat, muttered another thanks, and went to walk away from him. But Theodore Lockhart had other ideas.

"Hey, Rose," he said, softly. I turned back to him. My cheeks were surely tinged bright pink, which frustrated me. I wanted to seem cool and in control, so I took a deep breath to calm myself.

"Yes?" When I spoke my breath was clear in the air, wispy like smoke.

"Uh" – Theo scraped his fingers through his hair again, looking uncomfortable – "my mum wanted to invite you round to dinner."

I looked at him in surprise. "Invite me round for dinner?"

"Yeah. As a thanks," he explained. "For everything."

He looked at me then, his eyes filled with what I could only identify as regret, but I continued to stand in front of him in stunned silence.

He looked away a second later, hiding his face from me momentarily. "We just moved out of my uncle's place and into a new house, and Mum's insisting on having you round for dinner this Friday so she can meet you properly."

"Erm ... okay," I managed to croak, feeling a stray snowflake get caught in my eyebrow. It melted a second later, running down my flaming cheeks, as if trying to cool them down.

"You don't have to come if you don't want to, of course," Theo said hurriedly. "I can come up with an excuse –"

I didn't give myself a chance to think it over before I blurted out the next words, my impulses making the decision for me "No, it's fine. I'll come."

Theo looked at me in shock. Now he was the one who'd lost his train of thought, and he struggled to get his next words out. "R-really?"

I found myself smiling at his flustered expression, trying my hardest to remain as cool as possible. I raised my eyebrows at him, watching his neck turn a light shade of red. It felt like the tables had turned; now I was the one in control. It felt good. "Is that a problem?" I asked.

"No. It's amazing," he blurted out, the redness on his neck growing deeper and spreading up to the top of his jaw. "It's ... Never mind. Do you need me to come and pick you up at your house or –"

"It's all right. I can drive over," I said, shuffling my feet.

"Great." Theo smiled tightly.

There was another small burst of silence, as the bell signifying the start of the next lesson rang.

"So, what time?" I asked.

"Seven. My mum wrote down our new address on this card, and she added directions too," he replied, reaching into his pocket and plucking out a small card and a folded up sheet of paper. He handed it to me carefully, making sure his hand didn't make any contact with my own.

"Thanks," I mumbled. The snow suddenly came down heavier, some of it falling through the gaps in the top of my coat, making its way onto my clothes underneath and causing me to shiver.

"Oh shit, I'm sorry, are you cold?" Theo started to take his own scarf off. "Here, take my –"

I shook my head, stopping him short. I was suddenly eager to get away from him. My old feelings towards him were threatening to surge back to the surface after his small attempt at kindness. "It's fine, Theo. I'm fine."

"Oh. Okay." My heart clenched at the way his face dropped. "I guess I'll see you Friday then."

"Yeah, see you Friday," I said, walking off in the opposite direction. My head and heart felt heavy with every step I took away from him, reminding me that, despite being such a hot and cold person, Theodore Lockhart would always make me feel warm all over, even when the world around me was freezing cold.

Friday came around sooner than expected.

I spent far too long trying to pick out a suitable outfit; a dress seemed too fancy but jeans too casual. In the end I settled on a patterned skirt that reached just above my knees, and a long-sleeved top with a Bardot neckline that paired with it perfectly.

My mother stood in the doorway of my bedroom, hovering and watching me get ready. She crossed her arms over her chest, her eyebrows furrowing together. "Where did you say you were going again?"

I grabbed a pair of tights and bunched them up, sliding them over my feet. "Theo's house for dinner."

"Theo," she repeated, rolling his name off her tongue, testing it out for size. She hesitated. "So things are sorted between you two then, I guess?"

I took my time replying. I rummaged around in the top drawer of my desk for my make-up bag and sat down so that I could see into the mirror before asking, "What do you mean?"

"Well, I'd assumed he was the reason for the mood you've been in lately."

This time I chose not to answer, instead focusing on applying my foundation. I could see her out of the corner of my eye, looking like she wanted to say something else.

"I could have helped you plan your outfit if you'd bothered to tell me about tonight sooner," she finally muttered, before adding, "Not that what you're wearing doesn't look good."

There was silence as I applied a layer of mascara, before grabbing my lipstick and coating my lips in pink.

"You should have asked me or your father for permission to go tonight," my mother then said, her voice rising with authority. Her tone dared me to ignore her again, but I swivelled around in my chair and looked at her, my eyes narrowing.

"Neither of you have exactly been around to ask."

"We're around more often than we used to be. We both changed our schedules," she protested.

"Only because you're worried about me bringing another boy home to hide in my bedroom. Not because you actually want to spend time with me," I said.

"Rose!"

I was as surprised with myself almost as much as my mother was. I wasn't the kind of girl to argue with my parents; before the Theo situation, I had always agreed with what they said, and held my tongue if I wanted to argue with them. But something inside me had snapped. I could feel myself changing.

"You can't even deny it, can you?" I turned round to look at my mother. Her hair was still tight in its bun and her suit was flawless, despite the fact she'd been at work all day. On the surface, she was the vision of perfection, but the surface was where it ended. "You actually think I'm going to try the same stunt that I pulled before? Do you think I'm that stupid?"

"Well, I didn't think you were stupid enough to try it in the first place, so I clearly don't know you, do I, Rose?" she snapped back at me, her eyes wild with fury.

I was taken aback by her rage. I'd only ever seen her like this with Brent before, so to feel her anger directed at me was unsettling. But I'd had enough; I'd had enough of trying to please everyone, when I clearly wasn't able to make anyone happy any more.

"And whose fault is that?" I asked, my voice cracking.

My mother froze, the fury leaking out of her entire being. I pushed past her without another word, heading down the stairs and out of the front door, not bothering to say goodbye. Tears threatened to spill from my eyes, but I blinked furiously and forced the moment to pass.

I could feel my parents watching me from the front door as I walked through the snow over to my car. I brushed the snow off the windscreen, got in and slammed the door, then grabbed the sheet of paper with Theo's new address on it. I tapped it into my phone and waited for the directions to come up on the screen. The rear-view mirror was fogged with condensation when I looked in it, but I could see the single tear that had escaped and rolled down my cheek to my chin, and I brushed it away with my fingertips, removing all trace of the pain I felt in one swift move.

I took a final deep breath and started up the car, before driving away without another look back at my house. Because I could only face one form of torture at a time, and I was sure that being in the same room as Theo for an entire evening was going to be the worst torture of them all.

Fourteen

I pressed the doorbell.

I took a deep breath. Tried to compose myself. Pushed my hair back behind my ears.

The door opened.

Mrs Lockhart barely gave me a second to register what was happening before she gently grasped my arm and pulled me inside the house, her smile so wide it practically split her face in half. "Come in, come in! Let's get you out of the cold," she gushed before slamming the door and blocking out all of the cold air.

I forced a smile despite the uncomfortable feeling that was bubbling underneath my skin. I had thought I was ready for this, but I wasn't. I wasn't prepared for seeing Theo's mother after everything I knew and after everything that had happened. It made my head spin, and I felt a sharp twinge in my chest.

I felt a hand touch my arm, pulling me back to reality. "Breathe, Rose." Theo was suddenly by my side, whispering gently. "Just breathe."

I shut my eyes tightly for a moment as déjà vu washed over

me; an image of Theo holding me in my house as he whispered the same words into my ear filling my mind.

Mrs Lockhart was still standing there. A smile tugged on her lips as her eyes gazed at Theo and me standing so close together. I was hit with the sudden desire to tear myself away from him, but I couldn't do anything about it because his mum was watching us. His words had helped though, because now the pain in my chest had faded away until it was almost non-existent.

"It's lovely to see you again, Rose," Mrs Lockhart said, pulling me into a tight hug, effectively breaking Theo and me apart.

"It's nice to see you too, Mrs Lockhart," I managed to stutter out, my nerves getting the better of me.

She smiled warmly. "Please, call me Nicki. Here, let's get out of the hall and get warm. Theo, take Rose's coat?"

Theo turned to me, trying to catch my eye as he gently took the coat out of my hands. I turned away, following Nicki into the living room and leaving him behind.

"So, Rose." Nicki repeated my name, rolling the letters off her tongue. "Is that short for something? Rosalie, or Rosaline?"

"Rosaline," I answered. "My full name's Rosaline Valentine, but I've always just been called Rose."

Nicki's grin widened as Theo sloped into the room. I noticed that she seemed taller, livelier. Happier. I guessed it was all because she was finally free.

Nicki nodded thoughtfully, raising a hand to her chin. "Theodore and Rosaline." Her voice was sickly sweet. "They go well together. Did you know Rose's name was short for Rosaline, Theo?"

Theo cleared his throat. "Er, no, I didn't," he replied,

glancing back up at me and catching my eyes once more before looking away again.

"Everyone just calls me Rose," I repeated dumbly, my voice sounding hoarse and odd to me.

There was a pause, brief but noticeable, as we all stood in silence. I could feel Nicki's eyes flickering from me to Theo as she tried to work out what was going on between us, but I kept my gaze focused on the ground, not daring to so much as glance up.

"I think dinner's almost ready, if you want to head into the dining room," Nicki finally said. "I hope you like roast beef, Rose?"

I felt Theo's gaze shift over to me as I smiled brightly and nodded. "I love it," I said, allowing myself one more glance in his direction. Our eyes met again.

This time, he didn't look away.

"Do you like it?"

I finished the food I was chewing and took a sip of my drink. "It's amazing."

I focused on the plate in front of me, trying to get as much of the roast dinner onto my fork without looking too piggy. Neither of my parents had ever been one for cooking at home, and every time Brent had tried making a home-cooked meal for the two of us he'd managed to burn it, so having a meal like this cooked for me was a novelty that I wasn't used to – especially when the food was so incredible.

Theo looked up from his own dinner for a second, a glimmer of a grin on his face. "Mum studied at a culinary institute for a few years before she had me," he explained.

I opened my mouth to respond, but Nicki cut in. "Do you like cooking, Rose?" She raised her wine glass to her lips and took a sip, waiting for my answer.

"Yes, but I prefer baking," I admitted, shrugging. "I've always had a bit of a sweet tooth."

Nicki smiled. "It's just as well I made salted caramel brownies for dessert then."

My mouth practically watered at the thought. "Already those brownies sound amazing!"

The click of cutlery on plates filled the room, and I could feel my stomach fill up until it could hold no more. But I didn't want to stop eating; I didn't want to leave anything behind on my plate when the food was so good. I lifted my head to tell Nicki again how delicious it all tasted, but she beat me to it.

"I just wanted to say thank you," she blurted out, as if she couldn't contain the words any longer.

My mouth snapped shut, my words evaporating. Tension rose in the room, spreading through the air and thickening with every passing second. I shifted in my seat, feeling Nicki's gaze locked on me.

"Mum ..." Theo looked up at her, fidgeting uncomfortably in his seat.

"You did so much for Theo when he was in trouble," Nicki continued, ignoring him. "So much that I wasn't able to do. And even though I was so worried about him for all that time he was missing, I can't be mad at you for doing what I wasn't able to do. I can't be mad at you when you helped Theo out when he was so lost."

There was so much sincerity in Nicki's expression that I felt a wave of sympathy for her, and my emotions got the better of me as I realised how much pain she had suffered. My eyes burned and I blinked to stop tears from welling up. "Oh, Nicki, it's fine –"

"It's so kind what you did for Theo. I'm sure he's more than grateful." I realised she wasn't aware of the silent treatment I'd been receiving all this time. And, as if her words were a prompt, we both glanced at Theo expectantly, to see if he would agree.

He shifted in his chair. "Yeah," he said, shooting me a small smile, "I am."

The room froze. I was trapped in his gaze, unable to do anything but stare at Theo and only Theo. And, in that moment, I felt like I understood him and everything he was feeling.

But Nicki broke the moment. "I felt like I needed to invite you round for dinner tonight, because I felt so guilty for not thanking you for doing everything you did for us. Especially when I'm sure it wasn't easy for you."

I turned towards her, breaking all contact with Theo again. "I can deal with the negatives."

Nicki clasped her hands together on the table and sat up straighter in her chair. "Obviously, in an ideal situation, this wouldn't have happened." She laughed nervously, as if trying to joke away the awkwardness. "But with things so bad at home like they were, Theo did the right thing in going to someone else." She shifted her gaze towards her son, who looked extremely uncomfortable, his neck red and his eyes downcast. Then she turned back to me, a trace of a smile in her expression. "And it was even more right that he picked you."

There was a sudden scraping noise as Theo stood up from his seat. "I-I need some air," he said abruptly, heading out of the room.

"Theo, honey –" Nicki tried, but her words did nothing to stop him from leaving. A door slammed shut.

I hurried to my own feet. "Excuse me," I managed to get out, before heading off in the direction that Theo had gone.

He was sitting on the back step when I found him, staring straight ahead. His whole body was shivering.

I wrapped my arms around myself to keep warm as I walked over and took a seat on the steps next to him. He made no move to look at me as I sat down.

One of us needed to say something – *anything* – and yet we both stayed completely still, sitting together in silence. The wind picked up, causing my hair to blow wildly around me, and I reached up to push it back behind my ears.

"There were so many times when I tried to tell you," Theo said at last, his voice hoarse.

I turned towards him, surprised at the raw emotion in his tone. "Theo, you don't have to –"

"Every time I opened my mouth to say the words ... I just couldn't get them out. I couldn't sleep; I spent so many nights worried. I kept wondering what your reaction would be if I told you, but I ended up scaring myself too much ... I frightened myself out of telling you. I put it off for longer and longer ... and then it was too late. And you ... you found out from someone else."

My eyes tried to search his, but he was facing away, blocking himself from me. "Why won't you look at me, Theo?" I whispered, tenderly touching his arm. Our skin brushed and a spark of heat ran through my body, setting me alight.

"Because every time I look into your eyes, Rose, I see it. I see the hurt, the betrayal – everything that you felt when someone else told you what *I* was meant to tell you. What I should have told you. And it kills me," he admitted, glancing at me. It was just for a second, but it was long enough for me to see just how much pain he was feeling.

I struggled to think of the right words to say – the right thing that would fix everything that had broken apart. Theo waited, his body stiff and cold next to mine.

"Well, maybe it's not too late to share it with me," I said softly, my words so quiet I wasn't sure if he'd hear them.

He closed his eyes and took a deep breath. For a moment I thought he might close back up or push me away, like he was so good at doing. But he didn't – Theo realised just how much he needed to do this as I did.

"It wasn't ... often, I guess," he started, his voice shaking. "Only when I gave him a reason to be, I don't know, disappointed or something. My dad, he liked to use his fists whenever he was mad, so I used to try and keep away from him. But most of the time it didn't make a difference what I did. If he'd been drinking, chances were that me or my mum were going to get in trouble – it was the same for her too. I knew she felt helpless. And I felt so helpless too, because I couldn't do anything to protect her. I'd always have to go into school desperately trying to hide the bruises. But by hiding them, I felt like I was covering up for him." His words poured out, and I let them, finally understanding the boy sitting in front of me.

"I became so afraid ... and I pushed people away because I couldn't get too close to them. I was ashamed, I guess. I didn't want anyone to know my secrets so I did what I had to do to keep them hidden. It was easier that way."

He looked at me then, properly, for the first time in seven whole weeks. I saw every emotion he felt, everything he'd wanted to say to me, everything he'd been through. I saw it all. I saw it all in that one single glance and it was powerful enough to make the world suddenly stop still on its axis.

"When I was told at school that day that they were going to expel me, I panicked. I knew I couldn't go home, but I didn't know what to do. I-I couldn't think straight. So I did the first thing that came to mind: I packed a bag. I left home with nowhere to go, no idea where I could stay – and then, I don't know, I thought of you. I mean, I'd kind of assumed you liked me after you asked me to the winter dance, but it wasn't just that. I didn't really plan it, I just had this feeling you would help me if I asked for help."

He wouldn't stop looking at me and my heart wouldn't stop racing. I could feel it fluttering beneath my ribs, like a caged bird desperate to fly and sing.

"After I came back to school and saw you in chemistry for the first time since everything had happened, I knew straight away. I knew you'd been told about my dad, and I knew you were hurt that I didn't tell you. But I still didn't want to talk about it. I still wasn't ready for things to change. I wanted things to be normal. People like Hannah Marshall were paying me more attention because I was suddenly 'interesting', but I never wanted that. And I guess I used her as a way of blocking you out. Thankfully she lost interest pretty quickly too, and so I went back to being alone again. It's what I'd always done. Before ..."

He stopped, shaking his head, closing his eyes once more and turning away from me. But we'd come too far for him to stop now.

I raised my hand again, and gently pulled him back to reality with one single lingering touch to his shoulder. "Before what, Theo?"

He turned to me then, his eyes hollow. "Before you had the chance to actually care about someone as broken as me."

In that moment, I saw Theodore Lockhart for what he truly was: a damaged boy who'd gone through so much, and held onto too many secrets for too long. But what had happened to Theo, everything he'd suffered, while absolutely awful, didn't make him broken. He was one of the strongest people I knew, and hearing what he'd just told me only proved that in my mind. He didn't need fixing: he wasn't broken. And I wanted to tell him that, but I knew there would be time to do that later. So I just grabbed hold of his hand, grasped it tightly in my own, and whispered, "Too late."

And, as I looked into his eyes, and smiled softly at the spark that was still contained in them, I knew things were going to be all right for Theo. That things were going to be all right for both of us.

Nicki looked up as I walked back into the room, her face anxious as she tried to assess the situation.

"I'm so sorry. I shouldn't have brought things back up when they're in the past now," she said, shooting me an apologetic smile. "I just wanted you to know how grateful I am to you, Rose. I don't know what would have happened to Theo if he hadn't gone to you – I-I can't bear to think about it." Her eyes shone with fresh tears.

"I don't like to think about it either," I agreed softly. "Thank you so much, Nicki. The dinner really was amazing."

"Are you not able to stay for dessert?"

I was about to open my mouth and protest when a voice cut in before me.

"Yeah." Theo came back into the room, his hair messily swept back by the wind and a small smile on his face. "You should stay."

I found myself smiling back at him, my entire body relaxing. I shrugged. "All right then," I agreed, causing his grin to widen. "Maybe I will."

Fifteen

'd hoped I'd manage to get through winter without falling sick, but when I sat up in bed the Monday morning after dinner at Theo's house and felt my head spin at the sudden movement, I realised I hadn't been so lucky after all.

My nose was a blotchy red. My eyelids were heavy. My throat felt red raw even though I hadn't coughed much yet, and my skin felt like it was on fire compared to the cold air outside.

My mother came into the room a few moments after hearing me sneeze five times in a row, only to stand over me with pursed lips and confirm what I already knew. "You're sick."

"I'll be fine," I rasped. I pulled the covers off my body, pushing myself up to lean against my headboard. A wave of shivers ran down my back as the cold air hit my bare skin.

My mother clicked her tongue in disapproval. Then she left the room – only to come back with a thermometer a second later.

"Here." She handed me the stick and I slotted it under my

tongue for a minute before giving it back to her. Her eyes narrowed as she read the numbers on the screen. She checked the box then looked back up at me. "You've got a temperature."

I sneezed and she skidded backwards like I'd just breathed fire. "Great," I muttered as she hurried out of the room, and I snuggled back beneath my covers.

I squeezed my eyes shut and waited to fall asleep, the quiet only disturbed by the faint sound of my mother bustling around downstairs as she got herself ready for work. Just as I was about to nod off, she came back up and popped her head round the door. "I've called the school to let them know you won't be in."

"I could've done that," I protested weakly.

"Well, it's done now." My mother checked her watch and frowned at the time. "I need to get to work. Will you be all right by yourself today?"

"I guess I'll have to be."

"I can call Grace and Naya to come and take care of you after school finishes. I'm sure they wouldn't mind."

I almost laughed out loud when I noted that she didn't offer to stay behind to take care of me. Sickness to my mother meant missing work, and I knew she definitely didn't want to get too close to me in case she caught what I had.

"It's fine, Mum," I managed to rasp out, my throat now persistently hurting with every breath I took and every word that passed my lips. "I'll be fine."

She watched me for a moment, and I wondered whether she might change her mind and stay after all. I glanced up at her from my bed, watching as she clicked her tongue on the roof of her mouth again.

"Okay," she said slowly, moving backwards out of the door.

"I should be home around six. We can order pizza if you want."

The idea of food right now made my stomach churn, but I forced myself to nod in agreement. "Sure, sounds great."

I was so desperate for her to leave, and eager to fall back asleep and spend the rest of my day in bed. But my mother continued to linger, cautious and worried.

The idea that she may actually be concerned for me popped into my head, and I resisted the urge to close my eyes and fall asleep. Instead, I looked up at her again. Sure enough, she was still watching me, but I could now see the worry in her face, which was deepening the lines in her skin. She tried to smile but it wavered weakly, soon giving way to a frown.

"I'll be fine, Mum," I said softly, trying to comfort her. "Seriously."

My words seemed to snap her out of her trance, and she nodded curtly, her eyes drifting away from me. "Good," she said, and her tone was professional, business-like.

I couldn't help but smile at that, because that was the thing with my mother: she had two sides. There were only a few occasions when I got a glimpse of the woman she used to be – the kind, motherly, caring one. It was great that she'd climbed the ranks in her job, but it had changed how she was at home; it was as if she'd become the same person at home as at work – cold, aloof, distant. She'd certainly become a different woman to me, and it was only when I could see flashes of the old her – standing concerned in my doorway, for instance – that I realised she was still my mum, still the same mum I had known my whole life. But we'd both changed, for different reasons, and the old version of ourselves were now buried deep inside.

We'd always bash heads; we'd always clash. And I didn't

think she would ever change back to the mum I used to know. But it was nice to see this side of her, no matter how brief the glimpse was.

I closed my eyes and she started to walk away, stopping to gently close my bedroom door shut behind her. And before she'd even reached the front door I'd fallen asleep, drifting into oblivion once more, feeling slightly more comforted.

The persistent knocking on my door was starting to get on my nerves.

Someone had been ringing the doorbell for a while, and I'd been ignoring them, hoping whoever it was – most likely a salesperson at this time of day – would give up and go away. But the knocking had continued for at least five minutes and was showing no sign of stopping.

I felt weak and fragile. My head was pounding and my skin felt even hotter than it had in the morning. I didn't want to get out of bed; I didn't want to get up and make it all the way downstairs just to open the door to someone who I didn't want to speak to. But I managed to drag myself out, my feet thudding on the carpet as I made my way down the stairs still in my pyjamas, with my hair in a messy bun and my duvet wrapped around my shoulders.

When I opened the front door and saw Theo Lockhart standing there, a plastic tub in his hands, I thought I might be delirious.

"Theo?" I managed to get out, blinking once as though he might disappear before my eyes. He didn't.

Instead he smiled awkwardly, the dimples in his cheeks prominent. "Hi."

The cold air was flowing into the house, causing my skin to

155

prickle with goose bumps, but I hardly cared. "What are you doing here?" I breathed.

"Grace got a text from your mother asking her to come and check on you today during lunch break, but I offered to do it instead," he explained. He raised the tub in his hands. "Can I come in? I've got soup."

I wordlessly stepped aside, still dazed. Theo brushed past me in the doorway, our skin making contact and causing me to jump. He noticed and let out a small apology, handing me the container before he started to take off his coat, scarf and shoes.

"How are you feeling?" he asked as he took the container back out of my hands and made his way towards the kitchen. I followed him without hesitation. "Do you still have a temperature?"

"I think so," I said, barely able to think straight. Theo was here. Theo was *here*. The last time he'd been here, of course, was the moment he'd been found by my parents – the moment everything had been ruined.

The last time I'd seen him in this house he'd kissed me.

I felt my cheeks grow warmer at the memory and I averted my eyes, looking down at the floor and willing my heart to stop racing. Theo's eyes scanned me, full of concern like my mother's.

"You look a bit hot," he commented. Then his eyes widened in alarm when he realised what he'd said. "I-I mean you look like you still have a, err – a temperature, that's all."

"I'm fine," was all I managed to reply, my heart now beating at a fast, steady pace beneath my ribs. Despite my gross pyjamas and messy hair, I was glad that he was there.

He cleared his throat. "Do you mind if I go and heat this up for you?" He raised the container, nodding at it.

"Sure."

He pointed to the lounge as he headed towards the kitchen. "You can go and wait in there. I'll be back with your soup in a minute."

I collapsed onto the sofa as soon as I reached it, closing my eyes and listening to Theo crash around in the kitchen. A string of profanities soon followed.

Theo was here. Theo was here.

There was no way I was going to be able to relax now, especially with the racket coming from the kitchen.

"Do you need some help?"

There was another crash. He swore again.

"I'm fine," he said a moment later, his voice strained.

It wasn't long before he came into the room. He carried a tray with a pile of bread and a large bowl of soup carefully balanced on top.

"Here," Theo said, handing me a spoon before adding, "Eat the soup." He awkwardly sat down next to me on the sofa, facing towards me.

I decided to tease him. "God, demanding much?"

But he instantly recoiled, looking alarmed. "Oh, s-sorry, I didn't mean –"

"Theo," I said. "It's all right. I was just kidding."

"Oh," he mumbled, scratching the back of his neck. "Right."

There was a pause, filled with awkwardness and tension. *It's not the same*, I thought to myself, my eyes suddenly feeling heavy with tears. Things weren't the same. How could they be? I should have realised that we weren't ever going to be able to go back to normal – that so much time had passed now, a few months had gone by, and our relationship had changed drastically. But it was never normal in the first place, so I'd just have to hope that this new relationship of ours could be as good as the one we had before.

Trying to lighten the mood, I ripped off a piece of bread and dunked it into the soup bowl, not thinking before I popped it into my mouth. And then the memory of Theo burning my toast came back to me, and I suddenly regretted my actions.

Theo's eyes shifted to me, sparking with eagerness. "How is it?" he asked confidently, anticipating my answer.

"It's good," I said honestly, my tone full of surprise. "It's more than good, actually."

He smiled brightly, watching me as I grabbed some more bread and dunked it into my bowl. "Well, I am my mother's son, Rosaline."

Rosaline. He called me Rosaline. My heat skipped an entire beat.

"Mmm. Didn't you burn my actual toast when you were staying here?"

The memory of it made Theo laugh; he tilted his head back and closed his eyes. "I've been practising since."

He seemed to feel my gaze on him because a second later he turned to look at me with an emotion I couldn't quite place. I felt my whole body shake at that single look.

He broke eye contact and turned away from me. He scratched his neck and I saw that it was blotched with red. Discomfort was radiating off him.

"This really is incredible, though," I murmured, taking another spoonful of soup.

He shifted slightly, turning back towards me. "All right, I do have a confession to make," he admitted, smiling sheepishly.

"Yeah?"

"I actually got my mum to make it for me before I came over here. I just heated it up on the stove."

I let out a loud laugh and Theo tried desperately not to join in, his face still full of mischievous guilt. The awkwardness that lingered in the room drained right out of it, and Theo soon couldn't help joining in with my giggles.

"Theodore Lockhart, you liar!" I teased, nudging him in the side. I could feel my raw throat crying out in protest as I continued to laugh, but I tried to ignore it.

Theo's expression was glowing. "What?" I asked, my laughter dying away as I felt my self-consciousness rise to the surface again.

"It just sounds ... right," he said, his voice quiet but full of sincerity. "You calling me Theodore again."

I felt myself smiling, my heart flying with the emotions his words ignited. "I know."

"You're still the only one who calls me that," he pointed out.

"And you're the only one who calls me Rosaline," I shot back. I never normally liked anyone calling me by my full name, but from Theo it felt natural. It just felt right.

"I'll make sure to keep a note of that, then," Theo promised.

I noticed him glance at his watch, and I raised my eyebrows. "Don't you need to be going back to school now?"

Theo shrugged. "I've got some time."

I knew he didn't care too much about his education; he'd never been one to raise his hands in lessons or pay full attention to the teacher when they were speaking, but the idea of him missing his lessons because of me made me uneasy.

"Theodore, I don't want you missing school because –"

"It's fine, Rosaline. Seriously." He waved his hand in dismissal. "I can catch up."

"Oh right, and did you catch up from the entire week you missed thinking you were expelled?"

"I *was* expelled," he corrected me. "My mother just pulled some strings and got me re-enrolled. She told the headmaster about my dad, and they changed their minds. But, as for the work, I caught up in the week I came back to school."

I raised my eyebrows at him in disbelief. "You did? How is that physically possible?"

Theo let out a short laugh. "I only missed about a week of school, you realise. With the four subjects that I take, that really isn't that much to catch up on."

I let his words sink in, realising that he was right – it would be easy to catch up on the work. But then another thought popped into my mind. "Wait, you take four A Levels? Weren't you meant to drop one at the end of last year?"

He cocked one eyebrow in amusement. "You really do underestimate me, Rosaline Valentine. You weren't the only one the school let carry on with your four subjects, you know."

Surprise washed over me. "I'm sorry, I didn't –"

Theo's laughter cut me off. "It's really fine, Rosaline. I wouldn't have expected it from me either."

And then he looked at me, and my heart stopped. Because in that moment, sitting with me, he looked so happy. The happiest I had seen him in ages. And, I realised, I felt my happiest too.

I could feel heat creeping into my cheeks but I didn't look away so that he wouldn't notice. Instead, I let him see my blush spread, and from the visible outline of his dimples I could tell he noticed. "God, you seriously love my full name," I said softly, not wanting the silence to linger.

"It's beautiful," he said sincerely.

And then a moment later, his watch started beeping. He glanced down at it, frowning. "I guess I better be getting back to school then. Are you feeling all right now?"

I nodded, my heart deflating at the thought of him leaving. Theo smiled at me once more and grabbed the empty tray, moving to take it out of the living room.

"Theodore," I said softly. He turned around to look at me, waiting for my next words. "Why did you really come here?"

Theo smiled. It illuminated his whole face, making him look even more gorgeous than normal, and literally taking my breath away. "Because you're supposed to look after the people you care about," he replied earnestly. And then he tilted his head, looking at me with that same smile. "And, now that you're back in my life, I guess I can't stay away from you, Rosaline Valentine."

Sixteen

Life was hectic in the weeks leading up to Christmas. Mock exams were revised for, final lessons were finished, and university advice was given. I didn't have much time to think about anything other than school and the work I felt like I was falling behind on, so the idea of Christmas was lost on me.

But not everyone was as panicked as I felt inside – and ironically it was Theo, the one who had missed that entire week of school, who was the most chilled out of all of us. One day, he came into the chemistry room whistling 'Jingle Bells', and placed a box covered in wrapping paper in front of me.

"What's this?" I asked in surprise, dropping my pencil onto the table and gesturing towards the box.

Theo rolled his eyes, his smirk widening. "It's a Christmas present, Rose," he informed me in a slow, mocking voice. "God, I know you've constantly got your head stuck in those books at the moment, but I didn't think it had got to the point where you can't even remember what time of year it is."

I felt my cheeks flush as I carefully took the box into my

hands, my fingertips tracing each snowflake printed on the paper. "But ... I haven't gone Christmas shopping yet, so I don't have anything –"

"Don't worry about it. Just open your gift."

He watched me eagerly as I ripped open the wrapping. I pulled out *A Tale of Two Cities* by Charles Dickens and examined the front cover.

I looked up at him and smiled. "Thank you, Theo."

But as I was putting the book into my bag Theo cleared his throat. His hands started reaching into his pocket, and his neck turned red.

"I – uh, I also got you this as well," he mumbled, pulling out a long, rectangular box and passing it over to me. I pulled off the bow on it and lifted the lid, my eyes widening instantly.

"God, Theo –" I gently took the necklace out of the box, holding it up so I could get a better look at the light blue pendant that hung down, shaped beautifully and intricately wrapped around a long silver cord. I struggled to find the right words to say as I stared at it in admiration.

"My mum picked it out for you," he explained, scratching at his neck and averting his gaze. "She said it would suit your eyes."

"Yeah." I held the pendant up next to my face and batted my eyelashes, showing how well the colour of my eyes worked with the shade of the pendant. "A perfect match."

Theo looked at me then, his eyes raking over mine as a small smile lingered on his face. "A perfect match," he repeated.

We sat there looking at each other. The other students in the classroom chatted loudly as they waited for the teacher to come in, but I hardly noticed anyone else in the room. I stayed entirely focused on Theo.

He cleared his throat again. "Anyway, what are you doing after school today?" he asked. I raised my eyebrows, waiting for more, and he added, "Do you fancy going somewhere? Anywhere?"

"Er – yeah," I said, taken aback by his invite. "Sure."

Theo smiled, running his fingers through his hair, messing up his dark waves and pushing some of them into his face. "Okay. I'll meet you after the last lesson then?" he suggested.

I nodded in agreement, but I couldn't help wondering why he looked so eager to get away again.

Theo was waiting for me when I came out of my last lesson of the day, his back resting against the wall of my classroom and his feet sticking out so far that I was surprised he didn't trip everyone up as they came out of the room. But everyone noticed him – I saw people eyeing him, waiting to see what he was doing. I watched their eyes widen slightly as he pushed off the wall and headed over to me, a grin broad on his face.

"You ready?" he asked when I reached him, gesturing towards the exit behind me.

I nodded, shoving my hands into my pockets to keep them warm as I let Theo lead me out of the school building and towards the car park. But I stopped in my tracks when I saw where we were heading.

"Wait, you're driving?" I asked as we approached Theo's rusty old car.

Theo shot me a strange look as he walked round to the driver's side. "Well, I was planning on it, yes."

I hesitated, and he stopped opening the car door and raised his eyebrows, waiting for me to say what was clearly on my mind.

"Are you sure that's safe?"

A smirk appeared on his face. "Are you trying to call me a bad driver?"

"No!"

"You've never even seen me drive before, Rose!"

"You're just a bit of a reckless person, that's all." I paused for a second, thinking about it, then added, "Actually, you're probably the most reckless person I've ever met."

"Well, I can assure you that I'm the safest driver," Theo said in an exaggeratedly sincere voice, stepping forward and opening the door. "Don't worry, you're safe with me, Rosaline." And then he shot me a wink and got inside as if the conversation was over.

I hurried to clamber into the car after him. I quickly put on my seat belt, as Theo shoved his key into the ignition. And then we were off, driving out of the school car park and on to the icy road.

"Do we need to drive back here to pick up your car later?" he offered, as if the thought had only just occurred to him.

"It's fine," I replied, my voice light but my body shaking from the cold. Theo's car was so old that the heaters didn't work any more, both of them blasting out dusty cold air no matter how hot I tried to make them. I leaned forward to switch them off. "I didn't bring my car with me to school today."

"Thank God for that," he muttered, keeping his eyes on the road and slowing down when we came across a particularly large patch of ice.

"Where are we going?" I asked, staring out of the window at the scenery.

"Anywhere we want."

"You decide." I shrugged. "I don't care."

"Okay."

We sat in silence for a while, and I watched the scene outside my window. It was starting to snow again, flecks of white descending all around the car. Theo focused on his driving the entire time; his eyes never flicked away from the road and his speed stayed low. He didn't even seem distracted when the snow started to fall more heavily; he just flicked the headlights on and kept on driving.

"Can I ask you something?" I asked after a while, my eyes lingering on him.

Theo shrugged, his hands gripping the leather steering wheel. "Depends on what the question is."

"Are you trying to avoid going home?"

He sighed and I watched him, trying to gauge his reaction to my question. I felt myself tense for a moment, unsure if I'd crossed a line or brought up something he didn't want to talk about, but then he sunk down further into his seat, his hands loosening on the wheel ever so slightly, and I relaxed again.

"My mum's been driving me insane lately," he explained. "Ever since we left my dad she's been much more clingy and protective."

I understood where he was coming from, but I felt a pang in my chest for Nicki. I'd seen for myself her overprotectiveness, and while she may have been a bit pushy, she was also one of the sweetest women I'd ever met.

"She's only looking out for you," I tried to reason, my voice soft.

Theo sighed again, his face flashing with guilt. "I know. It's just too much sometimes, you know?" He shook his head, his lip turning red from where he had been biting it so hard. "God, I sound like such a dick."

166

"You don't," I assured him. "I know what you mean – well, I mean, I don't really, but ..."

I trailed off, feeling deflated as I thought of my own home situation. Theo's eyes held mine for a moment before he turned back towards the road. "Things are still bad with your parents?"

"They probably always will be."

"I'm sorry."

His tone was so sincere that it opened a floodgate of emotions inside of me, and I battled with myself for some control. "Don't be. It's not your fault."

"Yeah, but with the hiding thing –"

"That's not what they're even angry about any more," I interjected, cutting him short. "They're not angry, they're just ... distant. But they're not all bad, you know? Sometimes I'll see a different side to them – sometimes they'll actually come through for me. But I feel like we don't really know each other any more, and I doubt there's any chance of it getting better."

Sometimes a relationship you have with someone shifts, and you can never change it back to what it was again. That's what it felt like with my parents. They'd always be my parents, but they were never going to meet the expectations I had for them; they were never going to be like they used to be with me. I was learning to accept that.

"But you have that with Brent, right? That connection?" Theo prodded, his voice hopeful as he tried to make light of the situation.

"Yeah. I do," I agreed. "I'm lucky to have a brother like him."

"He's coming home for Christmas, right?"

"In a couple of weeks. Right before the twenty-fifth of

167

December. He wanted to leave earlier but he's fallen behind on some uni work."

Brent had actually mentioned that he wanted to meet Theo when he came home. The only things he'd heard about him were what I'd mentioned, and they were such vague details that he'd decided he just had to meet the boy I'd been hiding in my bedroom for days – the one who'd caused me to disobey my parents for once. But I didn't plan on telling Theo any of this. In fact, I was determined to make sure to keep Theo and Brent as far away from one another as possible. Putting them together would only cause trouble. I knew I could count on Brent to screw everything up between Theo and me with a single throwaway comment, when things were only just getting back to normal. Brent had always been overprotective, with a habit of saying whatever came into his mind, which had led to some awkward situations.

"Well, at least he's coming," Theo said, breaking me out of my thoughts.

"Yeah. It'll be good to see him." The car lurched forward as I spoke, and I sat up straighter in my seat, looking out of the window as we came to a standstill. "Wait, why have we stopped?"

He turned to me, smiling. "We're here."

I blinked, my mouth dropping open slightly. "We're at a park."

"So?"

"Theo, have you not noticed how freezing it is outside?"

"We have coats, don't we? Besides, walking will keep us warm." And then, before I could object any further, Theo got out of the car. If I didn't want to freeze in his death trap of a vehicle, the only option was to follow him.

"You're insane." I shook my head as he came around to me, grabbing my arm and leading me to the park entrance.

"And I'm also the only one who could be bothered to come up with an idea for a place to go. So come on, Rosaline."

We were the only ones in the park, unsurprisingly. Our feet made footprints in the snow and our hair caught all the little flurries that flew around us as we walked. Theo led the way. His expression grew excited as he grabbed some of the snow and rolled it into a tight ball, throwing it into the air. I scowled and wrapped my arms around myself, desperately trying to conserve all my body heat.

"You really are an idiot, Theodore," I scolded him when he stopped walking and waited for me to catch up.

He grinned widely, shooting me a wink. "And yet you tolerate me."

I rolled my eyes and continued walking, but his words played round and round like a broken record in my mind.

"I think I recognise this place," I said a moment later, in a desperate attempt to get Theo to stop staring at me like that.

Theo raised his eyebrows. "Oh yeah? From where?"

"I've been here before," I said. "With Xander."

He wasn't watching me now, his eyes instead focusing on the trees that were swaying in the breeze around us. We were walking around the large pond in the middle of the park, now frozen over in the bitter cold. "Oh, right." He paused, before adding, "Were you two dating at the time?"

"Yeah." I gazed around the park, taking every little detail of it in, noticing how it had barely changed since the last time I'd been. "We'd just started dating. Actually, this was where he took me on our first date."

Theo snorted, his shoulders shaking slightly. "To the park?"

"Hey, don't be mean." I jokingly shoved him in the side, and he stumbled over to the left, shooting me a mock glare. "The park seemed like a romantic place to be when we were fourteen."

"I can imagine," he commented dryly.

The way he spoke made me wonder what he was really thinking, but instead of asking him like I wanted to, I found myself distracted with another thought. "Well, where would you take a girl on a first date?"

"Anywhere but a park." When I scoffed, he glanced at me. "I have been on dates before, you know," he added pointedly.

"What?" I almost stopped walking in surprise. Surely the enigmatic Theo didn't do anything as banal as go on *dates*? "You have?"

"Yes."

The image of Theo with another girl – laughing with her, kissing her, adoring her – appeared as an unwelcome image in my mind. I pushed my jealousy down, swallowing to remove the bitter taste in my mouth.

"With who?" I desperately tried to act casual, but my voice sounded strangled.

I could see the smile playing on Theo's lips, proving he had noticed the way his words were affecting me. But he continued to be vague with his responses. "You don't know any of them."

"Them?" My mouth dropped open. "There was more than one?"

At this he started to get offended, his eyes looking at me accusingly. "Do you seriously think I'm so unappealing that I've never managed to get a girl to go on a date with me before?"

We both knew I was thinking the opposite of that – we both

knew he was baiting me – but I still let him do it, his words getting the better of me.

"No," I was quick to deny, my face flushed. "I just figured you didn't date or something. You aren't exactly the most flirtatious guy at school, that's all."

He let out a short laugh. "Ah, well, if it makes you feel any better, I wasn't when I was dating either. I'm not really a flirty guy."

"You are with me," I pointed out.

"That's because you're you, Rosaline."

I wasn't sure how to answer that. My mind went into over-drive as I turned his words over.

"Anyway, I bet I was better at planning dates than Xander ever was."

"Be nice," I scolded him. "Xander was a good guy."

"I'm sure he was."

I raised my eyebrows at him. "You never met him?"

"We all went to school together, Rose. I saw him around."

"No, but I mean you never spoke to him? You never had anything to do with him?"

Theo looked at me. His face shone with an indescribable expression as he answered, "No. Never."

Theo took me home after another hour of walking at the park in the freezing cold. By the time he pulled up outside my house, my feet felt like they were about to fall off.

"Sorry," he apologised as he turned the car engine off. "I didn't mean to keep you out in the cold for so long."

"It's fine," I said as I moved to pull the car door open. "Thanks for the trip to the park."

He opened his mouth to reply when my phone started

ringing, its blaring tones sounding all through the car. I pulled it out of my bag, shooting Theo a quick apologetic glance as I pressed it to my ear. "Hello?"

"You sound flustered," a voice commented on the other end of the line. It sounded a bit crackly, but the clear amusement in its tone still carried through.

"Brent?" I replied, surprised. Theo straightened up at the name, looking at me curiously. "Why are you calling?" I asked, grinning widely when he responded with a laugh.

"What, am I not allowed to call you spontaneously sometimes?" he asked, his tone teasing.

"Of course you are, but you never do." I paused for a second, before asking, "Are you in trouble?"

"What?"

"Do you need money?"

Theo was laughing now, his body shaking silently as he tried his hardest to be quiet.

"Why would I need money when I'm coming home in three days?" Brent replied, talking slowly like he wanted his words to fully sink in.

"Because –" I stopped when I finally got what he was saying. "Wait, three days?"

"That's why I'm calling," he explained as the line crackled. "I talked to my professor today, and he told me that the work I need to do doesn't need to be completed before Christmas – so I can come home early."

"Brent, that's amazing!" I felt a tap on my shoulder from Theo and tried my best to ignore it. But he continued to tap me, and as I tried to focus on what Brent was saying, I found my temper rising. I sent a sharp jab into Theo's side with my elbow to try and stop him, and he let out a small yelp of pain. I cringed as Brent stopped talking altogether.

It was silent for a moment, before Brent said, "What was that?"

"Nothing." I shook my head even though he couldn't see me, shooting Theo another glare. "Ignore it. So, why three days?"

"You and I both know travelling home isn't easy," Brent pointed out. "Especially in the holidays. Besides, I have a few more things to take care of over here."

"Well, call me as soon as you head back home."

"I promise I will. I'll see you soon, Rose."

I was about to end the call when Brent cleared his throat. "Oh, before you go, make sure you say hi to Theo for me," he said, and I could practically see him in that moment in his dorm room, laughing. "Tell him I can't wait to meet my future brother-in-law."

And, suddenly, I wasn't too sure I wanted my brother to come home any more.

Seventeen

The next three days went by incredibly fast, and school broke up for winter break on the Friday, much to everyone's relief. Then it was Saturday, the day of Brent's return, and I spent most of the morning looking out of the window for him.

Soon enough a car pulled up outside the house and I caught sight of Brent's wild and untamed hair as he stepped out of the vehicle. He took his time grabbing all his stuff out of the backseat, slinging three huge bags over his shoulder before heading up the drive, a wide grin already on his face.

He didn't get the chance to ring the doorbell – I tore the front door open and launched myself into his arms, causing him to drop everything he was carrying.

Brent let out a grunt at the excess weight that had been thrown at him but still wrapped his arms around my waist, hugging me back as I refused to let go any time soon.

"Hey, Rosie," he said when we eventually pulled away from one another, his grin widening at the sight of the scowl on my face.

174

"Four months," I replied, lightly punching him in the side. "I haven't seen you in four months and that's how you greet me."

Brent laughed. He picked up the stuff he had dropped, passing some of it to me as he started to make his way into the house. "Well, it wouldn't be me if I didn't use my favourite nickname for you," he shot back as he brushed past me.

"I missed you," I admitted, my words making him turn around to look at me. Then he dropped his things onto the floor again and came over to me. He grabbed me and pulled me into another tight hug.

"I missed you too," he said, his voice soft and sincere. But then he pulled back and roughly grabbed my cheeks, pinching them between his fingers. "You're growing up so fast," he cooed, his eyes alight with jokey excitement as I struggled to pull out of his clutches.

"Brent!" I shoved him away, shooting him a glare when he started laughing again.

"Sorry," he said. "You're still just so small. Have you even grown at all since I've been gone?"

He was teasing me, but I couldn't help but laugh along with Brent. "Says the giant. Just because you're taller than literally everyone else you know, it doesn't mean I'm small."

The scent of his aftershave left a trace everywhere he went, lingering in the air as a constant reminder to me that he was actually here. That he had actually come back. That he wasn't going anywhere.

Brent suddenly turned serious as he stood, taking in the house with a frown.

"Wow," he sighed. "Literally nothing has changed."

He ran his hands along the crack in the wall that he'd

filled in last year, which was still not yet painted over.

"What did you expect? I was never one for decorating," I said in response, before going back over to his things and starting to pick them up.

"That's very true." Brent chuckled as he came over and grabbed one of the duffel bags out of my hands, slinging it over his shoulder again as I led him into the lounge. "So where am I dropping all my stuff off this time?"

I made my way over to the sofa, slinging two of his bags onto it and gesturing for him to do the same. "I believe this is your bed for your stay, so you can just dump your things here."

I knew he'd be disappointed, but watching Brent's mouth drop open as he stared down at the sofa that he was going to have to sleep on for the next couple of weeks was still a priceless sight for me to behold.

"Seriously?" he groaned, dropping his bag onto the floor and running a hand through his hair. He thought about things for a moment, his mind most likely scanning through all of the other available options before he looked back up at me inquisitively. "What happened to the blow-up bed that was in my old room?"

"You burst it the last time you stayed," I reminded him, and his face fell. "And your real bed was demolished when we remodelled your room after you left, so it's either this or you go out and buy yourself a blow-up mattress."

Brent deliberated for a moment, then shrugged. "I guess the sofa will do," he finally muttered. "It's probably more comfortable than one of those mattresses anyway."

I was slightly surprised that he didn't pry into where Theo had been sleeping when he stayed here. The conversation I'd had with Brent about Theo had been short and awkward, and the subject hadn't been brought up since. I'm sure he had many more questions about what exactly had gone on when Theo was here, but he seemed to know his boundaries, and he understood the topic was still a tense one in this household.

"Are Mum and Dad home?" he asked.

"No, they're not," I said with a shrug. "Why?"

"They called me the other day."

The news shocked me. The last time my parents called Brent was to tell him about me hiding Theo, and that was almost three months ago. He'd been straight on the phone to me afterwards too, briefly telling me what they'd said and asking for himself if it was in fact true. From the grave expression on his face, and the guilt lingering in his eyes, I could tell that they'd discussed a much more serious topic this time.

I decided to play it cool. "Oh really? What about?"

"Uh" – Brent reached a hand up to run through his messy hair – "it may have been about you."

My breathing hitched. "What about me?"

"They were worried." There was a moment of hesitation – a moment where Brent almost seemed like he wanted to let the conversation drop entirely, or talk about something different. "Rose, your relationship with Theo –"

Three days ago. Three days ago my brother had been teasing me about meeting Theo, and now his tone had changed entirely. And all because of one conversation. Anger shot through me.

"It's none of their business," I said sharply, coldly – a clear sign that I didn't want to speak about it any more. But Brent was always one for pushing me further.

"At the end of the day, they're our parents. So if you live underneath their roof, then I guess what you do is actually part of their business."

I decided to ignore his comment. "What did they say about Theo?"

His feet shuffled along the carpet, looking uncomfortable. "That they aren't happy with you two being together. Mum mentioned that you've been very, uh – 'emotionally unstable' since he came into your life."

"Theo and I aren't together in that way," I was quick to explain. "And just because I'm not as polite to them as I used to be, doesn't suddenly mean I'm *emotionally unstable*."

I stopped for a second to think over what he was saying. Was Theo breaking me? It was true that having him in my life had never been easy, what with the lying for him, the hurt I felt when he pushed me away. But with Theo I *liked* the unpredictability. He was reckless, he was exciting.

He was Theo. And he was a breath of fresh air in my otherwise extremely dull life.

"They care about us so much more than you realise, Rose," Brent continued, unaware that I had spaced out. "I know that you're angry with them, you have every right to be. They haven't been there for us. But they came to me because they knew you wouldn't listen to them, and it shows they still care. They'll always care about us."

He leaned over to touch my shoulder, before heading out of the room with his washing, to let me mull over everything he'd said. And the conversation was dropped just like that.

Brent and I spent our Christmas Day together like always: both of us working together on the roast in the kitchen while our parents frantically finished wrapping our presents in the lounge.

I'd spent hours online looking for Brent's present and ended up getting him a stack of films just like I always did. But I didn't feel too guilty, as I knew I'd end up with more books from him, just like every other year. The presents our parents had managed to get us between work hours were put underneath the tree and present giving after a year of estrangement would probably feel a little awkward. But in the end it didn't matter; we stuffed our faces with good food and enjoyed our precious time together.

"Oh, by the way, I like your necklace," Brent said through a mouthful of turkey, pointing to the pendant hanging around my neck.

I absent-mindedly reached up to touch it for myself, a small smile making its way on to my face. I could feel both my parents' eyes on me, staring inquisitively. "Yeah?"

"It suits you," he said. I didn't comment because I didn't want to say anything to Brent in front of my parents, but I felt strangely like I'd lost my appetite, and I tried to hide my nerves by staring steadfastly at my roast potatoes.

The winter holidays were flying by, but we tried to ignore the date on the calendar that was marked as the day Brent had to leave once again, and focused instead on all the time left that we could spend together. Every night was filled with watching movies, until we could feel our eyelids dropping with fatigue, and every day was spent eating our favourite foods and walking outside in what would be the last bit of snow of the season. But by New Year, Brent had started to get bored of our precious routine.

"Let's do something on New Year's Eve," he suggested

one morning when I handed him a mug of hot chocolate and took a seat next to him on the sofa. His eyes glimmered with anticipation.

"What?" I crinkled my nose up in distaste.

"Yeah." He sat up excitedly. "We can go out – you know, celebrate with the other people in our life that we care about. It doesn't just have to be us two."

"I thought we liked our tradition."

Brent shot me an amused look. "Our tradition is the same as what we've been doing this entire week."

"But it's our tradition."

To be honest, I'd always been the type of girl who liked to stay inside in the evenings. While Brent, when he was living here, would be out every single night, I'd always be inviting Grace and Naya over for a night in stuffing our faces with popcorn and watching TV. Staying indoors was my comfort, and I hated being pushed out of my comfort zone.

"Don't worry," he assured me, "we don't have to invite anyone we don't like. Let's just ask Grace and Naya – I haven't seen them in ages. And hey, why don't you invite Theo as well?" Seeing my eyes narrow he sheepishly added, "It'd be great to finally meet him."

I quickly deliberated over my options, my fingertips anxiously playing with the hem of my pyjama top and ignoring Brent's eager gaze.

But I couldn't very well say no – and he knew that. He was the guest of honour after all, and what he said went. But he was sweet enough to make sure it was all right with me too, I guess.

"Fine." As soon as the words passed my lips Brent was in action, grabbing my phone from the coffee table and handing it to me.

"Just call them and ask," he said. "They may have plans already."

I was pretty sure none of them had any plans, but I called them up just to make sure, and soon enough I found myself getting ready for a dinner out on New Year's Eve, having no idea what to expect but telling myself that, with the four people I was going with, things were sure to be eventful.

Eighteen

We ended up going to a pub for a meal.

Brent and Grace had fought over where to eat, just like they used to before Brent went away to university. Brent had won, as he usually did.

"I told you this was the right choice," Brent said as the cab pulled into the car park. The pub he'd chosen was just on the outskirts of town. I turned around in the passenger's seat to look at Theo, immediately catching his eye. He'd been fairly quiet throughout the journey, laughing occasionally at Grace and Brent as they argued but being careful not to give his input. He shot me a small smile from the back seat.

Grace punched Brent in the arm as soon as we stepped out of the cab, and he wrapped an arm around her and laughed. He then grabbed Naya as well and pulled her into a hug. Despite it being so long since they'd all seen each other, Brent's relationship with my two best friends never seemed to change, and I watched them fondly.

The pub was beautiful – an old building covered in ivy

vines, growing upwards as if reaching for the sky. Inside it was filled with dark wood, and there was an open fire at one end of the large room. It had been our go-to place to eat since Brent turned old enough to drive, and now that he was home again it seemed like the obvious choice for getting the group back together.

As soon as we were seated, Brent loudly declared that we should all have champagne, and it was soon at the table.

"Here's to the end of this year," he called out once all of our glasses were raised into the air, the champagne sparkling in the light. "And to the new year coming around the corner, just waiting to be filled with memories that'll last us a lifetime."

We clinked our glasses together and I took a long sip of champagne, the cold bubbles dancing on my tongue and leaving the dimmest burn in my throat. I finished my glass and motioned to Brent to top it up again.

From that point onwards our table was nothing but raucous laughter. Brent had a lot of catching up to do with Grace and Naya, and I had to focus on not melting every time Theo said my name. As the first of our plates started to come out, Brent changed the direction of conversation, and leaned closer to Theo on the other side of me.

"You know, I have to say, I don't think I ever met you when I was at the school before leaving –"

"Actually, we did meet," Theo cut him off, a smile forming on his lips.

Brent blinked, clearly taken aback. "We did? When?"

None of us spoke now, all our focus on listening for Theo's answer. He cleared his throat next to me, and his eyes glimmered with amusement. "It was on your last day of school. You dumped a bucket of water over a group of us outside and I was one of the unlucky victims," he explained.

Brent laughed, but his eyes fogged over in confusion as he struggled to recollect that specific memory. "God, I can barely remember my last day." He shook his head as if to clear his thoughts. "Actually, all I can remember about you is all those rumours I heard when I was at school, Theo."

I almost choked on my drink. Grace and Naya exchanged a look, curiosity flickering in their expressions. Theo, meanwhile, kept silent.

I didn't know he was talked about at all back when Brent was still at school; I didn't think many people even knew his name. If he'd wanted to, Theo could have been the most popular person in our entire year – he definitely had the looks, and he could be charming and funny when he wanted to. But it just seemed like he'd always wanted to be invisible ... like he wanted to fade into the background.

But obviously not. "You did? Like what?" I nudged Brent in the side, interrupting his champagne guzzling.

Brent quickly swallowed and placed his glass down on the table. "Like that he rejected my little sister when she asked him to be her date to the winter dance all those years ago."

The whole atmosphere shifted at the table.

I turned to Theo, seeing the stiffness in his posture as he looked down at the table, and then to Brent, who was grinning and looking pointedly at the two of us. I honestly didn't know what to say. Of course I had never told my brother about how Theo had rejected me all those years ago, but I'd never expected him to find out about it from someone else. He'd known all this time then, but never mentioned it.

Grace leaned forward in her chair, and broke the silence. "What? How did I not know about this?"

I faced away from Brent and Theo's piercing stares, grateful for the distraction. "Grace, you were so head over heels for Naya that there was literally nothing else you wanted to talk about," I pointed out, and her cheeks flooded with colour.

Grace tried her hardest to ignore Naya's teasing smile and kept her eyes on me. "But you went with Xander?"

"Well, yeah. Theo chose not to go with me."

"I'd been asked by Hannah Marshall." Theo was quick to fill in this time, his words tumbling out of his mouth at an absurd speed. It was like he was desperate to explain himself, fearing that we would all judge him for his actions four years ago. "Well, more like Hannah Marshall came over and demanded I go with her."

Hannah Marshall's name being dropped evoked different reactions from everyone at the table. Grace rolled her eyes and Naya's face scrunched up in disapproval.

Brent, meanwhile, smirked and nodded his head at Theo approvingly. "Now, I remember *her*."

I dug my elbow into his side, and shot him a glare when he cursed and recoiled away from me.

Naya looked wonderingly at Theo as if she was trying to figure him out. "But you had a crush on Rose, didn't you? I was sure that you did."

Theo's eyes flicked to mine. Everything went still for a moment as I looked right back into his green irises, the light flecks of gold in them sparkling underneath all the restaurant lights.

"Yes," he said quietly, his eyes never leaving mine. "I did."

I knew I couldn't be drunk off the amount of champagne I'd had, and yet it felt like I was. Perhaps I was just drunk off Theo and his words instead.

185

Everyone was looking at me, I realised, but I had been too busy staring at Theo to notice. I broke our eye contact and looked down at the table, clearing my throat.

"And Rose?" Naya probed. Her voice was soft and cautious, but there was a hint of teasing in it. "Did you have a crush on him too?"

"Yes," I found myself mumbling before I'd even registered what she had asked. I looked back up again, focusing on Theo as I added, "I did."

The corners of his lips tugged upwards as soon as I said it, and I felt my heart beating faster at the sight. I suddenly wanted to lean over and grab his hand, to touch him. Because all of this was starting to feel like a dream, and I found myself getting swept up in the perfection of it all.

"It's funny how things work out," Brent suddenly said. He picked up his glass of champagne again, before noticing it was empty. "One minute your feelings are bolder than ever and the next they're gone, and it's just like they were never there in the first place."

Another bottle was ordered; we all had another glass.

"Oh, I don't know about that," Theo said, replying to Brent. "I don't think your feelings ever really do leave you."

"Yeah," I added, my eyes once again drifting back to Theo, who was already watching me. "I think they can spark back up again no matter how much time passes."

His lips once again tugged upwards. "Or maybe they just never went away."

And then I found my gaze dropping down to his lips for just a moment. But a moment was all it took, because when I looked back up at him, Theo was smiling knowingly.

I hadn't even noticed the others were still talking, but Grace

186

suddenly leaned over the table towards us, and the moment ended. "Hey, Brent, what happened to your girlfriend?"

I tried not to laugh at her question. "Which one are you talking about?"

Brent shot me a glare. "I haven't had that many."

"You've had at least ten since you went to university."

"That's nothing compared to some of the other people in my year," he said defensively.

"I still haven't met a single one of them. What happened to Natalie?"

The others were laughing now. Grace's rather significant intake of champagne seemed to be catching up with her, as she absent-mindedly traced her fingers around the rim of her glass. Her eyes grew unfocused as she drifted off into her own thoughts.

"We're still together," Brent said. He hesitated before adding, "For now."

A giggle escaped me. "That doesn't sound promising."

"Actually I'm thinking of breaking things off when I get back." He chewed on his lower lip, looking guilty.

"Seriously?"

I knew Brent treated his girlfriends well and didn't play with their feelings. And yet I couldn't deny that it did bother me a little that I'd never met one of them, or even heard much about them. I hoped that if he ever felt seriously about one of the girls, then he would bring her to meet me the first chance he got. Perhaps he just hadn't been lucky yet in love.

Brent shrugged, acting like it didn't matter that he planned to break up with Natalie when he got back to uni. "She's just not the one for me, Rose."

Grace shook her head, crossing her arms over her chest as she leaned back into her chair. "You're a pig."

187

"I'm not!" He glanced around the table, his gaze shifting rapidly and then stopping at the only other boy present. "Theo must know where I'm coming from," he said, looking at Theo for back up.

But Theo shook his head, watching Brent's face fall. "Actually, I can't say I do."

Brent scoffed, rolling his eyes mockingly at Theo's behaviour. It was clear he was getting tipsy himself – his eyes were glazed and his reactions to people were getting a bit odd.

"Oh yeah? You think it'll be easy to find that person who's the one for you?"

My eyes flickered over to Grace and Naya, thinking about how easy it had been for them to find one another. Brent also glanced over to them, and I saw his face drop just the slightest bit.

I could see it then: the longing to find someone special, the one who will always be by your side, no matter what. For all his bravado, I knew Brent was a hopeless romantic.

"Who knows?" Theo said, and we all looked back at him. "Maybe I've already found her."

If I'd been standing, the look Theo shot me right then would have had the power to melt me right down to the ground. I felt like I was going to burst with happiness, and I struggled not to become overwhelmed by my excessive giddiness.

"Hey, shall we toast for midnight?" Naya suddenly slurred.

Brent nodded his head so many times that I was surprised he didn't get dizzy. "I don't see why not."

"You guys go ahead," I said as I stood up, my chair scraping along the floor. "I just need the bathroom real quick."

As I hurried out of the room, I felt the eyes of one person at the table follow me until I was out of sight. I could hear the shouts and laughs of the others even as I turned the corner and walked past the toilet doors, heading instead to the emergency exit. I pushed the door open.

The cool air hit me straight away as I stepped outside, chilling me to the bone.

I was in the beer garden of the pub, a small area where you could sit outside in the summer. It was secluded, surrounded by trees that had been decorated for winter with hundreds of twinkly lights, which sparkled in the gloom. The tops of the wooden picnic benches were frosted, and the parasols that were usually up during the summer had been replaced by large jars with fat candles inside, flickering gently every time the wind picked up. My family usually sat outside when we ate at the pub, but it wasn't that part of the garden that I was interested in. No – it was the river running behind it, a beautiful stream that passed through the back garden and into the surrounding woods.

I'd always come out here every time we visited, no matter what the weather, just to see the river. There was something calming about the noise of the water swishing against the riverbanks as it flowed past. And the sight of the moon reflecting off it at night was magical.

It was frozen now, but just as beautiful. I walked over to the fence that separated me from the steep bank leading down to the water, gripping it as I leaned forward and took a deep breath. I was shaking from the cold, but I barely noticed. I closed my eyes and focused on my breathing for a moment, trying to relax myself and get a grip on reality.

And then I heard footsteps crunching on the icy ground behind me. I turned to see Theo standing there, a jacket in his hands.

"Hey," he said, his voice slow and cautious.

"Hi," I replied softly, shooting him a small smile.

He took a step closer to me. "You mind if I join you out here for a minute? It's loud in there."

In the distance I could still hear faintly the voices coming from inside the restaurant, and my brother's laughter rang clearly through all the other noise. "That's what drunk Brent is like, I'm afraid."

Theo came over, offering me the jacket before turning to face the river. "He's a good guy."

"The best."

I pulled the jacket on, slipping my arms into it and revelling in its warmth.

"Wow," Theo said as he took in the scenery. "I hadn't realised how beautiful it is out here."

"Yeah," I agreed. "Whenever we come here to eat I always have to make a trip out the back. The river looks amazing when the moon reflects off it."

He nodded, and we lapsed into a comfortable silence.

The noise of the people inside was still there, but it faded away with every passing second I spent with Theo, until all I could sense was him. Only him. He shifted a little closer to me.

"In the summer, I love to climb over the fence and sit right down there," I said softly, and Theo turned to look at me. I pointed to the bank just below us. "My feet can dangle off the edge without touching the water."

He paused for a second, glancing over at the spot where I had pointed as if trying to picture me sitting there in his mind. He chuckled, before asking me, "Do you think my feet would touch the water?"

I couldn't help but smile back. I leaned forward, resting

190

my elbows on the fence and cradling my head in my palms. Theo moved forward with me, waiting for me to speak again. "I don't know," I replied in a light tone, "you'd have to test that out."

"Well, we'll have to come back here in the summer again to see."

I couldn't help but smile at that: the thought that we'd still be talking like this in six months' time. Theo seemed to realise what he'd said as well, as his own lips curled into a wider smile.

"It's a date," I answered, before turning to him to see his reaction. He raised one eyebrow at my choice of wording but didn't comment on it; instead, he just moved closer to me.

"Rosaline," he said, closing the distance between us, reaching up to lightly touch my cheeks.

His eyes bore into my own, his gaze so intense that I could barely breathe. "I really want to kiss you right now," Theo whispered.

I tilted my head up towards him. "Then why don't you?"

Nineteen

He didn't hesitate.

Theo's lips instantly covered mine, soft yet firm, eager yet careful. I wound my arms around his neck, kissing him back without hesitation. He grinned into the kiss, his tongue soon snaking into my mouth.

It was the moment I'd been desperate for, ever since our first kiss three months ago. And, with everything that had happened in between, and all that we'd gone through, we both deserved this moment. So we relaxed and let the moment linger as long as it possibly could.

After a while, Theo reluctantly broke away from me to catch his breath, leaving his forehead pressed against mine. "You have no idea how much I've wanted this to happen," he whispered, and I let my body melt into his.

"I bet I do," I said back and he let out a light, happy laugh.

His mouth pressed against mine again, but this time the kiss was different. It was powerful, hungry. We were both so eager to make up for all the lost time, and we were starting to lose ourselves in the moment, so I pulled away, moving my head to the side when Theo tried to kiss me again.

"We should head back inside," I said. But instead his lips moved down, pressing soft kisses across my jaw.

"One more minute," Theo mumbled, and I gripped him a bit tighter as he lightly tugged on my earlobe with his teeth.

His lips were soon back on mine, and we stayed that way for who knows how long before I got back my sense of reality.

"Theo." I broke away again, but my arms stayed wrapped around him. "Let's not make this harder than it needs to be."

He growled into my neck. "Trust me, Rose, you're making all sorts of things hard right now."

I couldn't stop the laughter that escaped my mouth. "I just think we should keep this between us for now. Tonight is perfect and I don't want anyone else getting involved."

Theo nodded and grabbed my hand. "Okay," he said gently, interlacing our fingers. "But it's not going to be easy to keep my hands off you," he added teasingly.

I grinned and pulled him back towards the warmth and noise of the pub.

As it turned out, Brent, Grace and Naya had barely noticed we were gone. They were singing when we got to the table, and Theo and I exchanged a look of amusement as we took a seat opposite one another.

Another bottle of champagne had been ordered while we were gone and our glasses were topped up. The others started counting down the seconds to the New Year, and the whole restaurant focused on the TV in the middle of the room, which showed the countdown.

"Three ... Two ... One ... Happy New Year!"

And then people were screaming, cheering, shouting.

Laughter rang through the entire building as people celebrated another year of our lives ending, and a new one beginning. Grace and Naya threw their arms around one another as they shared a long, lingering kiss, and Brent got caught up in hugging a bunch of random strangers who were sitting at the table behind us.

I caught Theo's eyes as the people around me cheered, and he smiled widely at me, his mouth closed. But I could tell what we were both thinking as we saw Grace and Naya together: *I wish that could be us.* The desire to go over and kiss the living daylights out of him again was overwhelming, but I kept it down. Keeping our relationship on the down-low was the right thing to do for the time being. It was fresh and new, and we needed to figure out what exactly was going on between us before we shared it with everyone else.

"Happy New Year," he mouthed to me instead, shooting me a wink. I mouthed it back, my cheeks starting to flame red as he grinned brightly.

The celebrations lasted for a long time after that, but eventually they had to come to an end. Everyone started shuffling out some time in the early hours and we joined the mass of people pushing one another out of the way as they tried to catch cabs.

I felt an arm latch on to me as soon as I got outside, and I lurched to the side. My body crashed into someone else's as I was pulled away from the crowd and around the side of the building.

"Theo –"

He cut me off, closing the distance between us and kissing me senseless. He tugged on my lower lip with his teeth. His hands gently pressed into my hips, pushing me against the stone wall of the building and concealing us from view. My hands came up to lace through his hair. The kiss didn't last long – we didn't have much time. But to have just one more kiss from him was worth all of the worry of getting caught by the others, and I found myself smiling again as Theo pulled back and looked into my eyes.

"Happy New Year, Rosaline," he said softly, his nose brushing against my own.

"Happy New Year, Theodore," I said back, pecking him once more on the lips.

Grace and Brent's shouts suddenly rang through the air. They were most likely looking for us in the crowd.

"I'll call you later," Theo said, realising this was his last chance to talk to me properly before we joined the others.

"You better," I shot back, and his grin widened.

"I promise." And then he was grabbing my hand and placing it on his chest right where his heart was, letting me feel it pumping beneath his skin. Just like he did after our first kiss. "Hand on heart."

My heart somersaulted, but before I had a chance to reply Theo was pulling us both back into the crowd. We headed over to the cab where everyone else was waiting.

The cab was filled with chatter as we drove back home, but I couldn't bring myself to speak. No – I could only focus on my own heart, which had been beating out of control since Theo had kissed me earlier on in the evening.

Brent went back to university a few days later.

He stood in the doorway of our house, all of his bags on the floor around his feet, and pulled me in for a final hug.

"Call. Every single day," I mumbled into his chest, my body suddenly heavy with emotion.

He laughed buoyantly. "You'd get sick of me if I called every single day."

"I'll never get sick of you, big brother."

We pulled away from each other. He ruffled my hair once and slung the bags over his shoulder.

"Drive safe," I ordered as I opened the front door for him. He brushed past me and unlocked his car.

"I will," he replied, and then he tilted his head back towards me, a smirk playing on his lips. "Kiss Theo goodbye for me."

The smile that had been on my face disappeared, my mouth dropping open in surprise. I quickly collected myself though, shooting Brent a glare as he burst out laughing. "Shut up."

He winked and clambered into his car. And then he was off, pulling out of the drive and heading away as I waved him off. My parents had said their goodbyes earlier in the morning before they'd rushed off to work, so I was home alone once he'd left. I felt the loneliness settle in moments after I shut the door.

But the silence didn't last long, because the doorbell rang before I even got to the lounge. I couldn't help but shake my head at the sound, assuming Brent had left something behind and had come back to collect it.

The smile on my face still lingered as I threw the front door open. "How can you have forgotten something –"

I lost track of my words as someone pushed past me into the house.

He was wearing a hat, but Theo's brown, messy hair still spilled out the bottom of it. He had his back to me as he started sorting through the coat rack.

"Theo?" I asked, frowning at his back. "What are you doing?"

He hadn't called me since New Year's Eve, but I hadn't had

much time to brood over that fact during Brent's last few days at home. But there had been a nagging feeling in the back of my mind, making me wonder ... Did he regret what happened between us? Had he changed his mind?

But now he had turned up at my house. And that was enough to settle my worries once again.

"Where's your coat?" Theo asked, not bothering to look at me or answer my question.

"Why?"

He found it a second later, buried under one of my father's jackets. He let out a short shout of triumph before grabbing my scarf off another hook.

"Because we" – he thrust the clothes into my open hands – "are going on a date."

"We are?" I asked in surprise.

Theo also seemed to be slightly taken aback by his own confidence because he awkwardly scratched his neck, before muttering, "I mean – uh – if you want –"

I didn't give him time to finish. I was already throwing the coat on and winding the scarf around my neck. A smile blossomed on Theo's lips as he watched me, his expression the happiest I had seen it in the longest time.

"Where are we going?" I asked.

"That's a surprise."

It turned out that wherever we were going wasn't suitable to drive to, as Theo led me to our local train station, where we had to wait ten minutes for the right train to arrive. Still, he grabbed my hand as soon as he noticed me shivering on the cold platform, and his touch sent sparks down my spine and warmed up the blood underneath my skin.

We weren't on the train for long, but I fidgeted with

anticipation, tapping my feet on the floor of our crammed carriage as the train moved at what seemed like a snail's pace. But Theo soon tightened his grip on my hand and pulled me off at the right stop. We were hit by the wind again as we came out of the station.

"Hampton Court? What are we doing in Hampton Court?" I asked, as we joined the crowds of people crossing the bridge leading towards the palace that was once owned by Henry VIII. The River Thames ran underneath the bridge we crossed, just upstream of central London.

Theo laughed, taking my hand out of his so he could wrap his arm around me and pull me closer to him instead. "Isn't it obvious? We're going ice skating."

I turned to him, an excited grin spreading across my face. He took one look at me and laughed again. "I'm guessing you like ice skating then?"

"Of course I do," I replied. "I haven't been here in years."

Long ago, it had been a tradition of mine, Grace and Naya's to come to Hampton Court every year for the ice skating. We'd eat out at one of the restaurants on the other side of the bridge, and get some hot chocolate – and even though we'd end up queuing for hours and my feet would always kill me on the train ride back home after wearing the skates for too long, it was always one of the most fun nights of the year. But one year, when the weather wasn't cold enough, the rink had been closed. After that, we all seemed to let go of our little tradition.

"I've actually never been here," Theo admitted.

My eyebrows shot up. "You haven't? How have you lived this close to Hampton Court your whole life and never been ice skating at the palace in winter?"

He shrugged. "My mum's not very good at skating," he

said. "She always said she would embarrass us all if we went because she'd be falling over the entire time."

"Do you honestly think every single person who goes can skate? Trust me, you will see plenty of people falling over today and that'll be just when you're waiting to get on the ice."

Theo let out a gentle laugh that warmed me to the core. "I'll make sure to keep count then."

As it turned out, we saw about twelve nasty accidents before we managed to get on the ice.

Theo was more interested in the amazing skaters, though. There was always a group of people in the centre who would whizz around the rink effortlessly, either flying past everyone, or weaving between those who were moving too slowly. Someone would almost always try skating backwards, and they'd always master it beautifully – right up until they crashed into someone who was actually facing the right way.

And then of course there were the people around the edges – the ones who gripped the sides of the rink for dear life, desperate to not fall over and get ice on their jeans and bruises on their bums. Grace and Naya were always with these people, and even though we went for years and they had plenty of time to practise, they never seemed to progress from this group.

I was by no means a skating expert, but it became pretty clear from the moment that Theo and I finally got onto the ice that I was going to be the one leading him as we went around the rink.

Almost the second his feet touched the ice Theo slid too quickly; his legs moved in opposite directions and he let out a yell as he grabbed on to me to balance himself. I couldn't help but laugh and his face turned bright red. He was quick to grip on to the railings and regain his balance.

"It's slippery," he mumbled, looking up at me through his long lashes.

I bit down on my bottom lip to keep myself from laughing at him again. "It's ice. What did you expect?"

He looked back down at the floor of the rink, his expression now cautious and timid. I could tell it was going to be a while before he would want to move.

"Do you want to do a loop together?" I offered, holding out my hand for him to take.

But Theo shook his head, glancing back down at the ice before looking back up at me, fear flashing in his eyes. "I need a moment to get used to it. You go and do a lap and I'll be ready by the time you come back round."

Of course, I knew it would take him longer than one lap to regain his confidence, but when I flew past him on my skates for the fifth time, I started to wonder if Theo was ever going to get used to the ice. He'd barely moved an inch, trying to keep his balance but constantly slipping on the spot as he watched everyone else overtake him.

I could feel his eyes on me as I glided effortlessly on the ice. An embarrassed smile played on his lips every time we made eye contact. But I got so saddened watching his pathetic attempts to skate that I went over and offered my hand to him again.

"Come on," I coaxed, forcefully clasping his hand. "I'll lead you."

He took a deep breath and pushed himself off the railings, his hand grasping mine so tightly that I thought he might break it. We moved slowly but still faster than Theo had been before. My laughter at seeing him tense up every time he almost slipped echoed around the rink.

We got into the swing of things eventually and soon we were both moving at the same speed around the ice. Theo's hand was firmly clasped in my own and the cool breeze whipped our faces.

But that wasn't to say that Theo didn't look extremely relieved when at last we stepped off the rink – I saw his entire body relax once his feet touched solid ground.

"Come on," I said as we walked over to a hot chocolate stand.

"Well," he said, cheerful now, handing me a cup of hot chocolate and shooting me a smile, "that was interesting."

I couldn't help but let out an unattractive snort, cradling the cup in my hands as it warmed me up. "You clearly didn't enjoy yourself."

"I did!" he protested, his expression one of pure mock outrage. "Any moment I spend with you is a good one."

His words made my heart feel like it was going to explode, and I felt my insides warm up in a rush of emotion.

"Same here." I took a final sip of my hot chocolate, then looked up at Theo. "Thank you for an amazing date, Theodore."

He took a step closer to me. "Thank you for saying yes," he said softly. His eyes held mine as he added, "And I hope there's many more to come."

He closed what little remaining distance there was between us, and gently pressed his lips against mine, soft and sweet. He tasted like hot chocolate and peppermint, and I sighed as he pressed himself closer, pushing his lips more firmly against mine.

"So, uh" – he spoke between small pecks, his lips constantly seeking my own – "in case that wasn't clear just now ... Will you be my girlfriend, Rosaline?"

I smiled and pulled back only a little bit to let our noses brush. Theo didn't seem to breathe as I tilted my head towards his and pressed our mouths together once more, smiling as our lips met.

"In case that wasn't clear," I said, "yes, I would love to be your girlfriend, Theodore."

Twenty

One of the best things about a new relationship was learning new things about the other person. It was my favourite stage of a relationship – the one I had enjoyed the most when I dated Xander before. I loved getting to know Theo better. He was unlike anyone I'd met before, and I was learning new things about him every single day.

Things like him being allergic to bees. Or that he couldn't have the radio on in his car without singing along or drumming his fingers against the steering wheel. Or that he's addicted to mayonnaise, and has to have it in all of his sandwiches, no matter what other food he plans to put in there. Or even that his mum calls him "Teddy Bear" whenever his friends aren't around – I wasn't supposed to know about that one, but she accidentally let it slip once.

We had a week before we had to go back to school and every moment of it was spent together. I didn't know how the rest of our school were going to react to seeing Theo and me as a couple, but it seemed like Theo wanted to let people know, because he was waiting for me outside my house on the morning of the first day back after the holidays. He stood propped up against his car in a black puffa jacket.

"Was I expecting you?" I asked as I strolled towards him.

"What? Can't I offer my girlfriend a ride to school?" he shot back, before pulling me in for a long, lingering kiss.

"Of course you can," I replied when we broke away, my arms still wrapped around his shoulders. "It saves me having to pay for petrol."

I grinned wickedly as he rolled his eyes. We broke apart and he opened the passenger door for me. "At least I have some uses."

We drove to school in comfortable silence, Theo's fingers drumming against the steering wheel whenever we stopped. "You know, this is the first time at school that people are going to see us together," I said as we turned a corner and the school building came into sight.

"Oh yeah," Theo said, as if he'd only just realised it. His eyes flickered over to mine briefly, before turning back to the road. "Are you worried about it?"

I looked at him properly for the first time that morning. He seemed so relaxed. And I realised that it didn't matter what others thought, or if they kept staring at us, because he was one of the only people whose opinion actually mattered to me.

"No," I said honestly, "because I have you. The other students won't care about us for long anyway."

He smiled and pulled into a parking space, then reached over to squeeze my hand. "You're right – they won't. We'll be old news by the end of the day, I'm sure of it."

As it turned out, people did stare at us and whisper about it for the first half of the day, but the news of us dating was ancient history by lunch.

When we'd got out of the car together and Theo had put his arm around me, I'd felt everyone's gaze latch onto us. If Theo had noticed the attention he didn't say so; instead, he just led me towards my locker and gave me a fleeting kiss before heading off to his own lesson. I almost envied the way he could act so casual – so normal – when people's eyes seemed to follow his every move.

"Do you realise what this means?" Naya asked. We were sitting at a table in the canteen, Theo's arm around me. "We finally have a couple to go on double dates with."

I shrugged and Theo reached over and grabbed a chip off my plate. "Sounds fun. What did you have in mind?"

"I've always wanted to go into London to see something at the theatre," Naya suggested. "There are some amazing plays on at the moment."

Both Grace and I nodded enthusiastically and I looked at Theo for his reaction, but he was too busy picking chips off my plate and dipping them in ketchup. "Theo?"

He looked up and noticed us all looking at him expectantly. "I'm up for anything," he answered eventually, nudging me lightly.

Grace snorted loudly. "Oh, just you wait until she forces you to sing all the male parts in *Grease* along with her," she said. "Then you'll regret saying that."

Theo let out a short bark of laughter and turned to me, his eyebrows rising. "Seriously? You'd make me do that?"

The others all laughed as I blushed further and crossed my arms over my chest, shooting Grace a glare that only made her laugh harder. "It was just a joke," I tried to reason, but they weren't even listening to me any more, their laughter was too loud.

"It was all she talked about for a week after we watched the film," Naya elaborated, now joining in on the fun. "She was desperate for her future man to be a good singer."

"With a gelled quiff," interjected Grace, and both girls fell about laughing.

Every single part of me felt like it was dying. I wanted to sink deep down into the ground, or at least remove myself from the situation until Theo had stopped laughing. But he nudged me a moment later, snapping me out of my embarrassment with his reassuring grin. "Well, unfortunately my singing isn't up to scratch, but I'm not a half bad dancer."

I looked at him, surprised. "You can dance?"

Theo looked uncomfortable as Grace and Naya stared at him in interest, waiting for his answer. He leaned closer to me, keeping his voice quiet so that only I could hear him when he murmured, "I had lessons until I was thirteen."

"Did you like them?"

"No," he said flatly. "My mother forced me to go. Every Monday evening she had to physically drag me to ballroom dance classes."

My shoulders shook as I started laughing. Theo shifted in his chair uneasily, ignoring the curious gazes of Naya and Grace as they wondered what he'd just revealed to me that was so funny. His cheeks were tinged an adorable shade of pink.

"Well, I want to see these dance skills for myself," I said, leaning into him so our lips were almost touching. "Promise to take me dancing sometime?"

Theo smiled easily. "Okay. I promise," he whispered, his tone becoming teasing when he added, "but I'll warn you now, I'm *very* good. You might struggle to keep up."

"I'll take my chances," I replied and then gave him a small peck on the lips.

Sometimes, I looked at Theo and wondered if I'd ever really know him – if I'd ever really figure out the boy sitting right next to me. He was always surprising me, always saying or doing things unexpected, and always revealing something about himself that I never would have guessed. He was like one big puzzle, and I couldn't find all the pieces to put him together. But I liked being with someone who I couldn't ever quite figure out. With Xander, I'd been able to read him like a book. He was like me in so many ways, whereas Theo was my opposite. And I hoped we would never leave behind this stage of our relationship; I hoped I would always be finding out new things about him, because that was what made him so fascinating to me, and why he made my heart flutter just by smiling at me.

Theo Lockhart would always be a mystery to me, but I wouldn't have it any other way.

Twenty-One

I woke up locked in Theo's embrace.

Our legs were intertwined like two jigsaw pieces perfectly fitted together. His arms were around me, pulling me tightly into his chest. I smiled and closed my eyes again, relaxing into him as I inhaled his intoxicating scent.

He was still asleep, his breathing steady and his bare chest rising and falling. I'd tried to protest when he'd stripped down to his boxers as we were getting ready for bed the night before, but one glimpse of the toned muscles he was hiding under his clothes had my protests dying on my lips. He was insanely attractive and he knew it. The way he watched me catch my breath as he took his shirt off, a small smirk playing on the corners of his lips, made it clear that he had fully expected my reaction.

Theo started to stir next to me then, and I lifted my head off his chest to watch his eyes slowly blink open. Our gazes locked and he shot me a sleepy smile that made my heart swell.

"Morning," I said softly, starting to run my fingers along

the contours of his chest and smiling when he shivered at my touch.

"Morning," he replied, his voice gravelly from sleep. His eyes never left mine, not even when he pushed himself up so he was sitting upright. "You know, I could get used to waking up like this every morning."

My smile widened. "Yeah?"

Theo nodded and reached over to grasp my fingers in his own, locking them together tightly. "No better start to the day than your face being the first thing I see when I open my eyes."

His words made my head spin. But then, before I could even muster up a reply, he added, "Actually, you know what would make it even more special? If you were holding a bacon sarnie in your hands right now." He paused thoughtfully. "Or if you were naked, I guess."

I didn't know whether to laugh, blush or hit him, so in the end I decided on all three. "You'd seriously put a bacon sarnie on the list first before seeing me naked?" I accused, jabbing a finger into his stomach and meeting pure, solid muscle. "You didn't get a six-pack like that eating bacon sarnies, that's for sure."

He raised his hands up defensively, stifling a laugh. "Hey, food before girls every time. Besides, if I taunt myself with the idea of you naked any more than I have done already, I don't know what I'd do."

I have some ideas.

The words were on the tip of my tongue but I couldn't say them, they felt so out of character for me. And so, despite my eagerness to put his taunt into action, I pushed the words down and tried to change the subject. "Well, I gave up half of my bed for you last night, so I should definitely be first on the list."

Theo paused for a second, considering my valid point. "That's true, and for that I am very grateful." But another smirk appeared on his lips as he once again ruined the moment by adding, "Still, a breakfast of some kind would've been nice."

I was ready to bite his head off for teasing me so early in the morning, but my eyes drifted to an object beside him and a better idea popped into my mind. "Well, how about a glass of cold water instead?" I asked in a sickly sweet voice, reaching over to grab the glass on my bedside table and preparing to dump the contents all over his head.

Theo realised what I was going to do before my fingers had even skimmed the glass. "Rose!" My name came out in a strangled gasp as he lunged forward, using his body as a shield so I couldn't get to the glass. The next thing I knew I was being flipped so that I was under him. His arms were on either side of my head, caging me in.

My laughter died away, and the smile on Theo's face also morphed into a serious expression as our eyes locked, our breathing suddenly heavy.

His lips were on mine a moment later, filled with an urgency that I'd only encountered from him once before, when we'd had our New Year's kiss over two months ago. My arms wound around his neck, pulling him even closer to me as I kissed him back with the same amount of force.

I was aware of how quickly everything was moving, but at the same time it seemed like time had literally stopped. Since we'd decided to take things slow and not rush into anything, Theo and I hadn't gone that far, but in this empty house, and in this perfect moment, it seemed like there was nothing to stop us.

His hands touched the hem of my oversized T-shirt, then he

broke away from my lips to look into my eyes and wait for my consent to take it off. I nodded, raising my arms to help him. But before he'd even pulled the T-shirt up over my stomach the sound of noises coming from downstairs made both of us freeze.

And then my mother's voice rang out. "Rose, are you going to get out of bed soon?"

Both Theo's and my eyes widened as he pulled away to stare at me in horror. "Your parents are here?" he whispered, his voice a hiss.

I'm sure my own expression matched his. "I didn't know!"

It was a Sunday morning, but still I didn't expect them to be home. They were at work so much that I hardly ever saw them – so much, in fact, that they were the only people in my life who didn't know about Theo and me yet. The small period of time when they hadn't been keen on leaving me home alone in case I broke the rules again was over, and they seemed busier and more absent than ever before.

So, just like the good old times, I'd been sneaking Theo into my room again. Whenever he stayed over we'd go to bed before either of my parents came home, and they'd be gone so early in the mornings that we could go downstairs and have breakfast almost as soon as we woke up. The system had been working perfectly; but now, it seemed as if things were coming full circle, and they were about to catch us out once again.

And then, the horror continued. We shared another panicked look as we heard my mother's footsteps as she padded up the stairs.

"Please tell me you locked the bedroom door last night," Theo breathed, and I felt the dread inside me rise.

"I thought *you* locked it!"

211

"Rose" – my mother tried twisting the door handle, but it wouldn't budge – "why is the door locked?"

Theo and I both let out the breath we were holding in relief. "I'm sleeping, Mum," I managed to answer, desperately trying to keep my voice calm.

There was a pause. I could hear her feet tapping on the carpet outside my door. "Well, can you get up, please? Your father and I are going out for breakfast with some friends and then we need to go to work for a while, so I've left you a list of chores to do on the kitchen worktop."

Theo then removed his weight from me, rolling gently onto the other side of the bed. He grabbed his shirt from the floor and threw it on.

"Okay," I replied, and we both lay back, facing the ceiling and waiting to hear her walk away.

As soon as I heard the front door slam I sighed, swinging my legs over the side of the bed. The moment we'd been having before we were interrupted had been ruined, so I got up and headed over to my wardrobe to pick out something to change into. I could feel Theo watching me from his spot on the bed.

"When are you going to tell them about us?" he asked carefully.

"As soon as they're around long enough for me to talk to them," I replied, still shifting through my clothes. "Every time I try to speak to them they suddenly have other things to do – it's like they already know what I'm going to say."

He paused. "I'm know I'm not their favourite person in the world –"

I quickly turned around to look at him. He was tugging on his lower lip, an apprehensive expression lingering on his face. "That doesn't matter. I don't care about their opinion."

"Maybe we should have dinner with them?" he suggested.

"No."

He stood up and came over to me. "Rosaline –"

"It doesn't matter what my parents think of you," I stated firmly. "It isn't going to change anything."

He touched my arm. "I want them to like me," he admitted.

I felt myself soften. "I know. And I think it's really sweet that you want to make a good impression, but please don't bother with my parents."

He looked like he was struggling with something, and took his time to weigh his words carefully. "But the good boyfriends always get along with the parents," he protested a moment later.

I'm not sure that I wanted what my parents would consider a "good boyfriend". I only wanted him. But that wasn't the answer he was looking for, so instead I reached up to wrap my arms around his neck. "Then think of Brent as my parent. When I told him the news he was really happy for us."

"Okay," Theo agreed begrudgingly, and I smiled and pecked him once on the lips.

"Now we can go and cook some breakfast if you're still hungry?" I offered, letting out a little laugh when he nodded eagerly. He tugged me out of the room by the hand, pulling me closely into him, right where I belonged, as we headed downstairs.

Teaching Theo to cook was more of a challenge than I thought it would be.

He let out the most pathetic squeals every time the pan spat out a bit of oil when we were cooking the eggs, and if I left him on his own for more than thirty seconds he'd do something wrong. It was a surprise that we managed to make something edible at all, but we were soon piling our plates high with a full breakfast. The bacon was a bit crispier than I would've liked, but tasted good nevertheless.

"How does all of your food taste so good?" he asked after we were done, grabbing the plates and going over to the dishwasher.

I put my cup of tea back down onto the table. "I don't know." I shrugged. "But you helped as well, so it was a joint effort."

He scoffed, coming over to me. In the morning light, when we'd only just woken up, I swear Theo was more beautiful than ever; there was something about the messy look that just worked for him. And the sunlight coming in from the window shining on him gave him a glow that took my breath away.

"We both know you did most of the work. But it was incredible." He leaned in and kissed me once, pulling away all too soon. "Thank you."

An uncontrollable smile was spreading across my face. "No problem."

Theo then leaned back, stretching his arms and legs for a moment, leaving me transfixed on the movement of his muscles. "I'm going to go and grab my jumper from upstairs. Do you need anything?"

I shook my head, my eyes not leaving him until he was out of sight and heading back up to my room.

A bubbly feeling of giddiness rose inside me, making me happy and excited. I was so lost in my own little world that I barely noticed Theo's phone buzzing on the table next to me. Without thinking, I bowed my head towards it and tried to read what had appeared on the screen.

And then my smile slowly started to fade as I picked the phone up. I swiped to unlock it and filled in his password, desperate to check that what I had read wasn't my imagination. My eyebrows scrunched together as his messages came up, and I scanned every single one of them over and over again as each word sunk in.

When Theo came back down, he stopped moving as soon as he saw my expression. His eyes dropped to the phone in my hands and his body went rigid. He didn't say anything; there was no need.

And yet I still said it. I looked straight up at him as I murmured, "Your dad's been trying to contact you."

Theo's eyes closed for a moment as he nodded his head twice. "He has," he confirmed.

I sucked in a sharp breath. "How long?"

"Two weeks."

I didn't know how to react. Theo's dad was contacting him after months of estrangement? This was major, and I desperately wanted to ask him about it, to know how he felt and what he was thinking. But if he wanted to talk about it, he would have told me. And I hated how much that stung. I fidgeted in my seat, struggling to find the right words.

"I'm sorry I looked," I managed to say. "I did it without thinking."

Theo moved closer towards me. "Rosaline –"

"Are you going to see him?" I suddenly asked.

He seemed taken aback for a moment; I wondered if he'd been expecting me to berate him for keeping it secret. It was clear the question threw him. "I haven't decided yet," he finally got out, his voice strained.

I didn't know how to react, so I started to talk, numbing

down all of my emotions with words. "Is he allowed to see you? Is he even allowed to contact you? I mean, I suppose you should consider all your options. I mean, you don't have to see him for very long, it could just be a coffee –"

Pain flashed in Theo's eyes. "Rose," he mumbled.

"– you should probably see how your mum feels, though," I went on. "I mean, I'm sorry. It's none of my business. You don't have to talk about it with me –"

I knew I was acting crazy. I was overreacting about the whole situation. And yet I couldn't seem to stop myself.

I'd always been so driven, so in control of my own life, and now, with Theo, I was vulnerable. He was naturally chaotic and reckless – the complete opposite of my regimented personality. Being with him, there were no rules and I felt like I wasn't always in control.

"Rose." Theo said my name so firmly that I stopped altogether, allowing myself to break my composure a little bit.

"Yes?"

"Stop acting insane and just be mad at me."

The barriers to the flood of emotions building up inside me were becoming weaker. "I'm not mad at you," I said honestly, but my voice cracked slightly at the end. "I just ... You didn't tell me."

Guilt swept over his features again. "I didn't know how to."

"It just hurts that there are secrets between us. Again."

"I know."

"Especially now that we're together." I couldn't stop myself from letting it all out, the words tumbling from my mouth without a second thought. "And we've been dating for two months now. It's just the kind of thing I'd hope you'd talk to me about, or at least just tell me."

I knew that Theo struggled to open up about his dad. But wasn't part of dating someone being able to trust them? And I'd tried to show Theo that I was trustworthy. I knew he was entitled to his privacy and yet it hurt so much that he still hid things as if he was scared of how I was going to react, or what I was going to say.

"Our relationship is strong," he objected, his tone changing. "We work, Rosaline." He sighed and ran his fingers through his hair. "I wasn't going to see him without talking to you about it first."

"I understand," I said softly. "But why didn't you just tell me sooner?"

"Because I don't like bringing up the subject, okay?" he grumbled. And while I already knew this for myself, hearing the words come out of Theo's mouth struck me. "Every time I talk about him, every time I think about him, I bring up everything from the past. And I hate doing it, because it makes me feel weak. It brings up all these emotions I don't want to have anything to do with. And I didn't want you seeing that side to me again – not when everything has been going so well between us."

I took a moment to digest everything he said, the words spinning around in my mind. "Theo," I started slowly, waiting until he looked back up at me before continuing, "you can't just push your feelings down and hope they'll go away. You can't ignore these things; it's important to talk about them. I'm not going to feel any different about you for saying how you feel."

His expression softened. "I know that." He started to close the distance between us again, and I let him. "And I'm working on that, I really am."

I stayed silent, looking down at the dining room table where his phone lay. The phone was still unlocked, all his father's messages filling the screen. Theo gently touched my chin, lifting my face to look up at him.

"I'm not going to see him," he said. "He's not supposed to have any contact with me or my mum while the case is ongoing, but he's desperate to talk to me. I don't know what I'm going to do. I'm not really ready to talk about it, but I will get there." He stared deep into my eyes. "And you'll be the first person I talk to about it when I do."

I tried to smile. "I know it's really hard for you, I do. I'll be there when you're ready. I know it says more about me than you, but I really need to feel like you trust me, and that I can trust you too," I said.

"Rosaline." Theo looked at me with an expression that I'd never seen before. It was soft and gentle, and I felt like he wanted to take care of me, and treasure me for ever. "I trust you more than anyone else in the entire world."

"I trust you too." My eyes burned with tears. I blinked rapidly. "But you keep things from me," I persisted.

He let go of my chin, but I kept it in place as he reached down and threaded his fingers through mine. "I won't. Ever. No more secrets."

I gazed up at him through my lashes. "Promise?"

He moved one of my hands up and held it over his heart, just like he'd done before when we'd kissed on New Year's Eve. "Hand on heart."

I managed to tell my parents about Theo and me later that evening. They sat there, taking in every word in silence, exchanging looks with one another but not giving their opinion.

After I was done they both acknowledged what I'd said with a nod and muttered a few new rules that I barely paid attention to and wouldn't bother keeping, and then they went back to their bedroom to talk about it in soft, hushed voices.

But the walls were thin and I still managed to hear what they were saying as I came upstairs to go to my bedroom, my feet lingering on the landing so I could listen a bit longer. I could hear all the worries they had about Theo being too reckless. All the worries that I was going to put too much time into someone who wasn't right for me and how I would get badly hurt in the end, just like I'd got hurt before.

But the worst part was that all of their worries reflected my own, still swimming around in my head, lingering there despite our promise to be more open with one another and not keep secrets.

I just had to have faith that in the end, all this trust I'd put in Theo would be worth it, and that *we* were worth it.

Twenty-Two

Funnily enough, Theo got exactly what he'd wished for with my parents, as they invited him over for dinner only a few days after I told them about us dating.

I was used to my parents running hot and cold with me. One minute I could see the people they used to be lingering behind the cool demeanours that they showed everyone now, and the next they'd be distant with me, and only there to keep me in order and make sure the house was running how they wanted it to. But them inviting Theo over felt like a peace offering – a way of them showing that they respected my decisions, and that they wanted to be more involved in my life.

The dinner itself was terrible compared to the many that Nicki had made for me when I was over at Theo's. My mum had never claimed to be a master chef and she certainly wasn't one. There was no way around it – this roast dinner was borderline inedible. But Theo – who was desperate to make a better impression than he'd made before – was extremely polite, and even though I saw the grimace on his face when he tasted the oily and semi-raw roast potatoes on his plate, he still forced the whole thing down and brightly told my mother it was delicious.

After that dinner my parents seemed happier, and my mother even commented that Theo seemed like "a nice boy". I took this as the best endorsement I would get, and I was over the moon to sense that they finally approved.

He was trying. Theo was really trying. It was clear that he wanted to make amends for not telling me about his dad a few weeks ago and he was desperate to make sure I knew I could trust him – and trust him I did. We had jumped off that same metaphorical cliff together, hand in hand, facing everything together as we fell more and more for one another.

Theo was all about making every moment count, though. While I was the kind of person who liked to stay at home and watch a movie cuddled up on the sofa, he was the kind of guy who liked to be spontaneous. He frequently turned up on my doorstep demanding I come with him, and we'd hop on the train and go into London, getting lost in the crowds at Waterloo or among narrow market streets filled with flowers, street food and antiques. Or, if there was nothing better to do, we would just go to the park and sit on the swings with cold hands, talking about our parents, school, or nothing in particular. He always wanted to go out, anywhere. He was impulsive, easily excitable – everything that was opposite to me, but that was what made him even more thrilling. He knew how to take me out of my comfort zone.

I was addicted to Theodore Lockhart and I didn't mind one little bit.

As the year progressed into March, and Theo and I hit our two-month anniversary, the weather started to get much warmer, and life finally felt like it had truly gone back to normal.

"Well, that place sucked," Theo said one night as we left the tiny French restaurant where we'd just eaten. His arms were wrapped tightly around me as we walked down the street, along the river that ran through our town. The breeze blew softly and pushed my hair off my face for me.

I smiled, burying my face into his chest. "I told you fast food sounded better than snails."

"Not to mention the tiny portion sizes that cost more than the clothes I'm wearing," he grumbled under his breath. I stifled a laugh. After a pause he sighed in defeat, asking, "Big Mac next time?"

I smiled as he finally gave into what I had been insisting on for the last few weeks. "I'm more of a chicken nugget kind of girl myself," I admitted.

He laughed and tightened his arms around me. "Rosaline, babe, you can have whatever you want."

Babe. I wasn't normally the kind of person who liked nicknames – and neither was Theo – but that word coming from his lips made my heart skip a beat. We continued walking down the road, my heels clicking on the pavement, before we finally got to his car and clambered inside.

"Here," he said softly once we were both seated, reaching out to take my hands. He lifted them up to his mouth and blew on them softly. He rubbed them together a moment later, warming me up, both inside and out. "Better?"

My lips, coated in ruby red lipstick, beamed at him. "Perfect."

He smiled back and reached forward to turn on the ignition, glancing over at me again as his hands lightly gripped the

222

steering wheel. "So," he said in a slow drawl, as if we had all the time in the world – which we did. "Where to next?"

The March evening air was still quite cold, chilling me beneath my light dress, but I never wanted the night to end

So I smiled once more and whispered, "Anywhere with you."

Over the next few weeks, Theo and I were constantly at Grace's house, where she lived with her mum and two cats. She'd tripped on the stairs and had ended up badly hurting her leg and now we needed to look after her. She objected to doing anything for herself and demanded that someone be around to help her out as she lay in her bed all day. And, as much as Naya loved her, she'd soon grown tired of the incessant whining and asked for our help in making sure Grace didn't overdo anything and make her leg even worse.

But looking after her did have its benefits, as she was often sleeping during the day on the weekends that we were over, and her mum worked weekends, meaning we had the whole lounge and her selection of films to ourselves.

We got into a routine fast. I would check in on Grace to see if she needed anything and then wait with her until she fell asleep, while Theo picked out a film for us to watch downstairs and got the snacks ready for when I came back down.

"So," Theo said as we sat down. I rested my legs on his lap and he wrapped his arms around my waist and pulled me into his chest. "I blocked my dad's number last night."

I whipped my head up to look at him. "You did?"

"It feels final now," he said. "Like he's out of my life for good."

"You don't need him in your life," I said softly. "Even if he is sorry now. Not after what he did to you and your mum."

"I don't want to see him again," Theo said. "Not after everything."

I nodded and reached for his hand. I would have supported his choice either way, but it felt like he'd made the right decision.

Harry Potter and the Prisoner of Azkaban started playing in the background.

"I just didn't want things to end on bad terms between us, you know?" Theo said after a pause. "At the end of the day, the man is still my father. He didn't always act like one, but I hate leaving things unfinished." Theo paused to let out a small scoff. "But I guess with him things were always going to end badly."

"I know what you mean." My fingers found his and I intertwined them together. "And I'm always here for you, you know. If you ever want to talk about anything."

"Thank you," he said, his hand giving mine a squeeze. "It's nice to talk to someone who understands how I'm feeling."

He went back to concentrating on the film and I hesitated, unsure if I should say anything, before I admitted, "I know it's not the same at all, but Xander and I left things between us on bad terms too, and that still haunts me sometimes."

There was a pause. I could tell Theo really badly wanted to say something.

After a while he finally whispered my name. "Rose."

"Yeah?" My thumb was gently stroking the back of his hand, rubbing circles on the skin as my fingers clasped around his tighter.

"What happened with you and Xander?"

I shrugged, trying to keep my face blank. "There's nothing

much to it really. We had a fight the night he told me he was leaving, because he'd kept it a secret from me."

Even now I could still remember the details of that night. Xander's guilt-ridden face, the anger burning deep in the pit of my stomach, and then the tears afterwards. I was so angry about him leaving and not telling me one minute, then hit by sadness and distress the next and Xander had to watch as I broke down right in front of him. It was not a night I particularly wanted to remember and yet I couldn't seem to let it go.

Theo tensed underneath me before saying in a quiet voice, "You came into school crying the next day."

My eyebrows rose in surprise. "You remember that?"

I'd been so upset about Xander and everything that had happened the night before, that I'd started weeping almost the second I'd seen Grace and Naya in the lunchroom staring back at me with concerned expressions as they took in my puffy eyes and stressed-out face. I couldn't remember seeing Theo but he must have been there, witnessing me collapse into a puddle of tears for reasons unknown.

"I remember," Theo repeated softly, and I felt his grip on me tighten a little bit more.

I hesitated, reluctant to continue. "Well ... yeah. I was pretty upset about the way things had gone down between us, and I wanted to make things right. But after the fight we had I never saw him again."

"You didn't?"

I shook my head, feeling the back of my head rubbing against Theo's chest. "I tried calling him, I tried going around to his house. But he refused to speak to me – he said he didn't want anything to do with me. I never even saw his face after our fight, and he left without saying goodbye."

Some of the emotions were still there, I realised – feelings from my time with Xander that seemed to have never quite left me. They weren't feelings of love or longing, but more of sadness and regret. I seemed to have carried them around with me like a dark weight, making things feel unfinished.

I could tell Theo was still tense, and his fingers found their way to my hair. He played with plaiting it as he murmured, "I'm sorry."

"Don't be. It's not your fault." I raised my head up to look at him. His face was blank as he stared back, but his eyes softened as he noticed the sadness held in my own. I forced a small smile onto my face. "I just wanted to know why, you know? I didn't understand why he'd pushed me away like that, and I always wondered if it was something I'd done. I think that might be why I didn't have a boyfriend after that, until you. I was afraid of being pushed away and hurt like that again."

Theo smiled comfortingly back at me, leaning in so our faces were closer together. "That won't happen."

"I know," I said softly, leaning in further so that our fore-heads were touching.

We rested back on the couch again, both of us watching the movie in silence for a bit, enjoying the peaceful atmosphere we had created. Then Theo shifted on the seat, raising his hand to scratch his neck and manoeuvring our bodies so we were looking at one another again.

"Did I tell you about my first date?" he said, a smile linger-ing on his lips as he spoke to me.

I was suddenly extremely interested – albeit mildly jealous – and I sat up further and stared at him. "No, you didn't."

His eyes closed and he shook his head, still smiling faintly.

"God, it was bad." His striking green eyes opened and locked onto my own. "In fact, all the dates I've been on were bad."

A snigger escaped me. "Then why did you still date?"

"I don't know. I think deep down I just wanted to connect with someone. I should've said yes to a certain girl when she asked me to the winter dance a few years ago, but I was an idiot and didn't know what I was missing out on." He winked at me.

"Well, you did have Hannah Marshall to entertain you at least."

"And then you had Xander," he continued.

I smiled at him and snuggled closer.

"They can't all have been that bad," I mused, thinking Theo must surely be being melodramatic.

His eyes twinkled with mischief as he stared at me. "You sure?"

And then he proceeded to tell me every embarrassing story, every hilarious moment, and every cringe-worthy episode that had led him to me, from the time he was forced to go on a date with a girl his mother had set him up with, who refused to say a single word to him, to the time he tried to end it with a girl in a really hip café and it wound up with her throwing a fit – and a cup of coffee – right at him. And while we laughed about every story, tears streaming and my face aching from so much smiling, I realised Theo had in fact successfully distracted me from Xander and the past, just like he'd clearly wanted to. I also realised that I was falling harder and harder for the boy cuddled up beside me.

Twenty-Three

It was a knock on my front door that brought me out of my bed on a sleepy Saturday morning. With my dressing gown wrapped around my shoulders and my hair in a messy clump on the top of my head, I just about managed to trudge down the stairs and open the front door in my tired state, where I was greeted by a man holding a large bouquet of flowers.

"I'm looking for a Miss Rosaline Valentine," he said in a bored voice before glancing up at me and looking taken aback at my attire. "Is this you?"

"Yes," I barely managed to get out, my eyes still locked on the flowers in his hands.

Roses for Rose. Of course. A bubble of laughter rose inside me as I reached forward to take the flowers.

"Here you go."

The scent from the roses filled my nose as I buried my face in the velvety petals. I beamed – unreciprocated – at the deliveryman as he held out a clipboard for me. He waited for me to sign it with my free hand before walking back to his van, waving a hand behind him to acknowledge my shout of thanks before driving off.

The roses were a light pink – the colour Theo always loved me wearing – and as I started to pull them out to snip their ends and arrange them in the vase, a card fell out with the stems, tumbling onto the kitchen counter. I scooped it up and read the back.

Be ready at 8 for a surprise. Dress fancy. Thanks for making these last four months feel like a dream.

T

Theo. I tucked the card into the pocket of my dressing gown with a grin. Now, what on earth was I going to wear?

I'd been on many dates with Theodore Lockhart, yet as I smoothed down the silk of my light pink dress I felt nervous. I found myself scanning my appearance critically in the mirror as I waited for him to arrive.

I'd found it so difficult to pick out what to wear that Naya and Grace – who was determined to hobble around in assistance – had come over earlier that day to help me pick the perfect dress. They pulled everything I owned out of my wardrobe and muttered evaluations of each piece of clothing – "too boring", "too try-hard", "very 90s", "what were you thinking?". They tossed everything aside before they stopped at this dress – "perfect" – and thrust it into my hands, demanding that I try it on. I'd forgotten all about it, but already knew it was the one before it was on, especially considering the colour of my flowers earlier. Grace and Naya sighed at me and insisted there couldn't be anything more perfect to wear.

They carefully styled my hair into simple ringlets that

cascaded down past my shoulders, and painted my lips to match the colour of my dress – both Grace and Naya's choices, as they claimed I was hopeless at doing my own hair and make-up. I couldn't help but feel like I was in a different body as I stared back at myself in the mirror, like I was someone who had a whole different life to the normal, mundane one I normally led. I looked too sophisticated and too fancy to be me, and that made me feel like I was existing in a dream.

But as soon as the doorbell sounded and I went downstairs to open the door to Theo, everything became reality once again.

He was dressed in a suit, something I'd never seen him wear before. It fitted him to perfection, and when he smiled and let his eyes roam over me, I felt my entire body stop moving and my breath stick in my throat.

"You look incredible," he said softly, reaching to grab my hand.

I pretended to look him over more critically, and tried not to laugh when he narrowed his eyes at me. "You don't scrub up too badly yourself." My eyes stopped at his tie, noticing that it matched the colour of my dress. "Is the fact that we're matching a coincidence or an extremely lucky guess?"

He started to lead me towards his car, his arms wrapped around me just like always. "I had to get Grace's help with that one," he admitted as he opened the passenger door for me.

I smiled at him playfully. "You'll lose points for that, I'm afraid."

He got into the car and shook his head in mock disappointment. "Damn, already off to a bad start." I laughed and he joined in as he put his keys in the ignition.

"So where are we going?" I asked as I gazed out of the window, watching everything fly by in a rush. It almost made

230

my head dizzy to see that we were driving so fast; the streets soon became unrecognisable to me as we headed out of town and on to a road I didn't know.

"That's a surprise," Theo said smoothly, turning to shoot me a smile before focusing on the road once more.

We sang along to the radio together (it turned out Theo was also a big Destiny's Child fan) until we arrived. I still had no idea where we actually were when Theo pulled up outside a big building, stopping the car and turning in his seat to look at me expectantly as if I was supposed to understand where we were by just looking around me.

"What is this place?" I asked, scouring the car park as if it would give me some more clues.

Loud music from the building was filling the car park. It flowed into my ears, the beat thumping so loudly that the ground felt like it was shaking beneath us.

Theo's eyes were gleaming as he stared back at me, his pearly white teeth on full display. "I promised I'd take you dancing," he said simply, before getting out of the car and leaving me stunned. "Come on."

I hurried out of the vehicle, managing to stumble on my heels. I lurched forward and crashed into Theo's chest.

"Woah," he teased, his hot breath fanning my ear as he clutched me in his arms. "You all right?"

My cheeks felt like they were on fire and I refused to look into his eyes. "I'm fine. Thanks."

"Are you sure you're okay to dance? You seem a bit wobbly on your feet," he said, clearly trying to keep a smirk off his face.

I pushed away from him and rolled my eyes as he let out a loud laugh. "Shut up."

I turned away from him but he quickly pulled me back, wrapping his arms around me as we headed into the building together. The music became a lot louder as we stepped inside, and my eyes widened. The room was very different to what I'd anticipated.

I'd expected a ballroom of sorts – lots of people standing around and talking while a few others swayed from side to side in the centre for everyone to watch. Instead, giant lights hung over a dance floor that filled the entire room, illuminating the dancers as they all twirled and spun in time to the music. Not a single person was standing still, and they all kept dancing, even when the song changed to a new track. The women were all wearing the same sort of sparkly tight dress in various bright colours and patterns, and the men were all in suits. I barely noticed Theo as I took everything in. He grabbed my hand and pulled me towards the dance floor, to the only spot that seemed to be free – the constant shifting of everyone else twirling around was enough to make me dizzy.

"Theo," I blurted as he grabbed me and positioned our arms, ready to begin, "I have no idea what I'm doing!"

"Don't worry," he said, placing his hand firmly against the small of my back, "I'll lead you."

And then he was moving us, twirling my body around so fast that I had to shut my eyes to keep my balance. But to my amazement we managed to move in sync with everyone else. As I started to pick up the routine I felt myself begin to dance properly with Theo, keeping my eyes on him instead of the others so I wasn't distracted. I counted my lucky stars that I wasn't entirely hopeless at dancing, thanks to the classes I'd taken with Grace and Naya a few summers ago. On we went through the rest of the song, until the routine ended with Theo flipping me in the air, squeezing my waist as he brought me back down. I gasped at how close our bodies were.

"You've got the moves," he said, moving his lips to my ear so I could hear him over the loud music. "Although can you please be a bit more careful about where you put your feet? You almost crushed my toes a few times."

I laughed, throwing my head back. The song changed in the background, its tempo slower this time so all I had to do was wind my arms around Theo's neck and sway from side to side with everyone else.

"So, tell me," I started, looking up and scanning his eyes, "how did you find this place?"

Theo hesitated as if he didn't want to tell me the answer. "This is where I used to come for my dance lessons," he finally admitted. "In the daytime, this place is a dance school."

His light pink cheeks turned a deeper shade of red. An image of a younger, dancing Theo dressed in a costume popped into my head, and I couldn't help smiling at the thought of how cute he must have looked.

"Well, that explains why you're such an incredible dancer," I said, glancing down at the floor where Theo's feet were moving along to the song, every movement perfect. "I never realised you were this good, though."

Theo's arms tightened around me. I pushed my arms further around his neck, my hands dangling down at the top of his back as I shifted my face closer to him.

"I've won some competitions, but nothing to brag about," he clarified, and the look on his face warned me that it should stay that way. "I just never thought to tell anyone before."

"You've always been such a closed book," I said, my mind drifting back to over half a year ago. "That's why when you went missing no one had any idea where to find you."

He winked at me, and smiled knowingly. "I've come a long way since then," he said. "And so have you."

Then, before I had chance to reply, he was swooping down, claiming my mouth with his own. I eagerly responded, my lips moving in sync with his as we took our time kissing, as the bright lights above the dance floor twinkled brightly over us.

When at last we pulled apart, Theo cocked his head to the side. "Did I forget to say I think you're amazing?"

"I think your actions spoke for you pretty well there," I replied, matching his grin with my own.

Then I reached out to secure his arms around my waist, and I let him guide me back into dancing once more.

For the rest of the night we didn't stray far from the dance floor. We only used the bar at the back of the room when we needed to take a breather from dancing non-stop. I learned that if you were going to stand on the dance floor with everyone else, then it was definitely better to keep on moving in time with the others than to stand still and risk being knocked over by another energetic dancer.

I also learned that most people there that night attended the school during the week, and were therefore much more skilled at dancing than I was. But I didn't need to worry – because I had Theo to lead me, and I was more than happy for him to take the reins.

By the time we called it a night and Theo led me out of the building, I was dripping with sweat, my dress clinging to my body and my hair damp on my forehead. The night breeze gently hit my body as soon as we stepped outside, and instead of shivering away from it like normal I found myself closing my eyes and embracing the cool air.

Theo grabbed my hand and started to gently pull me to the car, guiding me as if he seemed unsure whether I could make it there on my own. My feet were blistering already, I could tell, but it was all worth it – as I'm sure anyone could tell from the exhilarated smile lingering on my face.

"So I chose well tonight then?" Theo still felt the need to confirm once we were inside the car. He hesitated over turning the key in the ignition as he glanced at me. "I mean with the date – and the venue –"

"Theo," I cut off his stuttering. "It was perfect. Thank you. I couldn't have asked for a more wonderful date."

His face lit up. And then he leaned forward, asking me the question all girls dream of hearing on such an occasion:

"McDonalds?"

"The perfect end to the perfect date," I replied instantly, my heart beating wildly beneath my ribs.

"And the best part?" Theo leaned even closer, his voice seductive as he drawled each word out slowly. "I'll even let you order whatever you want. It's all on me."

I stared back at him in admiration. "Theodore Lockhart, you are the most incredible human being to have ever walked this earth."

By the time we got back from McDonalds, my house was in darkness. It turned out that my parents still weren't home; the vacant spaces where their cars should be only proved that.

I turned to Theo when he pulled up right outside at the kerb. My hands were suddenly clammy at the thought of what I was about to ask, but the way Theo stared at me gave me the confidence to push on.

"Do you want to come inside?"

We both knew where that question was headed. And yet, Theo shrugged nonchalantly, as if it didn't hold an underlying meaning, before opening up his car door, walking up the steps to my house and waiting for me to unlock the door.

Once inside, he took his suit jacket off and rolled his shirt-sleeves up to his elbows. His top button was undone. We stood in the hallway, a sudden awkwardness lingering between us.

"Want some tea?" I offered, desperate to ease the tension.

Theo smiled warmly. "I'd love some."

How we ended up kissing instead of drinking tea, I have no idea. One minute I was filling the kettle up with water and turning it on, and the next Theo's arms were around me from behind, his lips pressing soft kisses to my jaw as he whispered sweet nothings into my ear, and I felt like I was melting. And then our lips met, in a moment filled with desperation and desire.

His hands gripped my waist, while mine were more adventurous, running over his body and feeling the taut muscles in his arms, the hard contours of his chest. I tilted my head in order to deepen the kiss, and moved my hands to the back of his hair to bring us even closer together.

"Rose." Theo suddenly broke off the kiss, trying to bring us both back to reality. "Shouldn't we stop before we get carried away?"

I knew we were so close to going beyond the point of no return; we were so close to taking that next step and changing things between us for ever.

But with him standing there, looking and being so perfect, I knew how much I wanted Theo Lockhart. He was my thrill, my excitement, my therapy. Being with him the last four months had been a rollercoaster of emotions – and saying no tonight would be like getting off the ride before it was over, and I never wanted that to happen. I really did want Theodore Lockhart, in so many more ways than I could have him. But that night, there was one way I could have him.

So I looked up at him with a challenging grin. "Maybe I want to get carried away with you."

He smiled at that, then pulled me back into him, his hand holding my face gently. He tilted my head while his lips pressed against mine. My hands moved from where they clutched at his shoulders back up to his hair. I curled my fingers into his locks and gripped tightly.

But Theo still needed confirmation. He pulled away from me again, breathing my name. "Rosaline." I didn't pay much attention to him as he tried to talk to me; instead I released my hold of his hair so I could trail my fingers under his shirt and feel his wild heartbeat and hot skin. "Rosaline. Are you sure you want to do this?"

My face was burning and my hair was tumbling out of its perfect ringlets. I was struggling to breathe, and I could see from the dramatic, uneven rise and fall of his chest that Theo was too. His eyes took in my face as he tried to gauge my reaction. I nodded my head slightly, a smile tugging on the corners of my lips.

As his lips came crashing back down onto my own, I knew that this was the moment that made us both so much more vulnerable to each other than we'd ever been before. The masks that we wore around everyone else every single day had been taken off, and our real selves were fully on display.

And seeing the truth of Theodore Lockhart, knowing him for the person he was under his mask only made me fall utterly and absolutely for him. I wanted to be nowhere else but here, with no one else but him in those blissful hours of dancing and love.

Twenty-Four

It was the harsh glow coming in through the gaps in my curtains that woke me up the next morning. My body was still cocooned in my covers and my face was squished into my pillow. I groaned and turned away from the window. My eyes were still tightly shut as I reached out beside me, only to grab empty sheets with nobody wrapped in them. I pulled myself up in my bed to look down properly at the empty spot next to me.

Theo was no longer here.

I hesitated, unsure of what to do. Then I caught sight of the slip of paper resting on the pillow next to me, and I reached over to pick it up. My fingers fumbled to unfold it and reveal the delicately written words in the centre of the paper.

Am downstairs, making breakfast and coffee.

I smiled as I stood up from the bed and grabbed my dressing gown, before heading downstairs to join Theo.

The sound of my feet padding along the floor of the hallway alerted him to my presence. He turned around from where he was standing by the stove and shot me a warm smile before he went back to turning over the pieces of bacon in the frying pan.

For some strange reason, I felt almost anxious as I looked at him, thinking over everything that had happened between us the night before. I had no regrets about what we'd done, but the worry that *he* might regret the night we spent together was lingering at the back of my mind and sending it into overdrive. I fretted over things changing between us. Nervously, I paused, hovering in the doorway of the kitchen, waiting to see if he'd speak and ease the tension.

"Hey," he finally said, glancing over his shoulder at me again and narrowing his eyes when he saw I hadn't moved. "Are you all right?"

I snapped out of my worries and shook my head, walking over to him. "Yeah. Sorry, I'm just still a little tired."

"Do you want to go back to bed?" Theo's smile was so carefree and easy that I felt myself relaxing instantly. "I can always bring you breakfast in bed if you want to get some more sleep –"

"No. It's fine," I quickly interrupted, my tone soft. And then I laughed and ran my fingers through my hair. "You cooked me a fry-up."

Theo's eyes glistened with amusement as he stared back at me. "Well, yeah." He leaned closer. "I got so tired of waiting for you to wake up and cook me some bacon that I decided to do it myself," he teased, and I rolled my eyes.

"How very grand of you," I commented dryly.

"Well, I did get to wake up next to you naked which I believe was the second wish on my list, so it's not all bad," he joked. Then his focus returned to the bacon still frying in the pan. He let out a string of curse words as he tried to get the pan off the flame before the bacon burned to a crisp.

I watched in amusement as he fumbled around trying to serve it on to two plates, before reaching over to give him a hand.

"Here," I said, holding my hand out for the pan, "I'll just wash that up –"

"No, you won't," Theo said, shaking his head sharply. "I'm taking care of everything. You sit back and relax."

I was more than willing. We ate in silence, crunching noises filling the room each time I put a piece of the burned bacon into my mouth. I tried not to cringe at the charred taste, and took long chugs of my coffee to get rid of it when Theo wasn't looking at me.

He still noticed, though. I had realised that, along with my constantly overthinking mind, I was also very bad at hiding things, and Theo could read me more easily than anyone else. He was almost as good as Brent when it came to telling if I was lying, and all it took was one look at my face when he reached for my plate to know that, once again, his cooking was horrendous.

"I'm sorry," he said, his expression chagrin. "I know I'm a terrible cook."

I desperately didn't want to dampen his spirits so I shook my head to try and reassure him that it was better than he thought. "It wasn't that bad," I said mildly, but the doubtful look he threw me told me he hadn't fallen for it.

"It was burned to a cinder."

"But I ate it all," I protested.

Theo discarded the plates at the sink and came over to me.

He pulled me into his arms and I closed my eyes and leaned into him, enjoying the warmth and comfort of his hold.

"That's because you're incredible," he said before pressing a light kiss to my forehead. "And I'm extremely lucky to have you."

"Likewise," I replied, smiling at him brightly.

Brent came back for a visit a few days later for the first time since the new year.

He had a weekend off with no classes or work to catch up on, so he decided it was time to come home to see his family. I couldn't wait to see him.

Theo had also asked to be with me to welcome Brent home; it was clear he was still eager to make a good impression and since this was the first time he was seeing Brent as my boyfriend and not just my friend he was all the more keen to put himself into a good light.

Brent was late, of course – because he had always failed to understand how time worked. His car turned up on the driveway closer to mid-afternoon than lunchtime, but none of that mattered as soon as he got out and smiled at me when I opened the front door.

I launched myself at him as usual, and he dropped everything in his hands so he could hug me back, preventing us from falling over as my arms wrapped around his neck like a vice. I could feel Theo's eyes on us as he stood in the front doorway, a smile on his face as he watched us.

Brent's laughter filled my ears and he ruffled my hair as I pulled away from him. "Hey, Rosie," he said and I shot him a glare as I yanked his hand away from my hair so he would stop messing it up.

"Don't call me that," I practically snapped, but I couldn't seem to stop the grin on my face from spreading. "And quit making me wait four whole months before you decide to visit me again."

"And you can't come up and visit me instead?" he shot back – and then his eyes fell on Theo and his focus shifted. "Hey, Theo!"

I'd never seen Theo look so awkward. He acted like a deer caught in headlights. His entire body went rigid and he clearly forced a smile on to his face as he waved back at Brent. My brother didn't seem to notice how worried Theo was about making a good impression, and strode towards my boyfriend to shake his hand.

"It's good to see you again," he said, and I watched as Theo started to relax, his shoulders dropping. "I didn't know if I'd get to meet you again now that you're Rose's boyfriend. I thought she'd be too scared I'd embarrass her."

I rolled my eyes while Theo let out a short laugh. "It's good to see you again too, Brent."

Then Brent's eyes swept over his appearance, taking in his still-messy hair and crinkled clothes. His eyebrows furrowed together as he looked back up at Theo's face. "Did you sleep over last night?"

Brent was only teasing, but Theo looked panicked, and I watched him in amusement as he struggled to come up with a lie on the spot. "N-no!" he managed to splutter out, shaking his head wildly as my brother continued to regard him with a coy look. "Here, I'll help you bring in your stuff."

Brent came to stand next to me as Theo rushed over to the spot where he'd dropped all of his bags and started to pick them up, eager to let the conversation drop. Brent's arm brushed mine as he leaned down to my ear, keeping his eyes on my boyfriend fumbling with his luggage.

"Did he sleep over?" he whispered, his lips close enough to my ear that only I could hear him.

I could hardly deny it so I simply elbowed him in the side and muttered, "Shut up, Brent," before walking over to where Theo was and helping him bring the stuff inside.

We decided to go out for Italian food for a late lunch – and we made it Brent's treat considering it had been such a long time since he'd last come home to visit.

He agreed, although he wanted to take his own car as he had things to do in the afternoon and was most likely going to have to leave the meal a bit early without us. I suspected it had something to do with job interviews, but he didn't mention it, and I didn't want to ask in case he felt I was prying.

By the time we got to the restaurant, I was famished. I practically ordered the entire menu as soon as we were seated, even though the waitress hadn't yet asked us if we were ready for our orders to be taken.

"You're still such a pig I see, Rose," Brent commented in a gently mocking tone after our orders were taken and the waitress had left our table.

I shot him a glare and opened my mouth to reply, but Theo cut me off with a laugh. "This is nothing compared to the carnival I took her to a few weeks ago," he said, his arm winding its way around the back of my seat as he spoke. "She made me buy her candy floss eight times in one evening."

Brent started laughing loudly, and I turned my glare towards Theo and crossed my arms over my chest. "Candy floss is a food I only get the privilege of eating when I go to a carnival,"

I reasoned. "Therefore, I'm going to make the most of it when I can."

"And refuse to share it with your boyfriend," Theo pointed out right away.

"Well, the next time we go out and there's food involved, I'll let you have a bite," I offered. "Happy?"

Theo's arms moved down from the back of my chair so they could grip my waist and pull me in closer to him. "Very happy," he said, moving his lips down to lightly kiss my cheek.

I found myself blushing as I caught Brent watching us, and I remembered where we were and who we were with. I knew I wouldn't like it if he was like this with a girlfriend and I was third-wheeling it on the other side of the table, watching *him* be all gooey and in love, so I instantly straightened up, pulling myself out of Theo's grip.

Our food came to the table then and we all eagerly tucked in. I assumed Brent was distracted from our couple-y moment, as we kept up light chatter while eating, but almost as soon as Theo finished off his pasta and took my hand firmly in his own, Brent's eyes dropped to our intertwined hands and then glanced back up at us.

"I don't know if I should be grossed out or extremely happy for the two of you," was all that he said as he continued to stare at us, but the smile playing on his lips showed he was leaning towards the latter.

"The happy option sounds like it would cause a lot less drama," I said.

"Well, this" – Brent gestured towards Theo and me with his hand – "is going to take some getting used to, that's all. This is your first real boyfriend, Rose."

It was the way he said it, like being seventeen and only

having one boyfriend in total was so pathetic, that made me raise my hands into the air defensively. "Hey! What about Xander?"

I knew Brent was only teasing me, trying to get a rise out of me like he always used to do, but the way he smirked at me right then made me want to reach over the table and punch that look right off his face.

"You were fourteen when you started going out with him." He shook his head. "It doesn't count. What do you think?" Brent turned to Theo, asking for his opinion. "Was Xander a serious boyfriend?"

To say Theo looked uncomfortable discussing my ex-boyfriend would be a massive understatement. I wished Brent would stop talking, or would move on to a less weird conversation to have with my new boyfriend, but he seemed to be enjoying making Theo squirm too much to stop now. I knew he meant no harm; he loved to wind me up, but sometimes he went too far. Theo shrugged awkwardly. "I wouldn't really know."

"You've met Xander before though, Theo, haven't you?"

I opened my mouth to correct Brent – to tell him that Theo had never interacted with Xander before, and to shut up – when his next words stopped me in my tracks.

"Well, actually, it's more like Xander met your fists if I remember the rumours correctly."

In shock, I whipped round to look at Theo. He wouldn't meet my eyes and continued to stare down at the table, but that was enough to confirm that what Brent had said was true.

I struggled to process what I'd just heard, feeling weirdly numb from the revelation.

Our silence was enough to wipe the smile right off of Brent's face, and his expression grew confused. "I'm sorry, did I put my foot in it –"

"No," I cut him off, my voice hoarse. "It's fine, Brent."

I looked away from both of them then, clenching my jaw.

Brent shifted in his seat. "Well, I'm going to head off because I've got a friend who lives this side of town and I promised them I'd stop by after this. But ... I'll see you back at home?" Brent asked as he stood up, before reaching into his back pocket and throwing a wad of cash down onto the table in front of me. "Here."

I sat up in my chair, shaking my head. "Brent, you don't have to –"

"I said it was my treat, remember?" He smiled at me, but I could see the concern in his features as he looked between Theo and me. His eyes sought mine. I knew he wanted to make sure I was all right before he left, and I nodded my head slightly at him.

"Theo, it was great seeing you again."

"You too," Theo barely managed to get out in response.

"Bye, guys."

We sat in awkward silence as we both watched Brent weave in and out of tables to get to the exit, his hefty body knocking into a few chairs as he struggled to not get in the way of anyone else. It was only when the door closed once again and he was no longer in sight that Theo looked over at me, his eyes pleading.

"Rose, I –"

A waitress came over, cutting him off as I handed her the money that was sitting on our table. She hesitated when neither of us moved to leave even though we were done paying. "Sorry, would you like anything else?"

"No thanks." I forced a smile at her and stood up, not daring to look at Theo. "I think we're done here."

"Rose!"

I was walking away at top speed now, eager to get away. I didn't know where I wanted to go – I knew I couldn't leave Theo stranded without a car or a lift back home, but all the same I wanted to put some distance between us; I just wanted to get away from him.

His hand grabbed mine. "Rose, please listen –"

"I don't think I can talk to you, Theo," I snapped, pulling myself sharply away from him. "Not right now."

But he continued on, his voice turning urgent. "You came into school crying the day I punched Xander –"

"I don't want to talk about it right now." My voice was firm but it didn't stop him from talking.

"I can't see why you're so upset about me hitting Xander. I did it for you. I'd been in a bad mood already that day, and when I saw that Xander had hurt *you*, I saw red. But I did it all for you. I hurt him because he hurt you – I told him to never speak to you again, because I thought it was the best thing for you. To stop him hurting you again."

I stopped in my tracks, whirling around to face Theo. His eyes were filled with so much regret and pain that it physically hurt to look at him, and I felt my breath getting caught in my throat once more. But I forced myself to speak; I forced myself to face the emotions I was feeling and to tell him what I was thinking.

"It's not just about you punching Xander – although you should know that was unacceptable!" I said, and I felt like kicking myself when my voice cracked at the end. "It's that you didn't tell me about it. When I asked you if you had ever spoken to him before, you lied to me."

247

Theo tried holding my arm again. I yanked it away before he could get a hold of it, hot tears pricking my eyelids. "Rose. I'm sorry. I wanted to tell you –"

"So why didn't you? Why do you always keep things from me?"

He was so desperate now – almost as desperate as I was to leave. "Rosaline."

"I need there to be no more secrets between us. I can't take any more secrets. I need to know that you won't bail on me again."

"You don't trust me, do you?" he whispered, and my eyes flooded with tears that I desperately tried to blink away.

"You ran away before when things got tough between us, Theo." Another question lingered in my mind but I couldn't bring myself to say it: *How do I know you're not going to do it again?*

He looked away from me, his jaw clenched. "I thought we'd moved on from that."

"We have."

"We clearly haven't if you're still hung up on it."

His words stung, but I forced myself to reply. "I'm not hung up on it! But you're still keeping secrets from me and you know how much I need to be able to fully trust you, Theo."

Theo's eyes snapped back to me, holding so much pain that I almost fell apart right then and there. It made me want to say, "Let's just forget this ever happened," and go back to the way things were, when they were good – and yet I knew I couldn't do that. He'd promised me that he wouldn't lie again, that he wouldn't keep the truth from me, and he'd broken that promise. And even though I desperately wanted to ignore it, I couldn't.

Because of Theo, Xander had never spoken to me again. My whole relationship with Xander had been tainted by the fact that I never knew why things had ended like they had. My confusion and anger had soured my happy memories of him, and now I saw that it was all because of Theo.

I thought I knew the boy behind the mask – in fact, I thought he had taken off the mask – but I clearly didn't. He was still hiding himself from me, and now it was time for me to stop trying to get him to open up.

Theodore Lockhart was an enigma. A beautiful mystery. But maybe that's all he could ever be to me.

"You can trust me, Rose. You can." He was begging now, his own eyes filled with tears. "I promise, no more secrets. Ever. Please believe me. Please trust me."

He looked at me like I was tearing him apart, seam by seam – and maybe I was. But my own words were also ripping *me* apart. Theo looked me dead in the eyes, like he was imploring me to see the pain I was causing him. But his pain was my pain, and I couldn't bring myself to see him fall apart too.

"But that's the thing, Theo," I said softly, my heart breaking in two, "I don't know if I can any more."

Twenty-Five

The next day started off exactly the same as it had the day before and every other day before that: with the sun peeking through the gaps in my curtains hitting my face and bringing me out of my deep slumber.

That normality almost tricked me into thinking that it was just like any other day. That life was normal.

But it wasn't. And rolling over in my sheets to see no Theo lying there next to me only reminded me of that harsh reality, and it ruined my mood before the day had even started.

But, despite my emotional turmoil, I had to keep going on as normal; I couldn't spend the day in bed wallowing in the conflict I was feeling and wondering what I was going to do next. I could keep feeling sorry for myself, or I could see this as a chance to regain control. To be in charge of my life, to go back to the old Rose, to have some normality once again. Now that there was no Theo, there were no more hidden secrets, no more highs and lows – I was back to being in control. But – and this was the worst part – I didn't know if I wanted any of that any more.

Nothing in fact seemed to go back to normal. I couldn't sleep, I couldn't think clearly, I couldn't eat. I'd left Theo in the car park all by himself without finishing our argument, and the rest of the night had been a restless one, filled with a mixture of guilt for leaving Theo stranded, anger at him about Xander, and total heartache at the thought of losing him.

I'd eventually managed to drift off to sleep, but had only been out for a couple of hours before I was woken again by the sound of someone cursing loudly downstairs, followed by a series of bumps and bangs.

Brent was fighting with his duffel bag, swearing loudly as he fought to get everything inside and pull the zipper up at the same time. I stood at the bottom of the stairs, watching him, until he finally sensed my presence.

"You're leaving," was all I managed to say, my voice sounding hoarse.

"Yeah," Brent replied, shooting me a small smile as he ran his fingers through his hair. "I still have my classes."

"It's fine." I shrugged him off. "Were you going to leave without saying goodbye?"

It was clear Brent didn't know how to react around me. He'd come home last night and I'd asked him to fill me in with the details of what happened on the day that Theo hit Xander, and all the pieces started to come together. Like Theo had said, he'd been in a bad mood, and when he saw me crying and found out that Xander had hurt me, he'd seen red. Brent said that Theo had warned Xander to stay away from me, to never speak to me again – but he didn't think Theo had picked a fight with Xander simply because he was in a bad mood. I'd always been nice to Theo, and he knew I liked him, which somehow made him think that fighting Xander was a way to pay me back for that.

Brent knew things weren't right; he only had to look at me to see my puffy eyes, so after he finished talking he immediately pulled me into his arms and let me sob into his shoulder for the rest of the evening. But that was when there had been no need for words. When it came to actually talking about emotions, Brent was always a nervous wreck, never knowing what to say and often saying completely the wrong thing, causing the other person to start crying again.

"You were asleep and I didn't know if you wanted me to disturb you," he finally admitted.

"Don't be silly." I stepped off the stairs and opened my arms to him. "Come here."

It didn't take him long to reach me and pull me in for a hug, his arms wrapping around me tightly as he tried to offer comfort with his actions rather than his words. I rested my head on his shoulder and closed my eyes, inhaling his familiar soapy scent and savouring the moment. Brent smelled like home. And especially now that I felt so lost, it felt comforting and reassuring.

"Study hard," I said as we pulled away from one another. To my horror my voice cracked, and I had to face away from him as I willed myself not to cry.

"Rose," Brent sounded wounded for me. "I'm sorry –"

"You have nothing to be sorry for," I quickly cut him off, regaining control of my emotions.

He paused for a second, and I could sense his desperation to ask more questions.

"What happened?" he finally said. "Was it what I said about Xander at lunch yesterday? Xander's brother told me about it when we met up at uni a few months ago, but I assumed your whole school knew –"

"It doesn't matter," I cut in, my voice firm. I was desperate to convince him – and myself – of that. "Things will be fine."

Brent hesitated, and his eyes flashed with caution before he started, "Are you and Theo –"

"Honestly, Brent?" I shook my head, pushing the fresh wave of pain back down and blocking it all out. "I don't know what we are right now."

Brent looked at me with a concerned expression – the same one that always appeared on his face when he was worried about me. He might wind me up sometimes, but he was also fiercely protective. After all that had happened with Theo it was a comfort to see that familiar look, because it showed someone still cared about me, and that someone always would.

"Call me. Anytime," he said into my ear as he hugged me one last time. "I mean it, Rose."

"I know you do."

I helped him pick up his bags; I helped him put them in his car. I stood waving to that same car that Brent drove away down the street, until it turned the corner and disappeared from my vision.

And then I was on my own once again.

The cashier at the till was getting on my nerves.

She wouldn't stop staring, even when I was rummaging around in my bag for some loose change to make up the right money for the food I was buying. Her eyes were practically burning a hole into the side of my head, and when a small "tut" escaped her lips for the fifth time in the space of thirty seconds, I decided to just give up on trying to buy the sweets and chocolate I wanted and to not bother buying anything at all.

"Sorry," I said. I picked the basket back up and walked in the wrong direction, having to push past all the people standing in the line waiting for me to just pay and leave.

"Have a nice day." The scripted response from the cashier was said to my back as I tried to get away as quickly as possible, and it sounded more like a death threat than anything else.

I cursed myself for not bringing enough money as I walked back to the sweets aisle and starting putting everything I had grabbed back into the correct slot. I was so distracted by willing myself not to cry that when someone came and stood next to me, clearing their throat to try and get my attention, I didn't even notice.

"Question," the person who was standing behind me suddenly said, "is eight bars of chocolate too much for one person to eat all alone, or is it not enough?"

I spun around as I recognised the voice. "Nicki."

Nicki Lockhart smiled warmly at me, pretending not to notice my surprise. She pulled me into a hug, her basket awkwardly bashing into mine as she wrapped one arm around me.

"Hey, lovely," she said softly, her tone full of affection. "Long time no see."

I was speechless, a thousand thoughts whirling around my head. I hadn't seen Nicki in a few weeks – Theo often came round to mine instead of me going to his because I had the house to myself and didn't love driving at night – but you'd have thought it had been months by the way she stared at me adoringly. She didn't pick up on the tension in my shoulders at seeing my boyfriend's mother at a time when things were critically bad between us; if anything, she seemed more excited than ever to have bumped into me at that moment.

"How are you? Are you good?" she asked as she examined

the chocolate bars on the display. Her eyes dropped to my almost-empty basket, her eyebrows rising slightly.

"I'm fine," I lied, trying my hardest to keep my tone neutral.

I paused, unable to think of anything else to say. Nicki kept looking at me, her eyes piercing, as she waited for me to elaborate.

"So, back to the question," she said when she realised I wasn't going to say anything else. She raised her basket in the air to present to me the eight bars of chocolate inside it. "Too much?"

I smiled, desperately trying to make myself relax. I had no reason to feel awkward around Nicki; she clearly didn't know anything about what was going on between Theo and me, and she didn't need to be dragged into it now. "Just the right amount, I'd say."

"Ah, finally, someone on my side." She winked and I let out a feeble laugh. "Theo's always saying that it's too much, but he doesn't understand my addiction to chocolate like you do, Rose."

"Well, my love for it is almost as strong as yours," I replied.

"It's the only thing I want to eat at the moment." Nicki shrugged. "I've been craving it every single day. You've got to listen to your body, that's what I say."

"Exactly. You've got to keep your energy and strength up, after all."

"You're right." Nicki laughed, her whole face lighting up. "Besides, I'm celebrating. My brother is having a baby – I'm going to be an aunty for the first time."

It was hard to believe that this was the same woman that I'd seen seven months ago, looking frail and worried as she stood with her ex-husband talking to the head teacher about her missing son. Now, it was like looking at a completely different woman. She was glowing; her eyes were bright and she looked healthy and happy. Her life – and Theo's life too – had changed so much over the last few months, and she'd finally found her happiness.

"That's great news!" I tried to sound as enthusiastic as possible.

Nicki's eyebrows knotted together. "Theo didn't tell you?"

"My phone's been off since last night," I said, cutting in. That was in fact true, but I didn't want to tell her the reasons for it being off. "But I'm so happy for you! Are you excited?"

"Extremely." Her smile widened and she looked at me fondly, her eyes shining. "Life feels so different now."

I felt my stomach clench with guilt. "Yeah," my voice was thick as I replied. "Things are very different."

There was a pause. Nicki shifted to the side to put some more chocolate into her basket, smiling at me as she threw a large Galaxy bar in with the ones already filling the bottom of the basket.

"Anyways, lovely," she said, glancing back up at me, "I should let you get back to your shopping. I've got a bus to catch."

"Wait, you're not driving?" I said. "I'll give you a lift."

She looked surprised at my offer but didn't protest as much as I'd expected her to, instead just offering to buy me a bar of chocolate along with hers as we left. Then we drove off in the direction of her home.

As soon as I got in the car, I knew offering Nicki a lift was a bad idea. Theo would most likely be home, and I knew coming up with an excuse to not see him when dropping Nicki off was going to be difficult, yet I didn't feel like I could face him. Not when the sight of him would probably make my heart crack into a thousand tiny pieces all over again.

Sure enough, when I pulled up outside Nicki's house and didn't make a move to get out of the car with her, Nicki's hands stopped on the door handle and she turned and narrowed her eyes at me in confusion. "You're not coming in for a bit?"

"I really have to get home." I tried my hardest to keep my face apologetic and to conceal all the other emotions I was feeling.

Nicki looked doubtful, but she shrugged and unlocked the door, before turning back to me again. "Well, thank you, Rose."

My smile stretched and I shook my head. "It's nothing –"

"No," she cut me off, "I don't just mean thank you for the lift. I mean thank you for making my son so happy. He's really opened up again." And it was the way she looked at me then – like I'd carved the moon and the stars into the sky and made her whole life complete – that caused my eyes to fill with tears, and for the walls I had put up to come crashing down around me. I turned away so she wouldn't see.

"I'll see you soon," she added, before she got out of the car, took her bag out of the boot and headed inside. She waved at me once more before the door closed.

I knew I should drive off, but still I just sat there for a moment, thinking about everything she had said and wishing desperately that I had been a bit braver and had gone inside with her when I'd had the chance.

Twenty-Six

Nicki Lockhart was sneakier than I thought.

The morning after we bumped into each other at the supermarket I woke up to hear the landline's shrill ring echoing through the house at an ungodly hour. I'd fallen asleep in front of the TV, covered in a layer of fluffy blankets, with the empty wrapper of the chocolate bar she'd bought me discarded on the coffee table.

I groaned and headed out of the lounge to the hallway. "Hello?" I practically grumbled as I picked up the phone, my voice still raspy with sleep.

"Rose? I'm so sorry to call you, but I couldn't get through to your mobile." Nicki's voice made me freeze.

"I – uh, I forgot to turn it back on," was the only lame excuse I could come up with on the spot, still in a daze from being woken up.

I could practically see Nicki raising her eyebrows. There was a long, lingering pause. She knew; she had to know. She'd surely only have to have said a few words to Theo about seeing me and his reaction would have told her the rest. And now that she knew we'd had a fight, she was obviously trying to work her own magic and fix things herself before it was too late.

"Ah," she finally said, her tone dry. "Well, I'm only calling because I think I left some of my shopping in the boot of your car? It was all those chocolate bars I bought."

My body tensed. I could see where this was going. "Did you?"

"Yes." She kept her voice light and breezy – as innocent as she possibly could. "And I was wondering – if you wouldn't mind, of course – if you would be able to just pop over and bring them to me? I'd go and buy myself some more but the car's still at the garage, and I'd have to get the bus ..."

I was meant to be revising today. We had the week off school for our final exams, and with the pressure to do well so I could go to my chosen university weighing on my shoulders, I really needed to do some last-minute cramming before my first paper tomorrow. And yet some part of me couldn't help but give in to Nicki, and I found myself nodding my head in agreement before I realised she couldn't see me.

"No, it's fine." I let myself be defeated easily. "I'll bring them round to you."

I was letting her win; I was letting her get exactly what she wanted, which was for me to see Theo again. But there was something in the back of my mind telling me that perhaps the reason I was letting her win was because I did, in fact, want to see him myself, despite still feeling furious with him.

"Oh, really? You're such a sweetheart," Nicki practically cooed. "I'm in bed because I've got a terrible headache, but Theo will be there to answer the door for you."

Of course. I couldn't help but smile at her words, despite

how obvious it was that she was setting us up. "That's fine. I'll see you soon."

I took my time getting ready, a flurry of nerves and excitement bubbling up inside me as I grabbed my oversized hoodie from the coat rack and threw it on to try and stop myself from trembling. The air outside was cooler than I had expected, and my hair was swept off my face by the wind as I locked my front door and headed down to my car.

Sure enough, the bag of chocolate bars was in the centre of my boot, in full sight and not easy to miss. I rolled my eyes as I grabbed the bag and placed it on the passenger seat next to me before heading off to Theo's.

I was hoping that Nicki had told Theo to expect my arrival as I parked on their drive and stepped out of my car, clasping the bag of chocolate. I didn't know how he'd react to seeing me, and I didn't know how I'd react to seeing him. After everything that had happened, I still found myself wanting to see him, wanting to be near him. And that scared me more than anything else – more than all the worries, the arguments, or any of the nagging feelings in the back of my mind.

I took a deep breath when I got to the front door, hesitating for a second before pressing the button. I needed a moment to gather myself before the door opened.

I didn't get a moment.

The door was yanked open almost as soon as I pressed the doorbell, revealing Theo on the other side.

"Hi," I managed to blurt out, my hands suddenly feeling clammy.

Theo's gaze held mine, his body stiff. "Hi," he said back, his voice hoarse.

There was an awkward pause. I held up the bag, urging my hands not to shake. "I have the chocolate."

He blinked, confusion flashing in his eyes. Then, everything dawned on him. "Oh yeah," he said, nodding his head and stepping to the side to make room for me to come in. "Mum mentioned something about you bringing chocolate with you."

"We bumped into each other in the supermarket. I offered her a lift home and she forgot this," I explained before passing over the chocolate to him, making sure to not let our fingers touch. "Although I don't know how she could've forgotten it considering how addicted she is to the stuff."

"Yeah." He let out a short laugh, raking his fingers through his hair. "She's been talking about rocky road bars as well, so I'm going to make her some."

I raised my eyebrows at him. "You're going to make her some?"

Theo smirked and opened his mouth to reply, but was cut off by the sound of footsteps. A moment later, Nicki called out, "Rose? Is that you?"

"Hi, Nicki," I called back, my eyes on the stairs as I waited for her to come down. "I have your chocolate."

I have never seen someone look so thrilled about being reunited with chocolate; her eyes practically sparkled in excitement.

"We were just talking about how I'm going to make you some rocky road bars from this stash," Theo added.

Nicki's face fell at the thought of Theo cooking for her. It was clear she knew about Theo's lack of kitchen skills just as well as I did. "Ah, yes," she muttered, and I felt a smile spreading on my lips. "Well, I've been thinking. If you've got some spare time, Rose, do you think you could help Theo out

261

a bit? Considering we both know how bad a cook he is."

The smile on my face dimmed slightly. Theo looked like he was cringing when I snuck a glance at him out of the corner of my eye. His mother's lack of subtlety was clearly making him uncomfortable.

"Oh, Rose, you don't have to …" he started, looking at me with unease etched on his face.

"I know," I said, unable to look back at him. "But it's fine. I know how to make rocky road bars."

"And cookies," Theo said. "Your cookies are exceptional."

There was a pause. Nicki kept glancing between Theo and me, her grin triumphant.

"Well, you can make some cookies as well then, if you'd like." She decided to fill the silence. "This headache's killing me – I'm just going to have a lie down for a bit, but I'll be back later to see how you're getting on. Thank you, Rose."

"No problem."

She sent us one last lingering look before padding back up the stairs, leaving Theo and me all alone once more.

He started walking towards the kitchen, glancing over his shoulder to make sure that I was definitely following before saying, "So, I – uh, I already have some of the ingredients weighed out."

"Okay," I replied and raised my eyebrows at him. "And have you weighed everything out correctly?"

He rolled his eyes. "I think I can weigh out some ingredients."

"Sure," I said teasingly. "We all know how great you are in the kitchen." I headed over to one of the bowls already out on the counter, peering into it. "How much golden syrup did it say we needed exactly?"

262

"Three tablespoons."

I lifted up the bowl so Theo could see the contents once again, and his eyes scanned the large amount of golden syrup swishing about. "And you think that this is three tablespoons?"

His eyes flickered from the bowl back up to me, and he smiled sheepishly. "I'm going to say no?"

I couldn't help but laugh. "Now grab the biscuits and start breaking them."

"And how do I do that?" he said, playing dumb, his expression deadpan.

I shot him a withering stare and he smirked. I refused to rise to it, turning away. I could feel his eyes on me, following me around the room as I started looking through the cupboards above the sink. I felt my heart start to race.

Finally, he asked, "Don't you need the recipe?"

I pulled open another cupboard, scanning the contents before shutting it again, remaining empty-handed. "Rocky road bars are easy. I've made them so many times that I basically know the recipe by heart."

"Okay." He still didn't move; he still didn't look away from me. "What are you doing?"

"Looking for a glass bowl that'll fit on top of the saucepan."

"Here," he said, finally stepping forward and coming up behind me. His body brushed up against mine as he leaned over me to open a cupboard and pull out the bowl that I was looking for. I could practically hear the smile in his voice when he added, "All the bowls are in this cupboard."

"Thanks," I could barely speak, my voice strained.

He lingered for another second, his body impossibly close to my own, before pushing back and heading over to the biscuits, to finally break them into a bowl. I could breathe again.

I tried to think of something to say as we both started to get to work, standing with our backs to one another as I melted the butter in a pan by the cooker and he continued to crumble the biscuits.

But I didn't have to worry about starting the conversation again, because Theo suddenly said, "So you've heard the news about Uncle Adam then?"

I turned my head to look at him. "Yes, I have." An image of Nicki in the supermarket, smiling from ear to ear, was painted in my mind. "You're going to be a cousin."

"And a free babysitter," he pointed out, mock-grimacing.

"Are you happy?" I reached over to grab the chocolate and carefully started to mix it in with the butter melting in the glass bowl.

He took his time thinking about it, before letting out a little laugh and reaching up to run his fingers through his hair. "Well, yeah. I'm pretty close to Uncle Adam. He was great after – after the whole thing with my dad. I'm excited for him, I guess. And Aunt Tina. I want to help out any way I can. I'm going to need some tips for looking after babies, though."

"I can't help you there I'm afraid," I said, biting my lip as I concentrated on stirring. "My parents stopped having babies after me."

"Do you wish they'd had more?"

The prospect of more siblings didn't need any thought on my part. "No," I answered automatically. "Not really. If they'd had another kid, that would've meant me looking after someone else when they were busy all the time, and I'm not that great at looking after myself, let alone another child."

I tried to picture life with another sibling in the mix: a life where I wouldn't have been alone when Brent went off to university. A life where I would have had to look after someone else other than myself when my parents didn't come home in the evenings A life that would have been completely different to the one I was leading. My parents had never wanted any more children – and, thinking about it, I was immensely glad about that.

Theo's eyes drilled into me once again. "You looked after me when I was hiding at yours."

"That was different. We're the same age. You could basically look after yourself," I pointed out. I thought back to that time – it felt like a distant memory as I remembered everything that had happened. "God, does that feel like a long time ago."

"It *was* a long time ago." Theo mused. "We've come on a long way since then."

"Yeah. We have."

An image popped into my mind then, of a seven-months-younger Theodore Lockhart, his hair a mess, his eyes wild and his clothes torn, standing on my doorstep with that smirk I love on his face as he told me he needed my help. He felt almost unrecognisable now as I snuck a glance up at him. Even though he hadn't changed much physically, I knew so much more about him and cared so much more for him now, and that made him almost like a new person to me.

He looked up and caught my gaze. "Rose?" he said softly.

"Yes, Theo?" I breathed back.

"Can I ask you something?"

I hesitated, not knowing what the next words out of his mouth would be. "Yes." Everything else in the world started to fade away as I focused on him and only him, waiting for his next words in anticipation.

But he only lifted up the bowl of biscuits and held it out to me so I could see they had been crushed so much they were basically a powder. "Am I doing this right?"

The rocky road bars didn't take long to finish after that, although Theo did have to break new biscuits.

I also made the same cookies I had done for Theo when he was staying at my house. He snacked on them as I cut the rocky road into pieces on the kitchen worktop.

"Well," I said as I put the bars into the fridge to set, "that wasn't as much of a disaster as I initially thought it would be."

Theo turned to look at me, taking a new cookie in his hands as he finished off the previous one. "Can you admit now that I'm not that bad a cook?"

I shook my head, smiling widely. "Oh no, you're still awful at cooking."

He stuck his tongue out at me, dismissing my comment. "Liar."

I laughed heartily and his eyes lingered on me. He didn't laugh though; when I looked up he was staring directly at my lips, his eyebrows pulled together. He snapped out of his thoughts when he realised I was looking at him.

His gaze held my own as he started, "Listen, Rose –"

"Something smells nice in here." Nicki walked into the kitchen and Theo trailed off. It took every ounce of my being not to tell her to go away so he could finish what he started, and from the look of annoyance on Theo's face I could tell he was thinking the same thing too.

I held out a cookie for Nicki and she eagerly took one off the plate, shoving it into her mouth and chomping loudly. She looked so much like Theo right then that I almost burst out laughing.

"These are incredible," she moaned once she'd finished her bite, eagerly taking another chunk out of the cookie. "Rose, you have a serious gift for baking."

I tried my hardest not to blush at her comment. "Thank you."

She turned to Theo, raising her eyebrows at him. "I'm guessing you helped stir a couple of times?"

He smiled cheekily. "And I kind of crushed the biscuits so much that they turned into dust."

Nicki still shook her head, but a tiny smile played on her lips. "Honestly. I don't know where you get your bad cooking skills from, but they're a burden to everyone."

We laughed for a moment before Nicki went over to the leftover chocolate, chose a bar and started to open it. Theo and I watched her for a moment, before our eyes drifted over to one another. A smile crept onto his lips as he held my gaze.

I wanted to ask him what he'd been going to say before he was cut off, but I could feel Nicki watching us carefully, making me more and more uncomfortable by the second.

"Right, well, I better be going," I finally said, my voice awkward and small. I straightened up. The smile on Theo's face dimmed.

But I didn't want to leave. I wanted to hear Theo explain himself. We needed to sort things out and try to make them better again, and that wasn't going to happen if one of us kept running away every time we hit a rocky patch. And yet I couldn't stay and do that, because Nicki was standing there and it wasn't the sort of thing I wanted to talk about with Theo while she was in the room.

"Oh," she piped up. "You can't stay for some tea?"

I bit my lip and reluctantly shook my head. "Revision calls," I said. "I really need to get back."

I hurried out of the room before I got a response. I made my way to the front door, but footsteps behind me stopped me from opening it. I turned back to see Theo standing there, awkwardly shifting as he tried to avoid my gaze.

"You followed me," I said slowly and quietly.

He gave up on trying not to look at me; his eyes snapped up to meet mine. "I followed you," he repeated.

"Why?"

I tried to read him, to understand what he was thinking in that moment, but I didn't need to wonder for long. As he came to a halt in front of me, he summed up everything he was feeling perfectly in two sentences, almost making my heart stop in the process.

"Because they say that if you love someone you should let them go," he said, desperation laced in his tone. "But, Rosaline, I'm so in love with you that I don't think I *can* let you go right now."

My eyes widened. My mouth opened. And suddenly, all the other secrets and lies flew out of my mind, because telling me that he loved me was quite possibly the biggest and best secret that Theodore Lockhart could share with me. Ever.

Twenty-Seven

He waited for me to speak.

The ball had been placed in my court, and there was nowhere for me to hide.

But the thing is, when you know you should be pouring your heart out with all those thousands of things that you need to say, your mind just goes blank and all thoughts evaporate.

Everything I felt for Theo – everything I had wanted to say to him since we first started dating, ever since I started falling for him – decided to leave my mind for a moment. It left me in a state of panic as I desperately tried to string some words together to tell him how I felt before he could give up on us because I didn't say those secret words back to him.

A few days ago, I'd panicked when I'd found out about Theo lying to me about Xander. My brain had gone into overdrive, sending me back to that same time before when Xander had lied to me and shattered my heart into thousands of pieces. And I had been scared that I was going to be hurt again; I was scared that Theo was going to leave me feeling broken, just like Xander had.

But he loved me. Theodore Lockhart loved me. And I knew he didn't mean to hurt me, just like I never wanted to hurt him.

Even as he waited there for me to reply, I could see the love shining in his eyes. I could feel it pouring out of him, along with the longing for me not to go.

Theo and I weren't over. We may never be over. Life hadn't been the same for either of us since the moment he came knocking on my front door asking for a place to stay.

"But, Rosaline, I'm so in love with you that I don't think I can let you go right now."

Theo shifted on the spot, clearing his throat as if trying to remind me that he was still there, waiting. I felt a smile light up my face.

I stepped closer to him. His eyes were full of hope as they met my own.

I took another step forward. I sensed his body tense in anticipation.

Then the sound of footsteps made me stop. Theo dropped his hands, which had been slowly rising up to touch my cheeks, and a sigh escaped his soft lips. He dropped his head to mask his disappointment.

"Oh, I'm sorry," Nicki said, stopping in her tracks and holding her hands up as she realised she may have ruined the moment. "Am I interrupting something?"

Theo glanced back at her, trying to keep his expression as neutral as possible. "It's fine, Mum –"

"Actually, please could you give us a minute, Nicki?" I interrupted.

Two pairs of surprised eyes locked on to me at once. I gave

a weak smile as a nervous feeling settled inside my chest.

But Nicki understood what I was doing, and her smile widened. She quickly headed up the stairs, not saying another word to Theo and me.

He turned to me once she was gone and whispered, "Why did you do that?"

"Because I didn't want to kiss you in front of her."

There was no beating around the bush this time, no covering up my emotions with confusing and vague answers, no trying to say something poetic to convey my true feelings and desires. I didn't even give Theo a moment to grasp my words before I was closing the distance between us for real this time, reaching up to find his lips with mine.

Theo didn't need to think about anything then. His hands came up on impulse, and his fingers caressed my cheeks as he kissed me back with urgency, acting like I was the oxygen that he needed to breathe. He let out a soft sigh as I pressed myself into him, deepening the kiss and clinging to him as tightly as possible.

Neither of us wanted to break away. Neither of us wanted the kiss to end. But breathing was getting in the way of our perfect moment, and soon I had to pull away to catch my breath, leaving my body pressed against his.

"You love me," he said softly a minute later.

"I love you," I replied happily, and he grinned wider than he ever had before.

And then he was picking me up and spinning me around in circles. I laughed, throwing my arms around his neck and holding on for dear life. His lips were soon back on mine, and I couldn't help but smile into the kiss this time, because I'd finally found the real Theodore Lockhart. And there was no way I was planning to let him go ever again.

Twenty-Eight

"Here." My mother thrust the brochure she was holding out towards me, one perfectly manicured fingernail pointing to the page she wanted me to look at. "Greece is meant to be lovely this time of year."

"Mum, you've never even been to Greece before," I replied, resisting the urge to roll my eyes as I sat back in my chair. Theo snorted quietly in the seat next to mine, his arm wrapped around the back of my chair.

My mother shook her head in objection and pursed her lips in obvious annoyance. "You don't have to go to a place to know how wonderful it is. A friend of mine went a couple of years ago and she told me it was lovely."

"Look, we said we were only thinking about going travelling in the summer. It was never a definite decision."

My mother rested her elbows on the table, nudging a few of the magazines out of the way. They were splayed out, covering every single inch of the surface.

"Well, you've only got one more exam left, Rose," she

reminded me. "And then you've got the whole summer ahead of you with no work. You'll have to think of something to do."

"But I'm saying we don't need to make any definite plans right now."

I knew my mother was trying to be helpful. When she'd heard Theo and me discussing our plans for the summer and he'd suggested going travelling, she had instantly jumped in on the conversation, offering her tips and advice on places to go. Travel was her biggest passion, but with work she wasn't able to do as much as she would like, so to help us plan out our trip was something she was more than willing to do.

"I still don't know if I'm able to go either," Theo piped up, his hand falling over the edge of the chair to rest on my shoulder, which he squeezed comfortingly. "My mum said as long as I can pay for most of the trip myself then it would be fine, but I'm not sure I have enough for Greece."

We exchanged a look then, both of us trying our hardest not to smile as my mother sighed and nodded her head almost in defeat, agreeing to drop it for now. "All right – but if you make any more decisions, don't hesitate to ask for my help."

"We will, Mum," I said honestly, grateful that for once she was actually taking an active interest in my life for once. "Promise."

A smile blossomed on her face. I couldn't help but return it.

But as soon as she was gone Theo's body flopped down on to the table in front of him. He closed his eyes and let out a loud groan.

"Three hours," he whined, rubbing his hands over his face in exhaustion. "We talked about bloody holiday destinations for three hours."

I tried my hardest not to laugh at his anguish. "What can I say? My mother likes talking about travel."

"That's an understatement."

I sighed, leaning forward to rest my chin in my hands. "She was just trying to be nice, Theo. She wanted to help us out."

Even so, I had to admit that it'd been unexpected when my mother came downstairs and offered us advice on each travel destination, promising to help us pick out the best places to visit. I didn't have the heart to refuse her offer when I saw the spark in her eyes. It had been the first time she'd looked excited about anything in a long time, and I would have done everything in my power to keep that smile on her face, and to keep her happy. Because, at the end of the day, she was still my mother – she was still someone I loved – and seeing her happy made me happy.

Theo looked up at me then, slightly guilty, as he propped himself up off the table, finally sitting properly in his chair. "I know. I just didn't expect it to take so long." He paused for a second, and I heard a low rumble from deep inside his stomach. He bit his lip to keep the smile off his face as the sound echoed round the room. "I'm starving."

This time, I chuckled. "Well, Brent's due back any minute now, so we can go out to eat with him."

He stood up, raising his arms above his head to stretch them, the muscles rippling underneath his shirt. "Did he have another job interview today then?" he asked, and I sheepishly refocused my gaze from his body to his face.

"Yeah," I replied. "Now that he's graduated, he's more desperate than ever to move back out again. I think it's finally dawned on him that in September he'll be the one left alone with our parents when I go off to university."

Theo shook his head in amusement. "Well, we can call Grace and Naya and ask them out too," he offered, shrugging. "We could make it a celebration of sorts, for the exam period drawing to an end."

I started to gather up the travel guides that my mother had left scattered all over the place. "Sounds good," I said, absent-mindedly opening up one of the guides and flicking through it.

My eyes caught sight of one of the titles and I quickly scanned the pages. Theo's eyes drifted over to me and widened in alarm as I continued reading. "Oh God, what are you doing?"

I started to walk towards the door my mother had left through. "I just have a couple of questions to ask about –"

"Rose!"

We ended up at the pub again.

There was another fight over food between Grace and Brent and Brent won again, just like he always did. That boy was never happy unless he got his own way, but this time none of us minded because we were more than happy to go to the same pub we'd gone to for our New Year's Eve celebrations. It held some precious memories, and there was something rather appealing about going back to a place after so many things had changed.

Of course, those memories were slightly fonder for Theo and me than for the others. The restaurant was the place our relationship had officially started. Considering everything we'd been through before and after New Year's Eve, it was a bit surreal to walk back into the restaurant hand in hand and see that absolutely nothing about the place had changed. We even sat at the same table.

"Let's have a toast to the end of another era," Brent

practically shouted once drinks were delivered to our table, and we all raised our glasses and prepared to clink them together. "And to new beginnings on the horizon."

Brent didn't order champagne like he had on New Year's Eve. We didn't need it this time.

"I would love to make a speech about my little baby sister and how quickly she's grown up, but I know it'll only make Rose embarrassed," Brent then said, shooting me a teasing look as my eyebrows started to pinch together in annoyance. He paused almost thoughtfully before adding, "But I think I'll do it anyway."

The others started to cheer loudly as he conjured up a long-winded speech at the table right there and then, going into extreme details about each year of my life and every embarrassing episode from our childhood he could think of.

Later, when the toast was over and the chatter was back to normal, I excused myself from the table, deciding it was the perfect time to sneak away from the others and go outside.

Unsurprisingly, this part of the restaurant hadn't changed either – no tables had been moved, no chairs shifted. It was like everything had frozen in place, waiting for my return. As my eyes flickered over to the river flowing, I felt a smile creep across my face and a feeling of ease settled inside me.

I walked over to the fence by the riverbank, but this time, instead of standing beside it, I swung one leg over it and effortlessly climbed over to the other side, my feet hitting the soft bank of grass.

I sat down and pushed my feet over the edge of the riverbank. My legs weren't quite long enough to reach the water but it was a comfortable position to sit in. I took a moment to close my eyes and take a few deep breaths, listening to

276

the water trickle past and thinking about everything that had happened in the past few months.

I heard the crunching of someone walking along the ground behind me, but I didn't turn towards it, even when the person started to climb the fence themselves, struggling in his efforts. I knew who it was anyway; I could tell from the sound of his footsteps and breath. I knew him that well.

"Rosaline," Theo drawled, his thigh pressing against my own as he came to sit down. He pushed his feet over the edge of the riverbank along with mine. "How many times have I told you not to go wandering off like that?"

"You knew I was here," I replied, rolling my eyes but smiling nonetheless. "You know I always come out here when we eat at this restaurant."

His feet moved closer to mine, his ankles entwining with my own. "You could've asked me to come with you," he reminded me.

I continued to look out towards the river, ignoring his gaze. "You were too busy trying to stuff your face with as much food as possible. I didn't want to disturb you."

He let out a barking laugh, his shoulders shaking. Then he wrapped an arm around me and pulled me close to his chest. "Very true," he murmured softly, his breath hot on my ear, "but I think I love you enough to give up food for you, Rosaline."

I raised my eyebrows, amused at his comment. "That's not what you said a few months ago."

"Well, that was then and this is now. And you're much more important to me than my dinner will ever be."

I snorted at his comment and buried my face in his chest, deeply inhaling his intoxicating scent.

We sat there together for a while, enjoying one another's

company, listening to the water flowing by. Theo gripped my hand tightly.

"You know," he piped up, his tone thoughtful, "I hear Paris is meant to be lovely this time of the year."

I stilled, my head snapping up. "Are you saying what I think you're saying?"

"We could travel by Eurostar," he suggested, talking slowly as though he was only just thinking it through in his mind. "We could stay for a few days –"

"How soon can we go?" I interrupted him eagerly and he laughed, throwing his head back and looking up at the sky.

"So you're up for it then?" he asked, grinning.

"Nothing sounds better."

I could practically feel the joy radiating off him, and he tightened his grip on my hand. "I'll look into buying tickets first thing tomorrow. Just promise me that you won't ditch me for some fancy French guy when we're there, okay?"

I nudged his side, saying, "Well, the French accent is extremely sexy. And I heard they can cook ..."

He groaned, reaching up to run his fingers through his hair as he shook his head at me mockingly. "God, I swear you're going to be the death of me, Rosaline Valentine."

I leaned closer to him, smiling when I noticed his breathing hitch. My lips brushed his and so our breath mingled for a moment before I pulled back and softly whispered, "Likewise, Theodore Lockhart."

He didn't give me a chance to pull back any further. He reached up to touch my cheek and then his lips covered mine. I sighed and kissed him back, giving in to what I craved all day, every day. He smiled into the kiss, and his hands slipped from my cheek and started to roam downwards.

278

He pulled away all too soon and I frowned. I reached forward to kiss him again but my lips instead met his cheek as he turned his head at the last second. "We better get back," he said.

I ignored his comment, instead trailing my lips down his jaw, planting careful kisses on his neck and sucking on his sensitive spot. He stifled a moan and I smiled again. "Do we have to?" I asked in between kisses.

"You know, if I remember correctly, the last time we were here it was me who didn't want to leave, and *you* were the one who kept saying we needed to go back."

I reached up and nibbled on his earlobe, just like he had done to me when I'd tried to get him back inside on New Year's Eve.

"Well, that time I was drunk and clearly out of my mind."

"Clearly you were," Theo replied, before gesturing towards his body and waggling his eyebrows at me playfully. "I mean, who wouldn't want to stay wrapped up in all of this for the entire night?"

I almost fell into the river I was laughing so hard.

"Are you sure you want me to drop you here, Theo? I don't mind driving a bit further up so we're closer to your house if you'd like."

Brent turned around from the driver's seat as he pulled up at the bottom of the road. All he got in response was a simple shrug.

"Here is fine, thanks."

And of course it was – Theo's car was parked right around the corner.

"Well, I guess this is goodnight, Rose." Theo turned to me,

trying his hardest not to laugh as he shot me a wink, reassuring me that the plan was definitely set in motion. "Sleep tight."

I leaned over and gave him a small peck on the lips, keeping it casual. "Goodnight, Theo,' I said softly, ignoring the immature vomiting sounds Brent was making from the front seat as he watched our exchange.

Theo got out of the car and slammed the door, before watching us drive off, his eyes meeting mine as Brent pulled away. They twinkled with mischief and he shot me one final grin before he was lost from our sights.

My parents were still waiting up when Brent and I arrived home, and both of them came out of the lounge as soon as they heard the front door slam. They stood watching us take off our jackets.

"Did you have a nice time?" my dad asked.

I shrugged, exchanging a look with Brent. "Yeah, it was fine."

It was quite surreal seeing them both standing there watching us, for us all to actually be in the house together for once. It was like we had gone back in time, to when Brent was living here before university, and they both put their family life before work.

My mother hesitated for a moment before asking, "Do you want to watch a film with us tonight? We were thinking a horror."

I was cautious of the time but I couldn't pass on the opportunity to sit with the rest of my family and watch a film together for the first time in years, so both Brent and I agreed. My parents set up the film and then we all sat together on the settee, squishing up to make enough room for the four of us.

The film was terrible; my dad wouldn't stop talking through

it, my mum wouldn't stop screaming at the scary parts, and Brent crunched his popcorn loudly in my ears, but I didn't care. We were all together, and we were all getting along. It was the happiest I had been with my family for a very long time.

The film ended, and my mother turned to Brent and me, her face bright with happiness. "Want to watch another one?"

Brent was already nodding, but I glanced at my watch and cringed when I realised the time. "I'm actually quite tired so I'm going to head on up," I lied, pushing myself up off the settee.

My parents nodded, looking slightly disappointed, and my stomach twinged with momentary guilt. So, in a moment of spontaneity (which were becoming all the more frequent these days), I walked over to their end of the sofa and gave each of them a goodnight kiss. "That was fun. We should do it again soon," I said, as they looked up at me with mild surprise.

Brent stayed sitting and I caught his eye as I turned and made my way out of the room. He was smiling knowingly, the expression on his face making it obvious what he was thinking. He knew. He had to know. After all this time, and after all the lies and secrets I'd had to keep, it seemed I still wasn't any better at fooling him. I guess there are just some people in this world that you can never lie to.

"Okay then," he said coyly, "goodnight, Rose."

I forced a smile and walked out of the room as quickly as I could without seeming even more suspicious. "Goodnight, Brent."

And then I was heading up to my room and shutting the door behind me. I quickly went to the window and threw open my curtains.

And, sure enough, just like every other night since Brent

281

had come back and my parents had been home more, Theodore Lockhart was waiting outside, his feet planted firmly on the window ledge as he waited for me to let him inside. He'd driven here in his car and parked it round the back, then scaled the tree right next to my window. The plan we'd formed weeks ago was now mastered to perfection, and we were acting it out every night.

Seeing him there, waiting for me to open the window for him, took me back to nine months ago. Because it was almost nine months to the day that I went running downstairs at the constant ringing of my doorbell, opened the door to see a scruffy, desperate boy with striking green eyes and an irresistible smirk, and was sent into a state of shock at the words that came from his mouth – the same ones he used seeing me right now.

"Rose Valentine," Theo Lockhart drawled my name out as he smirked at me, holding out his hand, "I need your help."

I knew I would always end up helping Theodore Lockhart. No matter what we were to one another, no matter when it was, no matter where we were, if he ever came knocking on my door asking for help, I'd help him. Because, even when we barely knew one another, he was still everything to me, and he would always be everything to me.

His green eyes twinkled in the moonlight as I grabbed his hands and helped pull him in. His arm brushed mine as he walked further into the room, like he owned the place. He caught me in his arms a moment later, positioning my head against his chest, right where I could feel his beating heart.

And, as my heart beat in time with Theo's, I knew I wanted to be nowhere else but here.

17.5.18

Acknowledgements

Thank you to all my readers, new and old, for giving this book a chance. I hope you enjoyed reading Rose and Theo's story as much as I loved writing it.

Thank you to my mum for always pushing me to do my best, and my dad for being full of pride. Thank you to my sister and my family for the support, and for keeping me smiling, even in the hardest of times.

A massive thank you to the team at Ink Road for making my dreams come true. Especially to Megan and Rosie for your expertise in helping me shape this book into what I had always hoped it would be. I couldn't have done it without you.

To my friends, thank you for putting up with my moans, worries and stresses, as it got closer and closer to publication day!

Finally, thank you to Charlotte Harvey, my creative writing teacher, who has taught me so much and whose encouragement gave me the confidence to believe that my dreams of being a real published author could come true – and come true they did.